# UNDER A Feral Moon

# L.A. DAY

ELLORA'S CAVE
ROMANTICA PUBLISHING

# *What the critics are saying...*

ɛͻ

### FERAL DOMINATION

**4.75/5 Rating** "*Feral Domination* was a super fast read. From page one L.A. Day had me enthralled with the story of Gionne and Jenna. I loved the how she brought more than one type of shape shifter into the story and how spicy the love scenes were. If you enjoy a lot of fire and domination in your books this is the one for you." ~ *Night Owl Romance Reviews*

### FERAL LUST

**5 Lips** "*Feral Lust* has to be one of the most erotic and passionate tales by LA Day that I have ever read. [...] It will leave readers breathless and tingly! *Feral Lust* is the sequel to *Feral Domination* but it stands on its own. I do recommend reading *Feral Domination* though, as it too is a wonderful read. I can hardly wait to read more about Ms. Day's shifters."
~ *Two Lips Reviews*

### FERAL INTENSITY

**4 Stars** "L.A. Day's *Feral Intensity* is a quick-witted, fast-paced morsel ripe for the devouring. I know I gobbled it up in record time. What more could a man-love fan require in a sweet little package like *Feral Intensity*? [...] Everything is presented, spun to fine sugar thread and tied in a neat bow in a mere eighty or so pages. [...] The love scenes are sweetly quirky and offer a refreshingly new perspective on two aggressive men falling for each other. This is one well worth pulling out again on one of those chilly winter days for a little "warm-me-up" reading." ~ *Sensual EcataRomance*

An Ellora's Cave Romantica Publication

www.ellorascave.com

Under a Feral Moon

# UNDER A FERAL MOON

ɞ

## FERAL DOMINATION
*~11~*


## FERAL LUST
*~131~*


## FERAL INTENSITY
*~219~*

# FERAL DOMINATION

৪০

# Dedication

🌢

*This is for you, Mom.*

*Even though you are no longer with me, your support and encouragement carries on. You taught me my love for books and for that and many other things, I thank you.*

# Prologue

With a low crackling rumble, a dark fury of clouds billowed toward the mountainside, mimicking the storm brewing within Gionne. Grimacing, he threw back his head, wanting to howl at the fates. Today was to be a day to celebrate but now it was a day to mourn.

Nearly exhausted from spending the last twelve hours at his father's bedside, he collapsed on a fallen log, his bare foot kicking at a pinecone. Wearily his head dropped into his hands, his heart heavy, his mind filled with doubt and grief. The surrounding forest was unusually quiet as if waiting anxiously. The long walk had cleared his head of some of the fog surrounding him. Reality was his duty to his people but his heart demanded he protect Jenna. If she knew of his father's illness, she would blame herself. It was best if he stalled their joining until his father recovered. Jenna, being a proper female, would be submissive to her alpha. She would do as he told her, wouldn't she? At the moment, he doubted his ability to process rational thoughts.

A misplaced foot sent up the smallest sound, alerting him to her arrival just a second before she launched herself at him. She hit him with the full force of her supple frame and he flopped backward off the log to land on his back in a bed of pine needles.

"Hmph." The sound erupted from his lungs as he hit the ground and Jenna landed on him.

"Gotcha," Jenna declared gleefully.

Gionne's breath hitched in his throat. For a moment, worries disappeared. Gently, his arms enclosed the sleek blonde female lying on his chest. Her scent wafted through his

11

senses, consuming him, enthralling him. The aroma was tangy and rich, her usual sweet scent enhanced. A low growl rumbled in his chest as his senses absorbed the difference. She was in heat.

He could smell the powerful fragrance of her musk and see the fire in her dilated golden eyes. She had dared the wrath of her father to leave his stronghold in this state. Did she not know the danger in such a foolhardy adventure? Her brother should beat her. He should beat her. Gio felt his body tightening in response, his cock engorging at the thought of baring the softly rounded globes of her ass to his hand.

"You got here early. I couldn't wait either." Her voice bubbled with excitement.

"Have you lost your mind to come to me in this condition?" he growled, anger and lust brewing in his gut.

Jenna shoved off his chest to sit straddling him, her face a flame of color. "I couldn't miss coming here today."

This position allowed her damp heat to sit directly upon his cock. He closed his eyes, swallowing back the lump forming in his throat. He called on all the restraint he had ever learned. Was she so naïve? Did she not know how easy it would be for him to fuck her? Hot and hard. He could shred her clothes and bury his aching shaft to the hilt in her wet, tight canal.

Opening his eyes, their gazes locked. A knowing smile tilted the fullness of her lips as she moved slightly against his engorged length. "I guess I don't have to ask if you're glad to see me."

She knew what she was doing to him. He recognized the desire in her heavy-lidded eyes.

The smell of heat and lust was heavy upon them.

His hands gripped her hips holding her still. A muscle twitched in the side of his clenched jaw, his cock jerked uncontrollably. The shift she wore was a small barrier and his fingers dug into the softness of her ass. His arms shook with the effort it took not to grind her against him until she came. What he wanted most in the world now sat straddling him but he couldn't have her. Not now.

*Think of your father, think of your father.* The chant rattled through his head in an attempt to still the surge of lust.

Jenna's light laughter rolled down his spine, sending shivers in its wake. "So what'd you get me for my birthday?"

He didn't reply, at the moment he couldn't speak. He thought of the adjoining room he had designed for her at his home. It was too large to pack, and now it seemed he might not be able to give it to her, at least not today.

Jenna's hands blazed a trail of fire down his chest. The silk of his shirt did nothing to shield him from her poker-hot fingertips. Shudders of desire shook him and he was helpless to resist. When her hot hands reached the snap on his leather pants, she hesitated.

His shy kitten reemerged before his eyes. Gleaming teeth nervously bit her lush, pink lower lip.

She surprised him with her next words. "Is this my present?" Her voice was whisper-soft. Her fingers hovered at his zipper. "Can I unwrap it?" The question nearly unmanned him.

He was burning alive. She was going to kill him. An unholy growl left his lips before he could silence it.

\* \* \* \* \*

Jenna was out of her depth and she knew it. She couldn't stop the need coursing through her. She was in heat. Her pussy was cum-drenched with anticipation. Her need for Gio was all-consuming. Primal urges erupted as he lay beneath her. His body, so hard and taut against her softness, ignited her desires. The hard ridge of his cock, nestled where she needed it most, nearly had her begging. He was always patient, gentle and kind with her and she was tired of it. She was of age to mate. He had promised her that today they would confront their families. The way she saw it, it would be much easier if he had already fucked her. Who could deny them if his seed had already taken root inside her?

When he moved it was so quick it didn't register until she found herself on her back with him standing over her. He loomed dark and dangerous, as always the alpha male.

Disgruntled, she pursed her lips. Not easily dissuaded, her hungry eyes traveled along her very own road to paradise. His stance emphasized the thick, taut thighs encased in black leather. Her gaze locked on a most impressive bulge between those legs and unconsciously she licked her parched lips. His arousal was so obvious he couldn't deny he wanted her as badly as she needed him. Raising triumphant eyes to his face, she could not help but notice his heaving chest.

After noting such obvious signs of desire, she was surprised and irritated to read hesitation and denial in his dark gaze. Had she been too forward? It wasn't really her nature. She preferred to be the hunted not the hunter, unless of course, she was in fur on the trail of a tasty morsel. Today though, her heat was heavy upon her and she needed her mate.

"Jenna, we must talk."

Rolling to her feet, she adjusted her shift. Intentionally running her hands along her hips, she tempted his eyes and senses. "I don't want to talk. Touch me, Gio. Feel how hot I am for you."

"We cannot rush into this," he told her, but the huskiness of his voice echoed her own longings. "We need time."

"Rush! We have waited a long time. The last time we were together, you said you couldn't wait to possess me. What has changed?" Jenna stepped closer, the rigid tips of her breasts brushing his chest. Dark eyes flashed fire before his lips forcibly took possession of hers. His hungry tongue invaded her mouth and she could not resist suckling that thick muscle even deeper. The sucking motion sent quakes down between her legs and her knees would have buckled except for his supporting arms.

He growled into her mouth and shivers slithered up her spine. Rough hands grasped her ass, spreading her thighs, grinding her aching flesh against his groin. Sinking to his knees, he carried her with him. The forest floor was cool beneath her heated flesh but she gave it little thought as he knelt between her parted legs. Her control was shattered and her thighs trembled violently.

She was innocent but the heat inside her made her brave. She wanted him, needed him.

Feral eyes watched her as his hand slipped beneath her shift to fondle her wet folds. The brush of his fingers coincided with a nearby strike of lightning. She quivered and it wasn't from the drop in temperature. Nervously she bit her lip, her vagina quaking with need.

She knew what to expect but the overwhelming urges took her by surprise.

"You are so wet for me." He brought glistening fingers to his lips. "So wet and so sweet." He groaned as his tongue darted out to taste her sweetness. "I want you more than I want my next breath." Dark clouds whorled overhead, the electrically charged air crackled around them, adding to the excitement of the moment.

His words engorged her clitoris further, allowing silky cream to ooze from her heated folds and run down the crack of her ass. Watching him lick her cream from his fingers had her begging for more. "Take me then, claim me," she begged as the thunder boomed.

His eyes shut and a shudder shook his frame, on a deep breath, he reopened his eyes but his gaze was now shuttered, emotionless. "I can't right now, it wouldn't be right."

"You bastard." Both fists slammed into the ground. She scooted away from him, tugging at her shift, preserving what little modesty she could. "Why not? What is different today? Is it because I'm in heat and you're afraid I'll get pregnant? You don't want a little mix-breed pup?"

"No. Nothing has changed between us. There are other reasons. We have our whole lives," Gionne stated in a tone that brooked no refusal.

"Is there someone else?" Her voice was shakier than she would have liked. She gained her feet and backed away, cursing her own foolishness for ever believing in a lupine.

"Someone else?" His voice sounded bewildered.

"There is, isn't there? You lupine beast, you've been stringing me along all this time. You never had any intention of a permanent relationship with a feline, did you? You Valde dog, you were using me. Did you think I would be easy, that I'd let you mate me without a binding ritual?" Jenna sobbed angrily. Blinded by her fury, it never occurred to her she was the one pressing to consummate the relationship.

Gionne stepped forward. "I'm just asking for some time to deal with a family matter."

She snorted dismissively. "Time's up. Either you want me as your mate now, or never." She panted feeling as if a vise was closing on her chest. Tilting her chin, she boldly met his fierce gaze.

"We must wait," Gionne ordered, his tone uncompromising.

Her lip quivered as she sucked in a shaky breath. "You may wait if you wish. I will return to my own kind and find a mate. I will mate with a real male. One that knows what a female needs." She tossed the lies at him and spun in her tracks, allowing her blonde hair to swoosh past his face.

Darting into the brush, she emerged in the hunched frame and cream coat of her feline form. All the while, he stood stock-still. With one last look and a swish of her long tail, she leapt over a small ravine and bounded for home.

It didn't take long for sounds of his pursuit to reach her ears and she increased her pace. Her heart pounded as his steps drew closer. The thundering crunch of his massive weight seemed at the tip of her tail.

A pleading woof reached her ears but she didn't dare stop.

She was quick, but he was large and closing fast. Abruptly, the threatening skies opened up and a mix of freezing rain and snow poured down upon them making the rocky terrain treacherous. Miscalculating a slippery rock cost her a chance of escape, and as she stumbled, he leapt pinning her to the ground. Arching her back, she tried to throw him off, but he was too heavy. His weight more than doubled her hundred pounds.

In wolf form, he appeared menacing upon her slighter figure. His front legs held her shoulders and head in place. Twisting, she snapped her jaws, trying to bite him, but he held her in place, bringing his elongated muzzle next to her smaller, more rounded one.

"Transform," the sound was more a growl than a word but she understood.

She hissed her negative reply, showing him the sharpness of her fangs. The beast within her did not intend to transform into the more vulnerable human form.

His panting and weight upon her was irritating. She was in heat and his proximity enhanced the ache between her legs. She was embarrassed to realize she could smell her own musk. She could also smell arousal and lust and was unsure if it was his or hers.

She knew he scented it as well. His frame tautened. His low growl mixed with the rumbling thunder overhead.

A mixture of anticipation and trepidation twisted in her stomach as he moved and she felt the prominent length of his arousal at her hip. The Dark Beast was going to take her. He was going to mate her even though he did not want her for himself. She knew she should feel fear, but she did not. Her anger and his rough treatment of her made her want it even more.

Maybe this would be the only time they mated, but she wanted him. She had always wanted him.

Bracing herself for the invasion of the large cock into her virginal passage, she was amazed when, with a powerful jerk, he threw himself from her body.

Trembling with desire and fear, she turned to look at the wolf. Her cat eyes darted to the massive erection jutting from his body and she shuddered. Pulling her eyes from that sight, she met his lust-filled gaze. Dark, hungry eyes with a hint of what might be pain returned her stare.

She ran as if the hounds of hell chased her. She wasn't sure if she was running from him or from something dark she had just discovered about herself.

\* \* \* \* \*

Gionne followed, the scent of her heat filling his senses until he was sure she made it to her stronghold safely. Only then did he allow himself to mourn the loss of his chosen mate. Why did this have to happen? How could he have made such a mess of things? Throwing back his head, he howled his frustration for all lupine and feline to hear.

"Someday, Kitty, somehow you will be mine."

# Chapter One
*Faldron Mountains*
*Two years later*

&

Finally, she was within his grasp. There would be no escape for her this time. Noon tomorrow. The words rang in his ears. Emil had just confirmed the time of their meeting. He had anticipated this day for two years. Yesterday he received the message from the Carbonesse requesting a meeting. Part of his duties as alpha was to monitor the other shape-shifting races and it gave him an opportunity to keep track of Jenna. In recent months, he had witnessed the struggles of the Carbonesse. Several years of drought had led to the inevitable forest fires. The Valde had been lucky in escaping any severe damage to their lands. The felines had not fared as well. Now they sought assistance, he might be willing to help for a price.

The night was quiet, almost as if all the creatures held their breath in anticipation. Wandering into his moonlit, private garden, he followed a winding cobblestone path lined with lupine statues to a hidden frost-brushed bench. With a sigh, he collapsed upon it. Overhead, the brightness of the wolf's moon drew his feral gaze. His mind was troubled. The future of his people perched squarely on his shoulders and sometimes the burden was heavy. Valde and Carbonesse. Lupine and Feline. They had shared this mountain for centuries. Coexistence required wary acceptance of one another's ways and respect for the other's territory. Ultimately, their goals were the same, to live in peace and to keep the outsiders, the humans, at bay. They needed each other to survive.

He needed Jenna to live, the past couple of years he had only existed.

Doubts plagued him, his father's death was a heavy burden to carry but he had to believe that his relationship with Jenna was not the cause of it. His sister Riza made him believe it. How could his father have resented his relationship with a feline when he had loved a feline as well?

Tomorrow he would look into his counterpart's eyes and judge his intent before reaching a final decision, even though he feared in his heart that his decision had been made long ago.

He had known Jenna's brother, Leon Muldrew, as a young male, rash, careless, always out for an adventure. The last couple of years they had met on rare occasion. They had both changed under the weight of leadership. No longer were they the best of friends, but he owed the Carbonesse ruler a personal debt. He would settle the debt tomorrow.

Ominously, a ring encircled the moon. Was it a warning or a sign? He judged he had about a sixteen-hour wait until the fruition of his dreams. It would be a long night.

Lunging to his feet, he paced inside the walled enclosure in an attempt to work off some excess energy. Suddenly, the walls seemed to close in upon him. The beast within him raged as he felt the need to change and let his baser side free.

His clothes now a nuisance, he ripped them off. A single beam of moonlight revealed a face stark with need. Slowly raising one hand, he trailed the tips of his fingers along the ridge on the underside of his erection. A grimace of pain and pleasure contorted his face. Tomorrow the ache that had gnawed at him for so long would end. He could still remember the taste of her sweet cream on his tongue. In his mind, he imagined Jenna's delicate fingers tracing the veins of his cock, her lips parting as he thrust between their lush fullness.

"Tomorrow," he gasped with a tortured breath, ripping his hand away. The familiar tingle of transformation glided up his spine as he threw back his head and howled.

* * * * *

On the other side of the mountain, Jenna Muldrew nervously paced outside her brother's private chamber. She had her hand suspended ready to knock again when Leon jerked the door open.

Anxiously, she asked, "Any news?"

"The messenger just returned; we have set a meeting for tomorrow."

"Where?"

"Noon at the Valde compound."

Jenna stroked a finger across her lips in contemplation.

"Of course you will accompany me. It never hurts to have a beautiful female on your arm while dealing with a Valde."

Jenna chuckled. "Do you think I can influence the Dark Beast?" Dark Beast was the nickname she gave the Valde ruler years ago.

"There was a time when the Dark Beast spent much time sniffing your tail."

"We were but children," she replied flippantly, refusing to give voice to the uncertainties and doubts that plagued her as she thought of seeing Gionne again.

Jenna spun away from her brother's curious eyes. They had never discussed what had caused the ruination of her childhood relationship with Gio. There was a time that the three of them had roamed this mountain as the best of friends. She had thought it more than friendship for Gionne and herself. It had all ended in one day. Leon had been inquisitive, and she wondered if he had gotten any answers from Gio. She certainly had not.

"Of course I will stand at your side but do not expect it to make a difference in his final decision." The exuberance of earlier faded from her voice as her thoughts shifted to another time, the last time she had met with Gio. She straightened and squared her shoulders. She was that child no more. She would not cower or beg.

"Unfortunately, I have learned there is little I can count on," Leon murmured. The last couple of years had been difficult for the Carbonesse, and as alpha, Leon bore the responsibility for it.

Unease churned Jenna's stomach as she headed back toward her private rooms. It had been a long time since she had seen Gio. She wondered if he had changed much. Had he taken a mate? She comforted herself with the knowledge that if he had she would surely know. Nausea rolled through her at the thought. Someone would have told her. She would have felt it in her feral heart.

Restlessness plagued her as she tossed in her bed. The thought of seeing Gionne tomorrow intensified the hollow ache within her womb.

Bolting upright, she flung perspiration-dampened covers from her nude body and ran to her window to perch on the window seat. She threw open the shutters. The view that greeted her was breathtaking, the dense pine-covered mountainside sprinkled with snow, but that was not what drew her from her bed.

The restless sounds of the night greeted her. There it was again. She knew his call. He was out there somewhere. It reverberated through her soul, making the tiny hairs at her neckline stand up. She felt the familiar tingling along her spine, her body's want of the change. When she was young, she had answered his call many times. However, she was not that young girl anymore. The full moon beckoned and she yearned to trot across the mountainside with the crunch of ice and snow beneath her paws. It was out of the question though, at least for tonight. It would be far too dangerous in her current condition. Instead, she curled her frame upon the window seat staring aimlessly out into the night. Dropping her hand between her thighs, her fingers tried in vain to provide relief to the raging heat within.

The howl of a lone wolf echoed through the valley. It was the call to mate. It went unanswered. Her lips curled in a smile. One way or another, tomorrow would alter her destiny.

L.A. Day

# Chapter Two

ॐ

The sun had barely crested the trees to burn off the dense morning fog as Leon and Jenna, accompanied only by two guards, rode on horseback into the Valde stronghold. Jenna drew in a shaky breath at her first glimpse of the Valde home site. Curiosity drew her gaze to the many homes littering the hillside and the ridge above the focal point. Butted up to the mountainside sat a stone palace with detailed architecture rising three stories high. The opulence of the royal household was staggering.

She remembered how Gio had referred to it as "the shack". A shack indeed.

Many of his pack milled about in the courtyard. Two males at the end of the clearing were returning with a fresh kill. One male had long blond hair tied back. He was shirtless and even at this distance she could see his muscles rippling as he adjusted the weight of the deer thrown over his shoulder. It was a reminder of how different the two species were. Never had she seen a half-dressed feline male strut so boldly.

A few children stopped to stare as Jenna and her party grew closer but no one seemed surprised by their arrival. Obviously, they were expected.

The Carbonesse and the Valde were not enemies, but they rarely intermingled. The childhood relationship of Jenna and Leon with Gionne was an uncommon thing.

With destination in sight, Jenna's heart began to palpitate irregularly. Gio was within those walls. With a sense of doom, she realized they were about to come face-to-face. A cold knot of fear formed in the pit of her stomach and she felt a moment of panic as her mind jumped ahead—what if he was indifferent to her? After all this time, the years wasted in hoping, wishing things could be different. What if today she discovered it was truly over? Swallowing back her fear, she lifted her head proudly. If it were over, she would move on and make a life for herself. She would not grovel before this lupine race and certainly not before their pack leader.

Jenna's feline inquisitiveness overwhelmed her good judgment as they ascended the steps to the royal palace. Her childhood meetings with Gio had always taken place in the neutral territory of the forest. She had always wondered about his home.

Two bronze wolf statues stood as guard at the palace entrance. Their artistry was precise, lifelike. Without conscious thought, she reached out a hand to stroke the head of the large male, but at the last moment, she jerked back. Continuing into the massive foyer Jenna noticed several curious members of Gio's pack watching them but when she returned their gaze, they all turned away except for one.

A handsome older male approached and extended his hand to Leon. "Leon Muldrew, I assume."

"Yes." Leon clasped the male's hand before nodding in her direction. "This is my sister, Jenna."

The male's nostrils flared as he scented her. His eyes gleamed before nodding his dark head in her direction. "Please follow me."

Silently they followed the male. To Jenna's surprise and delight, she discovered the long hallway lined with paintings of the past and present Valde rulers. Her astute gaze had no problem identifying Gio. The painting was a masterpiece. Hesitating before the portrait allowed her a moment to peruse the work of art. The piece took in his long flowing hair and masculine features. The artist had managed to capture the feral beauty of the Dark Beast. Over his right shoulder was a rendition of the mountainside in full fall splendor. Atop of the mountain stood a large salt-and-pepper wolf howling at the moon, both man and beast held a remarkable resemblance to the Gionne she had known.

At last, they reached a study that reeked of wealth, from the expensive leather-bound books gracing floor-to-ceiling shelves to the gleaming mahogany desk. "Please wait here, Master Valde will join you shortly."

Left alone to await Gionne, Leon reclined in a leather wing-backed chair. Thus, Jenna took the opportunity to peruse the selection of books. The selection varied from ancient rare texts to technical guides and mystery novels. One particular cover caught her eye. *How to Tame a Wildcat!* A chuckle escaped her parted lips. She would bet this volume belonged to Gio.

The hairs along the back of her neck prickled suddenly and she realized they were no longer alone. Turning, she met the fathomless gaze of the alpha male of the Valde wolf pack. Hungry, brown eyes bore into slanted golden ones. Little had changed in the years they were apart. He had matured. The promise of manhood fulfilled with devastating effects.

Gio's salt-and-pepper hair had always fascinated her. It was longer than she remembered, hanging loosely past his collar, framing a face that was, in a word, beautiful. Thick, dark lashes enhanced eyes the color of rich chocolate. Full, sensual lips softened his high cheekbones and chiseled jaw.

Jerking her gaze from his, she couldn't resist scanning his body. A loose, white silk shirt was partially undone to reveal a tantalizing glimpse of a muscled chest silky with hair. Lowering her gaze farther to his skin tight, black leather pants was a mistake. His stance emphasized the force of his thighs and slimness of his hips and the proud ridge of arousal only enhanced her desire. Her eyes darted back to his face to witness his nostrils flare as he scented her from across the room.

Always the dog.

Her lips curled in a rueful semblance of a smile.

* * * * *

Gionne hardly noticed Leon, as his gaze was riveted on the sleek beauty that was Jenna. Her long blonde hair and cat eyes had always drawn him but her now fully developed female form stirred his untamed blood. As a youth, she had a slim, wild beauty but now her curves had ripened. The clingy shift she wore did little to hide her bountiful assets. Two of which were puckering beneath his gaze, their pebbled crests outlined by the golden, satiny material. As his lupine senses absorbed her essence, his heart hammered. His gaze hadn't missed the hungry way her eyes traveled over him. If it wasn't enough that she was here in his home, his keen senses detected she was coming into heat. She was ripe and unmated. The later was a condition he intended to remedy at first opportunity. Never had a female's scent fired his lust so.

His gaze flew to the other male in the room, Leon, her brother. Of course, Leon realized her condition and brought her to torture him. In the past, the feline male had always enjoyed taunting and tormenting him. He couldn't blame him since he knew the power Jenna wielded over him. Stepping into the room, Gio shut the heavy, wooden paneled door behind him. He did not want her alluring scent to draw a crowd, for he wasn't in the mood to share. "Leon, Jenna, it's been a long time. Welcome to my home." His voice seemed unusually raspy to his own ears.

As he moved to take a seat behind the desk, Jenna scurried to take the chair next to her brother. Gio's lip curled in a mocking smirk. Soon she would be unable to run from him.

"Gionne, thank you for taking time to see us," Leon said.

Gionne inclined his head. His long hair slid forward but he remained quiet. At the moment, he didn't trust himself to speak. Jenna's feminine scent inundated his senses and he struggled to control the beast within. His jaw locked and teeth gritted as blood flowed relentlessly to his cock.

Leon cleared his throat before proceeding with his request. "As you realize, things have been difficult for us these last two years. Much of our hunting grounds were destroyed by the forest fire and then with the drought there hasn't been an abundance of regrowth." Leon hesitated. "We need to expand our hunting grounds," he hurriedly added, "just until the growth is sufficient to draw game back into our areas."

"This is all you seek—additional land to hunt upon," Gionne asked, arching a brow at Leon before running his dark eyes over Jenna. Seated as she was with her legs crossed her shift had risen to mid-thigh. Her pale creamy legs were a delicious sight for a hungry male. A dimple in her knee drew his gaze. He wanted to smooth it with his fingers. He imagined kneeling at her feet and spreading those silky thighs, his tongue lapping the cream he knew was there waiting for him.

She shifted uneasily beneath his gaze. He lifted his eyes to meet hers. Dilated eyes returned his stare but it wasn't fear he read in their depths before she demurely lowered her gaze. Shaking his head, he tried to focus. It was difficult for him to concentrate on anything besides the scent of the female and the heaviness of his groin in his suddenly too tight pants.

"Winter is fast approaching and our supplies are low. I thought perhaps you would help us," Leon offered. Gio realized the other male sensed his plight and would use it to his advantage.

"We aren't here for charity, we will repay you when our part of Faldron Mountain prospers once again," Jenna added. In these male-dominant societies, it was rare for a female to speak in a meeting but neither male objected.

"And if prosperity is long in coming?" Gio quipped.

Leon met Jenna's gaze before looking back at Gionne. "If need be we'll leave the mountain to live among the humans until the area thrives once more."

Gionne's inner beast roared at the thought of Jenna leaving the mountain retreat. The feline race was not always easy to deal with but at least they helped to keep the humans at bay. If they left the mountain, his guards would have more area to cover. In addition, if they lived among the humans their secret was at risk. If discovered, they might reveal the secrets of the Valde as well. He would help them but the cost would be high.

"I will supply you what you need but I ask for something as collateral."

"What do you wish?" Leon asked, his tone suggesting he was suspicious.

Dark, gloating eyes turned to Jenna and a purely male smile appeared revealing strong, white, gleaming teeth. "I will hold Jenna as collateral until I am repaid."

"No," Leon roared.

Gio snarled, "Your choice."

"Boysss," Jenna hissed and two pair of male eyes glared at her. Neither having forgotten how she used to address them both as boys when they thought themselves men. "Enough." The oval pupils of her cat eyes dilated until just a rim of gold was apparent. "Gio, you realize this is impossible. I will not be your captive."

"Why is it impossible? Is there an anxious male awaiting your return?" Gio questioned.

"Several actually," Jenna purred the lie too sweetly. "But that is not the issue, it would not be appropriate. What would my status be, your hostage?" Narrowing her slanted eyes at him, she continued, "Or your bitch?"

Gio cleared his throat. "Think of yourself as my honored guest."

"There must be another solution," Leon replied.

"You do not trust me to host your sister," Gio challenged.

Mocking laughter rang out through the room. "Trust you with my sister." Leon turned to look at Jenna. "It is not that I do not trust you but I doubt your ability to handle a feline female. Jenna may appear submissive but believe me she has a mind of her own."

The insult was evident but Gio chose not to rise to the bait. "I believe I can handle her."

"Ahh, but that is just the point. To honor the deal, my sister would have to remain in the same condition that she is given. So you see you will not be allowed to handle her, after all," Leon replied smugly, his smile catlike as he toyed with Gio.

Gionne's gaze narrowed at the other male. He knew of what he spoke. If he took his sister's innocence, the deal would be broken. He would not be bound to repay any debt. Leon was no fool. He realized it would be impossible for Jenna to stay under Gio's roof for any length of time without him possessing her. Gionne considered the predicament for only a moment. He made his choice the moment he saw her again. Possessing Jenna was worth any price. "Nonetheless, the offer stands."

\* \* \* \* \*

Jenna feared her people would not survive if forced to live side by side with the human race. She would do anything to protect them, even sacrifice herself to the Dark Beast. She would not fool herself. If she stayed here with Gio, their long-buried passions would explode. There was a time she would have willingly become the mate of this Valde ruler but he had spurned her love and shattered her heart.

Observing him closely, she knew he still desired her but in what capacity? To her knowledge never had a lupine and a feline of the royal class mated.

"I accept your offer to remain here as your unwilling honored guest. I do this for my people," Jenna replied before her brother had a chance to speak.

"Jenna, this is a matter for discussion," Leon hissed.

"The decision has been made. I will send an envoy to your stronghold on the morrow. They will bring supplies and advise you of the areas you will be allowed to hunt upon," Gionne declared, relaxing back in his chair. To Jenna's chagrin, an air of wolfish confidence emanated from him.

"You will expect Jenna to return with them," Leon stated.

"No." Gionne rose from his seat and stalked around the desk.

Jenna gaped at him as he approached, the realization of what she had committed herself to dawning on her fully for the first time. She swallowed deeply, desperately trying to force moisture down her parched throat. The tightness of his pants did little to disguise the thick ridge of his arousal and she shifted nervously under his gaze. Breathlessly, she stared up at the male towering over her. Her nipples tightened painfully. She had forgotten the effect his nearness always had upon her. Now that she was a mature female, the effect was even greater. She clenched her thighs against the wetness that had been weeping from her pussy since he walked in the room. Meeting Gio's gaze, she witnessed his nose twitch and she realized he scented her arousal. She damned her body's betrayal.

"She will stay now. They may return with her belongings."

She realized that now he had her within his grasp he would allow her no opportunity to escape. Her hands were shaking; was it fear she felt or something else?

"You will take great care with my sister." The two males stared at each other over her. She witnessed a strange look pass between them. They were both dangerous, predatory animals, alphas of their own clan. She supposed it was a male thing.

"I will treat her as if she were my own," Gionne promised.

"Your own sister?" Leon asked, arching a brow sardonically.

Gio's feral grin was his only answer.

"You will walk your brother out," Leon demanded instead of asking.

"Of course," Jenna said, hurrying to her brother's side, anxious to put some distance between her and the dominant male that would be her host for the time being.

Gionne stalked behind the retreating Carbonesse, stopping at the top of the palace stairs, allowing the siblings a moment alone but not letting Jenna out of his sight. She could feel the hungry eyes devouring her.

"Jenna, it is obvious there is still much feeling between the two of you. It is up to you to make sure that your virtue is not compromised."

"Leon," she rebuffed.

"Jenna, I am serious. Do not mate with that male without a binding ritual. You are a royal, you deserve the honor of being a lifemate not a conquest."

"He is lupine."

"And you are feline and never the two shall meet. Except." Leon glanced up at the male pacing impatiently at the top of the stairs.

"I know that you loved him once. But his father would not accept you."

"You know nothing," Jenna insisted.

Leon drew her into his arms and kissed her forehead. "He wants you now more than ever. If you want him, make him wait. His father is no longer between you. He will take you as his lifemate if that is the only way to appease his hunger."

"I do not wish to be the lifemate of a male who only desires me. I wish to love my mate and be loved in return," Jenna replied. She wondered where Leon had gotten his information since it had not been from her. It must have been

Gio, but did he use his father as an excuse so Leon would not blame him? Or had his father been at the root of their separation? She had no way of knowing since Gio had never bothered to discuss it with her.

"As it should be but desire is a large part of love especially for a male. I have known you both my whole life, he is the only male you have ever responded to with anything close to passion."

"It is not my feelings in question, brother."

With feline grace, Leon vaulted onto the back of his horse. "Remember my words, little sister. I will see you soon."

# Chapter Three

❦

As she watched, her brother disappeared behind a stand of pine trees. She had a sudden urge to call out and stop him. She couldn't stay here alone with Gio. Taking a step forward, she opened her mouth but before she could form a sound, she felt Gio's presence close behind her. Large hands descended onto her shoulders. "Come, Kitty. I will show you to your room."

His breath was a heated caress on her flesh and she melted until the words sank in. Defiantly, Jenna stiffened. Kitty was the nickname he had given her years ago. It reminded her of all they had been to one another and how easily he had let their love wither and die. She shrugged his hands off. She would stay but she would allow no male to be her master. She dashed up the stone stairs of the palace ahead of him.

She hated to admit the palace was impressive. She had grown up in the lap of luxury herself but the lupines lived excessively well. Curious eyes tried to absorb her surroundings as he led her through a maze of hallways but it was difficult to concentrate with his firm fingers grasping her elbow.

As they walked, his thumb leisurely caressed the tender flesh of her inner arm and she realized she was even more susceptible to him than she originally thought.

The massive room he escorted her to was lavish to the extreme. The furnishings appeared to be hand-carved from the many pines that graced their mountainside. The décor was a jungle theme of green and gold, the kind of room she would design for herself. She wondered who had decorated it.

"Through that door is your private bath." Gio gestured with one hand.

"What does this door lead to?" She opened the thick paneled door and Gio's raw male essence engulfed her. The adjoining room was masculine, dominated by the largest bed Jenna had ever seen. A faux fur spread, the exact shade of her feline pelt, covered the bed. Interesting!

She could detect the faintest aroma of a female scent in the room. Whether it was a servant or a mate, she was unsure but jealousy burned in her breast.

Gio followed her into the room. "Your room, I assume," Jenna said.

"Yes. I want to keep you close for your protection."

"Do I need protection?" He rounded on her, closing in, and she backed against the wall. He moved close, his heavily muscled body nearly pinning her. She struggled to break free all the while enjoying her confinement. She was hungry for him and hated herself for it.

Dark, famished eyes watched her then dropped to her shift-covered breast. Desire had her taking rapid, shallow breaths. Her chest heaved and he inched forward allowing her pert nipples to drag against his thick torso. With the wall at her back she couldn't move. Using both hands she shoved at his chest but instead of moving back, he shuffled forward, pinning her against the wall. She felt his heavy arousal as he rolled his hips suggestively. The hot juices she'd been holding at bay began to flow down her thighs. Her heat was ripe upon her.

He licked a path from her collarbone to her ear and then growled. The vibrations shot the length of her spine. She was coming apart.

He grabbed the globes of her ass, lifting her onto his thigh and she lost it. She bucked wildly on the leather-covered steel, her own cream making it a slick ride. Arousal cramped her wet pussy in a wicked spasm of delight as she squirmed in pleasurable agony. She cried out as pulsing release washed over her. She gulped, unable to breathe, the searing, potent pleasure unlike the gentle relief she had occasionally been able to give herself.

Strong arms supported her as she recovered. From beneath lowered lashes, she glanced at his taut, hungry face and he permitted a corner of his lip to rise with amusement.

Embarrassment flooded her checks as she slid from his thigh. It grew worse when she saw the thick cream coating the black leather.

Two fingers gathered the juices and brought them to his lips. Her thighs clenched as she witnessed his long tongue greedily lick every drop. She thought of telling him where he could find more. A whole lot more.

Edging her way into the open doorway, she hesitated.

"Chicken," he said mockingly as he witnessed her retreat.

"I'm not a chicken," she replied, standing straighter.

"No, I guess not. You taste more like a pussy — cat."

She gasped.

"My pussy to be precise," he murmured.

"I don't belong to you."

"You think not." His hand stroked the thigh she had just ridden. "You felt like mine while you straddled my leg." His voice brimmed with sensual promise.

"Please, a log would have worked as well," she snorted.

His brows shot up before settling in a scowl. His hand dropped to the button of the pants riding low on his hips. Another button popped, revealing a trail of dark hair. She gulped.

"Stop." She held up a trembling hand.

Grasping the doorknob, she fiddled with the lock. "Does it lock?"

He arched one dark brow at her comment. "Of course. But tell me, is it me you do not trust or yourself?" His eyes gleamed determinedly.

Arching her back and purring in a purely feline way, she replied, "It's time for a catnap and I learned the hard way never to trust a dog unless he was on a leash."

Jenna enjoyed the sight of his mouth dropping open in shock before she firmly shut the door in his face and flipped the lock into place. There was a lock on both sides of the door but she was willing to wager he would never lock his side. Jenna shimmied out of her gown before curling up on the bed and allowing her body to take what she considered one of its natural shapes. The form was of a beautiful blonde leopard. Her ears twitched at the sound of the low curses from the next room. Anyone watching would have sworn the cat smiled.

\* \* \* \* \*

Gionne cursed himself. "Why the fuck did I ever place a lock on that door?" Stepping into the hallway, a menacing growl emanated from low in his throat. There were too many unattached males wandering about, drawn by her scent. He would have to claim her as his own before one of the others attempted to. There was nothing more dangerous to a wolf pack than an unattached female in heat. Brothers turned on brothers and subordinates could turn on their ruler. When a female reached her age of maturity without taking a mate, she was especially tempting. The older the unmated female was, the more alluring her scent. The feline males must be half impotent and for this, he was thankful.

He stalked back into his room, unwilling to leave his future mate unprotected. Changing into his lupine form, he once again stalked into the hallway. This time the path was clear. Gracefully he padded to her closed door. He rubbed his massive shoulders against the doorframe. Lifting a back leg, he marked the doorway, staking his claim.

The leopard on the bed lifted her regal head and sniffed the scent drifting under the door. She snorted and shook her head then began to preen and fluff her cream-colored coat.

* * * * *

In a darkened doorway down the hall an unseen presence stood. Dark, malevolent emotions engulfed the being. The scent of heat, lust and arousal that drifted into the hallway only antagonized the creature. "No. I won't let it happen again. The Valde bloodline will remain pure. I have done too much to ensure it. That feline bitch has no right to come here and sashay her hot pussy under our alpha's nose."

# Chapter Four

**ɛͻ**

Awaking once again from her nap, the feline was surprised to find the other side of her bed occupied by Gionne.

The feline tilted her blonde head as she distrustfully eyed the male. When he raised a hand, she hissed.

"Don't be scared, Kitty."

The feline jumped from the bed, grasped her shift in her mouth and trotted to the bathroom.

Moments later, Jenna nervously soothed the shift over her curves. Gionne was on the other side of that door. Did she dare open it? She raised her chin. She was a feline. A princess of her people, she would not hide in the bathroom.

The bathroom door creaked as she cracked it open. His lounging form still graced her bed. His eyes were melted chocolate and his smile pure sin.

She squared her shoulders and stepped into the room. "I thought this was my private chamber," Jenna stated.

His lip curled in a purely masculine way.

He patted the bed next to him. "Why don't you come here and we'll talk about it."

"I can talk from here." Jenna perched on the edge of a heavy pine dresser.

"You're in heat," Gio stated matter-of-factly.

Jenna's mouth gaped open. She couldn't believe he would broach such a subject. "I know that."

"You need me."

"I've been in heat before, many times. I've always managed without you."

"I remember the first time you were in heat and we were together. You begged me to take you."

Jenna's insides quaked. She couldn't do this right now. "I don't want to talk about it," she huffed.

"I should have taken you. I should have claimed you and filled you with my seed."

"No."

"You wanted me," he hesitated briefly, "desperately."

"I was a naïve fool. I was young and in love but things change."

He gracefully rolled from the bed. Stalking across the room, he stopped just in front of her. "You still want me."

"Like you said I'm in heat. I have needs. You're not the only male that can give me what I need."

Gio grasped her upper arms and pulled her to him. His thick ridge of arousal pressed into her belly. He dropped his head to her neck. She could hear his ragged breath as he scented her. She clenched her thighs.

"Your scent is pure. You have no mate but you will."

"Is that a threat?"

"A promise." His sinfully wicked voice sent a chill down her spine.

"Promises are made to be broken."

"So are hymens."

"You have a deal with Leon."

"To hell with the deal," Gio roared.

"You won't help my people."

He waved his hand. "Of course, I will help your people and I will help myself." He shifted her against him, dragging her taut nipples across his chest.

Jenna moaned internally.

"You are mine. You've always been mine. Tell me you want me."

She shook her head.

"There's no use denying it. Your lips say no but your pussy weeps for me."

"I'm in heat, any male would do," Jenna lied.

"Don't lie to me. You are pure. If any male would do you would have already fucked one of the felines."

"I didn't want a mate yet. I don't want to answer to any male."

"You'll answer to me. I'm the alpha here."

"So, what does that mean?" she gasped.

"It means if I want to fuck you, I will."

"I have no say in it," Jenna questioned but her unruly body tingled in delight at his words.

"I won't rape you if that's what you mean. You'll have to be willing but I think you are."

"You're wrong." The lie was barely audible.

"Your eyes are dilated and your pussy is hot, wet. The scent of your arousal is driving me crazy."

Jenna tried not so successfully to glare at him.

"You need to be fucked. A thick, hard cock burrowing through that tight cunt. Your juices easing the way as I thrust in and out. You'll tremble around me, stretched to capacity and still I'll give you more."

Jenna whimpered. *Damn, did that pathetic sound come from her?*

"After I've fucked your pussy raw I'll move to that sweet ass of yours."

Jenna gulped.

"It will be so tight. I'll use my fingers to work your cream inside your tight hole to ease my way. Slowly, I'll stretch you but only so much. It will still be a snug fit. Your tight ass will milk my cock much the same as your pussy."

She shuddered at the erotic description his husky voice painted in her mind. She licked her suddenly dry lips. It wouldn't do to let him know what his words were doing to her.

"And that rough little tongue, you don't want to know how many dreams that tongue has starred in. I can't wait to feel its raspy caress on my cock. I want to fill your mouth and throat with every straining inch as I pump my seed into you."

"Gio, please, I can't." She shuddered.

"You can, Kitty. We can. You want me and I need you. It's been so long." He moved against her, notching his erection in the V of her legs. "I can't wait much longer."

"I need time. I have to think," she stalled.

"You had two years. Tell me you want me."

She whimpered.

"Tell me."

She bit her lip. "I—"

\* \* \* \* \*

A knock at the door had Gio growling. "Gionne, are you there? I need a word with you," Emil's voice droned through the door.

"Fuck!" The protest burst from his lips.

"Gionne." The voice grew louder.

"Okay." Gionne raked his hair back and sat Jenna away from him. He felt like his head was about to come off. Did his people not realize he needed to claim his mate?

Gio cracked the door open. "This had better be good," Gio grumbled.

"Pack business."

"Is this urgent because—"

"There are invaders close to our lands. The guards await you."

Gionne shut his eyes, cursing. The fates obviously conspired against him. "Give me ten minutes."

With a deep breath, Gio turned back to Jenna. She now huddled near the window with her arms wrapped protectively around herself. He had probably lost all the ground he had fought so hard to gain with her.

"I guess you get your reprieve after all." He tried to smile but it was more a grimace.

His cock raged in objection as he stomped into his room in search of cold water or possibly ice.

* * * * *

The feline awoke alone in her room. The scent of the alpha male was strong but he was not around. However, her senses detected the presence of others. Crossing the room to the window, she hopped onto the sill. A cool breeze from the open window ruffled her coat. It was a two-story jump, well within her means. She had the need to stretch her limbs. With feline grace, she landed with a crunch as all four paws contacted the frosty ground only to realize her mistake. Several large male wolves surrounded her. The largest one was solid white. There were two black male wolves and one smaller male in shades of brown. None were the salt-and-pepper color of Gionne. She knew she was in grave danger.

The two black males approached her from the front, flanking her. The immature brown hung back as if he were unsure of his role. The white male was close behind her. Her sensitive ears detected the sounds of him sniffing her scent. She knew she would only have one chance before they were on her.

With the lightning speed of a cat, she spun and whacked the largest white male across the nose with her fully extended claws. A bright stream of blood spurted in the wake of her paw. As he yelped, momentarily stunned by the attack, he jumped back. That was the opportunity she needed to sprint to the closest tree. She was perched on a limb well out of their reach before they could react. Her long tail thumped against a limb as she watched the outsmarted wolves circling below. Suddenly a commotion to the right caught her eye. A massive salt-and-pepper wolf was on the scene. Snarling and growling his displeasure, he was a remarkable sight. Immediately, she recognized Gio.

Fierce chocolate eyes observed her on her perch for a moment before he turned back to the others. The young brown male tucked tail and ran, two of the wolves bowed their heads. It appeared the white male thought to challenge but eventually he submitted to his alpha as well.

The leopard curiously observed the wolves below, pleased the younger wolves submitted to their leader. She had no wish to be the cause of violence within the wolf pack. Soon, there was only one wolf remaining at the bottom of the tree regarding her with concerned eyes.

If he thought she would meekly climb down the tree to his side, he was mistaken.

With no thought of modesty, the Dark Beast transformed to Gionne.

The leopard's eyes dilated at the sight, to her knowledge felines never transformed in public. Jenna never changed in the presence of another, not even her brother. Unblinking eyes stared, and even as a leopard, she knew an impressive male when she saw one. His shoulders were broad his chest thick but narrowed to trim, rippling abs. A fine pelt of dark hair narrowed to a strip at his waist then spread out once again to surround the large, jutting shaft of his maleness. The feline wondered if it was wrong to admire the human side of this male.

\* \* \* \* \*

Stalking on two legs to the tree, Gio effortlessly swung himself up onto the first branch. Her unblinking eyes never left him as he shifted closer to her. He stopped when he was within a foot of her and reclined in the fork of the tree. "Here, Kitty, Kitty," he crooned.

Jenna hissed at him, baring her fangs. She didn't appear to be in a playful mood.

Inching closer, he extended his hand, intending to stroke her downy coat. She growled low in her throat and her fur stood on end. Slowly, he lowered his hand. He did not want to scare her. In his present form, he was very vulnerable to an attack from an angry, distrustful feline. Obviously, the lusty males had frightened her and he couldn't blame her. Terror had left him motionless for a moment when he saw them surround her. He feared he would not arrive in time to save her from a brutal, forced mating. It was not the usual way of the Valde males to force their females but Jenna was in heat and an outsider. She did not garner the respect of a pack member. That would soon change.

"It's all right, Jenna, I'm here now. I will allow no one to harm you."

As he watched, her fear dissolved by degrees. First, her fur relaxed and then her eyes resumed a less dilated state. Finally, she stretched her front paws, brushing his leg. When she extended her claws and flexed, two pinpricks of blood appeared on his thigh. He did not utter a word. For at heart, he was feral as well and knew of the games she played.

She arched and stretched before padding forward. She stopped at his side, lying next to him and placing her head on his bare lap. He smiled at this submissive act. She had always been more affectionate as a feline than as a human.

As soon as she settled, he began to stroke her luxurious pelt. He remembered the many times the man in him had petted her and the times the wolf had playfully rubbed against her, longing to lay claim to her. The feel of her soft coat beneath his palms called to the beast within him. Her warm breath and the rumble of her purr against his naked thighs did not help the situation but he could not allow the beast loose while they perched precariously in a tree. He felt certain anything else would shock her senseless.

Jenna laid her head in his lap as if she were a contented housecat. Rolling over, she allowed him to stroke her underside. As his fingers threaded through her pelt, he noticed puckered nipples beneath her coat.

Gionne sucked in a sharp breath.

He always wondered if she was attracted to him while she was in feral form.

She purred deeply and rubbed the back of her head against the burgeoning flesh of his arousal. He would take that as a yes. A rough lap of her tongue across his lower thigh nearly unseated him from the tree.

His cock throbbed and he eyed her tongue longingly but those gleaming white fangs brought him to his senses. He didn't trust her that much—yet. Besides the fork of a tree was not the place to indulge his carnal urges.

"Jenna, I need to get you inside where I know you are safe. Will you climb down for me?" Gionne was not concerned about the young males returning but she was in serious danger from him. This was definitely not the place to pursue her, but the longer they stayed entwined in the tree the more his resolve would weaken.

She sighed. Rolling over, she stretched then with graceful agility she bounded from the tree. Sitting on her haunches, she waited for him to climb down. When he stood at her side, her long, rough tongue darted out to lick the two fine streams of blood from his thigh.

That raspy caress of her tongue sent a jolt of lightning straight to his groin but before he could react, she trotted in front of him toward the palace. He watched in rapt fascination before slowly trailing after her. The beast within watched the sway of her hips and the twitch of her long tail. The feel of her rough tongue licking his thigh had ignited an inferno that threatened to burn out of control.

While he followed behind her, his initial anger at her for leaving her room unprotected resurfaced. Taking her up the back stairs, they encountered no one on their way. He assumed much of his pack was currently hiding from his wrath. He opened the door to her room, and then followed her inside.

* * * * *

She trotted toward the bed. Suddenly, a lupine Gio pounced from behind, pinning her against the bed frame.

The more Jenna struggled the more weight he pressed against her. Finally, she stood still. She would concede this battle. Abruptly his weight shifted and he placed one massive paw across her front shoulders, forcing her to the ground. She arched against him, trying to break free but quickly found herself pinned beneath his bulk.

After asserting his dominance, he lay quietly half on top of her with his muzzle very close to hers. His brown eyes bore into hers until she thought he tried to mesmerize her. She began to struggle again and he growled low in his throat and nipped her shoulder in warning.

The bite wasn't truly painful but regardless she settled once again. This time he began to lick her face and neck. When she tried to shake him loose, he growled and nipped her again.

Okay, she got the picture. He expected her to submit to him. If she chose to struggle, he would punish her. She would allow him his victory to a point. She lay submissively while he licked her upper half. When she felt him rise, she was unsure of his intentions but she didn't move until he made the next move. He shifted position, nudging her tail and she knew what he intended.

The leopard hissed in outrage and tried to spin on him but he dropped his weight onto her. They struggled for position and she sunk her teeth into mostly fur. Then she felt the tingling sensation come over her and without her consent she shape-shifted back to her human form. Jenna was horrified, she'd never shape-shifted spontaneously before and never in front of another being, period.

Spitting the wolf hair out of her mouth, she found herself eye to eye with the lupine Gio. Of course, Jenna had met up with Gio in this form before but never at this proximity and certainly never while she was unclothed.

The massive wolf was heavy, pinning her to the floor. His warm, wet tongue darted out, licking her cheek with a long, slow drag. Swallowing nervously, she placed her hand against his chest and shoved. He didn't move. Silky hair enclosed her hands. That same silky hair rubbed against other parts of her body. Other naked parts of her body. She squirmed and he shifted. This wasn't good, especially since it felt a little *too* good. She hoped he couldn't feel her erect nipples poking into him. His muzzle nuzzled her ear. Hot breath sent shivers racing down her spine.

"Hungrrry," he growled in a guttural tone against her ear. Understanding the word, she froze beneath him. What exactly did he mean? Jenna didn't have long to ponder the question. She felt more than heard his low growl. Then, before her eyes, he transformed until the human half of Gio lay naked on top of her, still pinning her to the floor.

If she thought she was in a predicament before now she was in true danger.

# Chapter Five

**ഇ**

Gionne grinned and slid his body rhythmically against hers to confirm that they were both completely naked. Her distended nipples poked into his chest and he forced one leg between her thighs before she could clench them shut.

"You can get off now," Jenna demanded, attempting to twist free before he noticed the cream seeping from between her thighs.

Gionne threw back his head and roared with laughter. "So you give me permission to get off. How nice of you," he purred, lowering his head to nuzzle her neck. "Do you wish to get off as well?"

Jenna's body suffused in color from head to toe. She realized her mistake as soon as the words left her mouth. "You know what I meant."

"Mmm, I doubt that you even know what you meant."

"Gio, this isn't funny anymore," she gasped, not disguising the panic in her eyes. She shoved against his chest, trying to dislodge him. He shifted his leg between her thighs and his eyes flared at his wet discovery. That solid thigh rocked against her pussy and she tried not to whimper.

"Was it ever?" His voice was a sexy rumble.

His nearness swamped her senses. His male vitality seeped into every pore in her body. With every breath, his silky chest hairs tickled her erect nipples. She couldn't breathe and she thought she was beginning to pant. It had to stop now or it would be too late. "Gio, please," she begged, her lower lip trembling.

"I will," Gionne groaned.

"No, Gio, we can't." Her mouth was dry, her throat ached.

"You are wrong—we can. We must, it is the only way to ensure your safety," he growled these words.

"You will rape me to ensure my safety," she cried.

"It will not be rape. I will not force you." His voice bespoke confidence and she feared he was right. After all, she was in heat, aroused and he was Gionne. Her Gionne.

"What do you call this?" Her strained voice held a note of humor.

"Persuasion," he purred, his hot breath caressing her face, the scent was spicy, male, Gio. It reminded her of his untamed taste.

"I want you so much. I need you, Kitty." His words melted something inside her but she refused to give in. With a hiss, she willed herself to transform. She would slice him to ribbons.

He seemed to sense her plan. Grasping her wrists, he forced her arms to extend fully above her head. Gio's mouth took full possession of her lips, forcing them apart. His tongue demanded entrance and devoured. Probing the depths of her mouth, he licked and stroked the sensitive tissue. Sharp teeth grazed her lips, nipping then suckling the tender flesh. She moaned deeply into his mouth and he shuddered atop her.

In this position, it was impossible to transform and his mouth distracted her, scattering her wits, not allowing her to focus on transition—as if she even would at this point.

One large hand held her smaller ones over her head, leaving his other hand free to roam. Deepening the penetration of his thigh between her legs, he rubbed the corded muscles against her softness and she felt dripping juices greet the intrusion. His free hand engulfed her breast and his rough thumb flicked the aroused tip. Long fingers massaged the aching fullness and they swelled even more. Lying fully upon her for the first time, she felt the steely length of his erection along her stomach. Her legs involuntarily clenched against his thigh.

At the sound of her whimper, he asked, "Do you concede?"

Jenna's body was on a slow meltdown and the heady flavor of arousal filled her senses. It appeared he was going to take her and she was ready. More than ready. Then his words registered. How dare he ask her permission? If he wanted her, he would have to take her by force. She would not submit to him willingly, at least not verbally.

"Never."

"Never is a long time." His deep voice filled with regret.

Before she could reply, he leaped to his feet, dragging her with him. Twisting her arms behind her back, he allowed her no opportunity to transform. The position was not painful but it wasn't comfortable either. Forcibly, he walked her in front of him into his adjoining room.

"You mentioned putting me on a leash but I think I'll reverse the positions. I'll leash my little pussy cat." As he spoke one hand caressed her ass then thick fingers slid between her legs, running through her folds. With a satisfied grunt he withdrew his fingers, spreading her thick cream all the way to her rectum.

"You wouldn't dare," she cried in outrage, or was it excitement? Her body trembled with desire. Shame filled her to know such dominant behavior aroused her.

Holding her arms behind her back, he forced her to bend over the bed. Her face buried in the fur covering, leaving her ass tipped up in the air. She felt exposed, vulnerable. Thickly muscled thighs pressed against her bottom and his torrid cock brushed her lower back. Expecting to be ravaged, she was surprised and quite possibly disappointed when he reached beneath the spread and ripped the sheet from the bed.

She struggled as he began tearing the sheet into long strips. Pressing her farther into the bed, his arousal now rested against the crack of her ass. She groaned. He shifted, the silky head of his cock brushed her anus teasingly.

Jenna was unsure exactly what he planned but she feared she was going to enjoy it too much. The feel of that thick, hard length nudging her bottom had her on edge, almost ready to beg.

A hand caressed her ass again. "You deserve to be spanked for your little stunt earlier." His hand came down firmly on one cheek.

"Obviously, your father did not teach you to obey as he should have."

His hand came down to deliver a stinging blow to her other cheek. She gasped. That one had stung but it also caused her pussy to throb in need. "Stop, Gio. That hurts."

His hand connected once more to the sensitized flesh of her bottom. She cried out, blinking rapidly.

His hand once again caressed the susceptible flesh of her bottom. His mouth joined his hand, kissing and licking the tender mounds. "Your skin is pink and hot." He nibbled. "Endanger yourself again and I will blister this flesh before I fuck it raw."

She squeaked.

Suddenly he flipped her onto her back on the bed and tied one wrist and then the other to his bedposts with the satin strips of sheet. This effectively stopped her from attempting to transform, but he was not finished. He strapped each of her legs as well. Adjusting the straps, he made sure they were tight. Struggling was useless. She lay spread as wide open as possible for him to peruse.

A flush of embarrassment covered her. The heat of excitement quickly followed it. He stood at the foot of the bed, all male, honed muscle, unashamedly naked and aroused. Jenna had never seen a naked, aroused male before. She had vague memories of watching him transform earlier while she was in feral form. Those memories did not do him justice. She couldn't tear her eyes from his erection. It was long and thick with an enormous blunt head. Fear began to tinge her arousal. He would hurt her with that thing. Her fearful eyes darted to his face. His eyes gleamed.

"Gio, I demand you untie me." Her voice didn't even sound convincing to her own ears. Damn, how could he do this? Her ass still stung but her pussy throbbed anyway. How could he make forced intercourse so appealing? Certainly, her enjoyment of this must be a character flaw.

\* \* \* \* \*

Gionne arched a dark brow but he didn't reply. He felt a twinge of remorse at the necessity of binding her but it was not enough to deter him. What he did, he did for both of them. He feared Jenna's proud spirit would not allow her to submit willingly to his dominance.

"You are a beast, I named you well."

"I never denied it." His eyes devoured her. His heated gaze drank in the sight of her hairless, soft pink folds. They were plump and glistening with arousal. When they were young, Leon told him that feline females had no hair on their pussy. At the time, he thought it was odd but now looking upon her naked folds, he found it extremely sexy. Her flesh lay bare, begging for his tongue, mouth and cock. Finally, his gaze was able to leave the fount of his desire and travel over the rest of the treasures he had uncovered. Abundantly full breasts with rosy peaked nipples drew more than a passing glance. However, it was on the beauty of her face that his gaze ultimately rested. He sat down on the bed next to her, close but not touching.

"You won't really force me. Will you?" she asked.

"There are many kinds of force."

"If I am unwilling, will you force me?" She demanded an answer.

"Force is too strong of a word. I prefer persuade," he replied, his voice laced with intent. She would be his one way or the other.

Moving as slow as his raging hormones would allow, he raised a trembling hand and brushed the smooth blonde hair back out of her face. The pale color blended into the faux fur spread upon his bed. "Do you feel this fur beneath your skin? I bought it on impulse. I couldn't resist covering my bed in a fur so similar to your pelt. Don't worry though, it's not real; I didn't kill one of your breed to adorn my bed."

"You're sick, you know that," Jenna stated.

Gio chuckled. Leaning close, his breath was a caress on her heated flesh. "Sometimes I lie naked on this fur and run my hands through it as if it was your pelt. I imagined that it was you lying beneath me." He hesitated a moment. "Do you want to know what I did next?" He thought to describe taking himself in hand and finding release as he dreamed of her.

Jenna hissed, showing the sharpness of her teeth. She closed her eyes and groaned. "Shut up, just shut up."

Gionne enclosed a breast in his hand, testing its fullness. The tight peak jabbed at his palm. Her skin was so soft, softer even than her luxurious feline pelt. "But unfortunately it wasn't you." His thumb lazily stroked her nipple. "Did you know that even in feline form when I stroke you, your little feline nipples harden?"

"That's disgusting, you — beast."

"You won't think so soon. And you haven't met my true beastly self — yet." His chuckle ended in a growl.

"Is this the only way you can get laid? You have to kidnap and tie up females."

A low fierce growl erupted from his lips. "I did not kidnap you."

"No, but you know I'm not here willingly." She looked at him then continued. "Duh, I'm tied to your bed."

"Your words say you are not willing. Your body speaks differently." Knowing fingers tweaked a taut nipple, before tracing a pattern across trembling abs. Reaching her female core, he inserted a finger, teasing her clit. She was hot and wet, in need of a good fuck. Raising cream-covered fingers to his lips, he suckled the moisture. "Delicious," he murmured then dipped his fingers again. She bucked beneath his hand. This time he brought his fingers to her lips. "Do you want to taste how delectable you are?" She clamped her lips together and tossed her head from side to side. He ran his fingers across her lips then he leaned forward, his tongue lapping behind his fingers. "Sorry, you taste too delicious to share."

"Look, you lupine bastard—"

"If I were you I'd shut my mouth before I decide to fill it with something." He issued the low warning with a husky chuckle.

"Well, if I were you I wouldn't place anything of value in my mouth because I might bite it off." Her slanted feline eyes flashed at him.

"Enough," he roared, tired of this verbal sparing match.

Jenna gulped and a look of fear filled her eyes.

Gionne's nostrils flared as he scented her. He knew mentally she resisted him but the female essence of her body called to him. She was a mature feline in heat and needed a mate. He would be that mate.

\* \* \* \* \*

He stretched out alongside her, leaning over until his long hair cascaded forward to brush the tips of her breasts. She hissed but not in outrage. The long silken strands tantalized her pebbled peaks.

His skilled fingers rolled the tip of one breast between his thumb and finger, while his ardent mouth dropped to the other breast. He suckled her, nipping her with his sharp canines. At first, the suckling was gentle, and then he drew her nipple deeper into his mouth and pulled powerfully upon the tip, sending arcing currents of electricity straight to her clit.

Jenna could not speak. She could only gasp for air to fill her burning lungs. Tremors shook her thighs and the muscles of her stomach began to contract rhythmically. She strained against her bonds trying to get away — to get closer.

Slowly, Gionne pulled back to kneel between her wide-open thighs. "Don't fight it."

Jenna gulped as she looked at him. From the nest of dark hair between his thighs, his shaft jutted long and hard. The length and girth was enormous and it bobbed in a sinful rhythm. Raising her gaze to his face, she met his eyes.

Intent fierce eyes gazed with hunger but his voice was softly coaxing. "Accept me willingly and I will fulfill your every want and desire."

She knew what he asked of her. Her consent. She couldn't, wouldn't give it. She wouldn't give him that power over her. Tied to his bed, spread-eagled, her sex dripped at the thought of Gio dominating her. How did he manage it? It was humiliating but she would not verbally surrender. "No," she muttered between her clenched teeth.

A feral gleam ignited in his eyes before he blinked and shuttered his gaze from her. Lowering his eyes, his long thick lashes hid the hunger burning in his gaze from her.

He perused her splayed body as if it were a banquet and he a starving male. He licked his full male lips.

Jenna flinched and shut her eyes tightly when she saw him move. She expected him to try to shove that thick shaft between her virginal nether lips. Her eyes popped open at the touch of his soft lips nuzzling her so intimately. "No, Gio— no," she pleaded as she watched his face disappear between her spread thighs, this was too much. She wanted — no, needed — the pain of his possession so she could hold on to her anger, not this soft caress. The gentleness of his lips contrasted with the rough stubble on his face and the effect was mind-boggling. His long tongue lapped and her juices flowed. Large hands engulfed her ass, spreading the globes as he slurped his way from anus to clit and back again.

She begged and pleaded but he ignored her requests. He seemed as if he didn't even hear her he was so absorbed in his task.

She had thought his lips and tongue a sweet torture beyond endurance until his fingers joined in the play. His lips suckled her folds, his tongue flicked at her clit and a finger inserted into her tight canal. Her back arched, straining her muscles. This was too intense, and she tried to break away.

Slowly, the finger progressed, deeper then deeper still. His sharp teeth grazed her clit and she felt her inner muscles begin to flex around his finger. Swamped with emotion she was startled when he slowed his ministrations, leaving her hanging on the edge.

"Gio, please," she begged, unashamed for the moment of her need.

He pulled back, letting his finger dance along her wet heat. Her head was frantically tossing from one side to the other. Long perspiration-damp hair was sticking to her face. "What do you want, my little pussy cat?" His voice was husky with desire but his feral grin was smug, taunting and confident he would get what he wanted.

"Stop…I want you to stop," she lied.

"Stop." He snorted in disbelief. "Stop what…this?" he asked as he added another finger. "Or this?" His thumb found her clit and he worked the nub in a circular motion. Tighter and tighter, he coiled the tension in her untried body. Her clit was hard and erect beneath the callus-roughened pad of his thumb.

An unladylike moan escaped her lips. Then she bit down on her lower lip, trying to stop her groaning vocalization.

Unable to help herself, she cried out.

"Ask me, damn it," he demanded, losing what little patience he had.

"Gio, please…"

"Please what?" His thumbnail flicked the tight nub.

"Me…please me," she begged on a whispered breath as she lost the will to resist.

*  *  *  *  *

With a feral growl, he descended upon her. He kissed her deeply and she responded, her tongue meeting every thrust. The large, blunt head of his cock probed the virgin passage. She was wet but tight. He knew he was going to hurt her. He nudged her opening and crooned sweetly to her.

"Relax, little one. You're so fucking tight and I don't want to hurt you." He groaned.

"I'm in pain, Gio. I ache."

"I know, Kitty." He edged an inch into her and felt her tight confines stretch. Their eyes collided and he fought for control over his emotions as he witnessed pain cloud her luminous eyes.

Using his thumb, he rolled her clit, bringing her once again to the brink of orgasm. With a series of retreats and thrusts, he managed to deepen his penetration. Her legs quaked and her inner muscles contracted around him.

She gasped as he butted up against her maidenhead and her eyes widened. Leaning forward he kissed her deeply, thrusting his tongue into her mouth much the same way his cock thrust within her.

With a flick of his knowing thumb, she shattered beneath him and he thrust through the proof of her innocence. His thighs quaked with the restraint it took to lie still within her hot depths.

When her shudders subsided, he slowly thrust farther, still seeking the deepest penetration.

"Gio, I can't take any more."

"You can take it. You can take me." He grasped her hips, pulling her toward him as he rammed forward. She arched, allowing him better access. Her eyes rolled back in her head and once again, she spiraled over the edge into an abyss of pleasure.

Tight inner muscles spastically milked his cock and he had to grind his teeth to stop himself from finding his own satisfaction too soon.

Tentatively, he withdrew and thrust deeper. Her tight, sopping heat enveloped him and spurred his ardor. He could feel the beast rising inside him but he fought to stay in control. Her moans of delight were his undoing and he began to stroke deeply, powerfully within her.

Soon, he felt her body begin to spasm again and he thrust harder, convulsing within her, releasing his seed deep into her womb. Slowing his thrusts, he smiled into the side of her neck.

She was his.

After all the wasted time, she was finally his. He had taken her, marked her, hopefully planting his seed. No one could dispute his claim.

Leaning back, he looked at his beautiful mate. She had her eyes closed so he was unable to gauge her reaction. Her body's reaction had been explosive but he feared her feelings might be more difficult to sway.

A shudder shook her frame as she opened misty eyes to meet his. The golden pools were full of wonder, shock, longing and a little horror, before she blinked and shuttered her gaze.

"You can release me now that you're done."

"I'm far from done." He enclosed her breast and the stiff nipple jutted into his palm. "I'll never be finished," he murmured in a hoarse voice as he dipped his head, his mouth descending on her already sensitized lips. Plundering, his tongue licked at her teeth and the inside of her mouth. He would never tire of the taste or feel of this female.

\* \* \* \* \*

*Holy fuck*, she thought as her vagina jerked in response. How could her body betray her again so soon? Losing the battle not to respond, she arched up, seeking closer contact.

"What is it you want, my tongue or my cock? Or both?"

Jenna tossed her head, unwilling to answer.

"Tell me. I want the words." He bent his head, nipping a turgid nipple then powerfully sucking it until she screamed. Thick fingers probed at her sex but it wasn't enough.

"Gio," she gasped ardently.

He shook his head, salt-and-pepper hair sliding over his shoulders. "I need more than that," he demanded.

Feeling his fingers slip out, she thought he might end her torture until she felt them slide down an inch or so. "No, Gio, no."

"Yes," he insisted.

The blunt, broad tip of one finger slipped into her anus and she felt the tight hole contract around the penetration. Jenna gasped a shaky breath at the slight discomfort. The finger slid deeper. "What are you doing?"

"Teaching you. Teaching you your body belongs to me. Your pussy is mine to take. Your ass is mine and I will take it, and you'll love it."

"I'm my own person."

"Be your own person but your body is mine." Leaning back, he ripped first one then the other ankle restraint from the posts. "I am your alpha and your mate and you will obey me in all ways, especially sexually or there will be consequences." Kneeling between her thighs, his hot cock rubbed against her folds and she moaned and wiggled against him.

"Now," she pleaded.

The tip of his cock perched at her entrance. She wanted so much to pull him forward, burying him to the hilt where she needed him most but she couldn't move her hands.

"Tell me who owns your body."

She bit her lips and hesitated. The blunt tip of his cock nudged her clit. "I'm waiting."

"You do," she cried and he plunged fast and deep before she could finish telling him. He angled her hips and withdrew achingly slow. Bringing her legs together in front of him, he wrapped one large hand around her ankles, the other under her ass, holding her up off the bed. His slow, deep thrusts whetted her appetite.

His thumb buffeted her clit before sliding down the dripping trail to her ass. When his thumb drove into her tight hole, his rhythm changed, increasing in tempo. "You're so wet and tight, you're killing me."

Jenna panted, trying her best to thrust back against him. She was full, stretched, the pleasure unbearable. The muscles of her stomach clenched as pleasure exploded and waves of orgasms rolled over her. She couldn't have stopped her feral cries of satisfaction if she wanted too.

Floating back to consciousness, her body was empty but the throbbing cock now lay against her stomach. Looking from his distended member to his gleaming eyes, she knew he was far from finished.

\* \* \* \* \*

Gionne's cock throbbed as he waited for her recovery. As her eyes fluttered open, he licked his lips. Lifting her hips, he spread her flesh and flicked his tongue over her. Her tasty cream a sweet treat that he had earned. Her taste only made him hungrier and he devoured. Her cries echoed in his ears but he refused to stop until the throbbing ache between his legs demanded release. Kneeling between her thighs, he eyed the reddened, swollen folds that still gleamed with her release.

Dipping the head of his cock into her cream had her moaning. He knew she was tender but his cock demanded release. The rosebud opening of her anus drew his eyes. His cream-coated cock nudged the entrance.

Jenna's eyes popped open wide and her body went rigid.

"Relax, Kitty," he soothed, inching inside the tight channel. Holding the beast at bay, he willed himself to edge slowly. Her eyes dilated. "Breathe and relax. You can take me fully this way." Withdrawing to the tip, he thrust forward. Her eyes shut, and her mouth sucked in with a little "Ohhh" sound.

"Are you all right?" he asked.

She gulped and nodded. Her eyes glimmered golden.

He slid farther. Her breath left her body in a lusty hiss. He pulled back until just the head of his cock filled her tight passage. He rotated his hips. She groaned.

"I'm going to take you now long and hard." She whimpered and he surged forward.

Her slick canal parted, accepting his domination. "You are so fucking tight I could come right now but I won't." He spread the globes of her ass farther. "I'm going to pound your ass until you scream." He withdrew and plunged. She whimpered little kitten mewing sounds that nearly drove him wild.

"Mine," he announced as he pumped his hips. "Mine, all mine." Once he had hilted himself in her heat there was no stopping him. He pounded back and forth in an age-old rhythm.

"Gio," she screamed. Her back arched and her legs wrapped around him trying to pull him deeper.

Her body clenched around his cock, milking the torrid flesh. He bit his lip, fighting for control over the raging beast within. Using one hand to support her hips the other was free. Two fingers plunged into her weeping vagina and she bucked again as another orgasm racked her body.

Her hair was perspiration-dampened and clinging to her face, her eyes dilated, and her mouth hung open in a gasping pant. She was the most beautiful sight he had ever seen.

"Gio, no more…no more," she pleaded.

He thrust forward and held his ground, deeply embedded in her as a constant pressure. His fingers fucked her pussy. His balls tightened to bursting. His cock throbbed.

"Come with me, Kitty," he groaned.

His hips fired as if by pistons, his fingers kept pace.

Her body clenched as his seed spurted free. As the dam burst inside him, he threw back his head and howled.

Yanking loose the remaining ties, he rolled bringing her to lie on top of him. His sweat-covered chest rose and fell rapidly as he tried to catch his breath. He had won this battle of wills but he feared there was war ahead.

# Chapter Six

ᔥ

Jenna felt the restraints release and found herself on top of Gionne. She wasn't ready to talk. Without looking at him, she rolled off him and his bed and bounded to her room on legs barely able to support her. Scooping up her shift, she tugged it on over her head. Shaking hands smoothed the fabric into place.

Gionne quickly followed behind her. His rasping pant made her shiver. Grabbing the jungle print comforter, she wrapped it around her as a shield as she scooted up the bed. Her accusing eyes flashed his way.

"If you expect an apology you will be disappointed. I did what I needed to. As alpha, it is my right to make decisions, and I will make them as I see fit. You are mine and I had to claim you or there would be more incidents as before." His voice was hoarse, the torment evident.

"What would you have done if one of them…if one of them…" She couldn't vocalize the question.

"If one of them had taken you first and claimed you I would have killed him. They are of my pack but I would have killed the male that claimed you. Then I would have taken you and claimed you and any child you conceived."

"And if you weren't the father?"

"I will be father to any child you bear." He sat tentatively on the edge of the bed. "I will father your offspring. I may have already."

As she parted her lips to speak, he pressed his fingers lightly against their swollen fullness. "Don't say anything now. It has been a stressful day. Prepare yourself for dinner and I'll return for you in an hour. Don't be afraid, I'll post a guard at your door. After tonight you will be safe."

"Don't you see this is wrong, we are wrong?" Jenna asked, gesturing with her hand.

"There is nothing wrong with a male and a female mating."

"But you tied me up and I—"

"I'm sorry, if I scared you. But you seemed to enjoy it." His hand cupped her chin, lifting her head. "Look at me. Didn't you enjoy our coming together?"

Jenna's eyes darted away. Of course, she enjoyed it and he knew it but she couldn't admit it. "You forced me," she whispered.

"In the end, you begged me," Gio replied tersely. "I could make you beg again."

Jenna jumped. "So, is that what you enjoy? Force?" She had to know if he liked it as well, or if it was only her.

"It is not required, but I have to admit I enjoyed having you at my mercy. Can't you be an adult and admit what you want?"

That irked her, just because he was three years older and a lot more experienced didn't mean she was a child. "Fine. I liked it. Is that what you wanted to hear? I enjoyed the ties. I liked feeling helpless, dominated. So, what does that make me?" Jenna all but sobbed.

Gio pulled her close. "It makes you perfect, desirable. I am an alpha male. I enjoy a submissive, willing mate in my bed."

"Is there something wrong with me?" she questioned.

"No. You're fine, perfect in fact."

"Just one thing, I enjoyed what we shared. I like to be dominated in bed. Here I can accept..." She lowered her eyes demurely. "Even enjoy being the sex toy but when we walk out that door I want to be your equal."

A grin tugged at the corners of Gio's mouth. "You mean I can't dominate you in the bathroom. Because I have this fantasy of you…"

Jenna forcefully jabbed him in the ribs, and was pleased to hear him grunt. "That's not what I meant."

"I have no desire to master you, but at times for your own safety you must obey me. Otherwise, you may do as you please, within reason as long as you respect the fact that I am alpha of the pack." His voice was a sexy rumble. "However, when we mate I prefer to take control. If I tell you to suck my cock, I expect you to drop to your knees."

Jenna blinked rapidly. It was disgusting how much such words turned her on.

A finger lifted her chin. "You like to be talked to like that, don't you?"

Jenna felt heat flush her face.

"Admit it."

Jenna nodded her head, letting her hair slide around to cover her face.

"Don't hide from me. Nothing that we do together is wrong as long as we both want it."

Relaxing against him, she began to feel as if this might work. Suddenly she felt him stiffening and pulling away. "What's wrong?" she asked looking at his scowl.

"Earlier, when you were surrounded, did that excite you? Did you want them to fuck you?" he asked curiously.

"I have to admit, they were handsome wolves." She had been scared when they surrounded her, but excited as well. She didn't want them to force her but the thought of four males touching and licking her the way Gio had wasn't unappealing and that thought was somewhat frightening.

"Yeah, I was kind of hot for them. That's why I gouged Whitey and jumped into that tree," she finished mockingly. Gio need never know her fantasies.

"It is good that I was your first. Of course, no other will ever please you as much."

Jenna wondered at his words, he spoke of mating and claiming and in the next breath, it sounded as if he thought she would mate with another.

"Gio, I don't know where we are going from here. You say I am yours but what we did, is that normal?"

Gio chuckled. "Normal? Fuck no. Who wants to be normal? It was fucking unbelievable. I get hard just thinking about dominating you. There are so many things I want to do to you. There are so many combinations to try."

Jenna gulped nervously and shifted on the bed. A gasp escaped her parted lips as little-used muscles protested.

"Are you sore?" His hand glided along her comforter-covered bottom.

She nodded nervously.

"Don't worry. I'll give you a reprieve for a little while. I have business to attend. I'll place a guard at your door and be back to get you for dinner. After tonight, you'll have nothing to fear from my pack."

Gionne returned to his room to dress, and then left. Alone, Jenna was able to examine her feelings. Gio was the same male she fell in love with all those years ago and yet so different. She had never seen the lusty side of him, except for maybe that last day. His animalistic side excited some dark part of her but she was afraid of total submission to her alpha male. In a way she was jealous of him, he wasn't afraid to let his inner beast free in a way she never could. Inhibitions had always held her back but she was beginning to think that with Gio she could be herself, discover her true self for the first time in her life. This might be the place for her if his pack would accept her and if Gionne could love her.

Resigned to waiting for his return, she scooped up her shift and tried to restore some order to her appearance. Hearing a noise at her door, Jenna approached, sniffing the air.

She could scent feline and lupine. Of course, the scent of her and Gio's fierce mating clung to her, making it difficult for her to distinguish the scent of the visitor. She glanced at her image in the mirror and grimaced, she hadn't had time to wash.

The scent seeping through the door was an unusual combination. Refusing to cower in her room, she yanked the door open. She gasped in surprise. Lounging against the opposite wall was a female. A beautiful female. She was small in stature with long black hair and startling green eyes. Jealousy overwhelmed Jenna as she recognized the scent as the same one from Gionne's room.

"Hello, you must be Jenna. I am Riza." The dark-haired female held out one immaculately manicured hand.

Jenna grasped her hand briefly. "You're my guard," Jenna asked suspiciously.

"I may look harmless but I'm far from it." Riza pulled a pistol of some sort from the back waistband of her well-worn jeans, and waved it for a moment before replacing it.

"I never thought you were harmless." In fact, she feared she was anything but harmless. "You would shoot one of your own kind."

Riza snickered. "Just a dart gun. Put them right to sleep. Of course Gionne might kill them."

Jenna wasn't sure what this woman's angle was. She was beautiful. Obviously, close to Gio, so why would she protect her? Why would Gio ask her to? Moreover, why did she have a combination feline-lupine scent? "Are you of Gio's pack?"

"Yep. Half sister."

Relief flooded Jenna. She didn't have to dislike this female. "Are you mated to a feline?"

Riza's grin revealed sparkling teeth. "No. I'm half feline, half lupine but unmated as of yet."

"What! Gio never told me he had a half feline sister."

"He didn't know I was his sister until right after our father died," Riza explained.

"Oh. Uh, sorry, I shouldn't be so nosy. You know what they say, curiosity killed the cat."

"Hey, that's all right. I'm rather curious myself, being half feline and all."

"I guess if we're going to have a conversation we should get comfortable in my room," Jenna invited, swinging the door wide.

Riza followed her into the room, shutting and locking the door behind her. "So, I guess you knew Gionne before?"

"Yeah, we met in the forest years ago but I hadn't seen him in several years," Jenna supplied.

"And the two of you were—friends?" Riza asked slyly.

"Yes, the two of us and my brother Leon were friends. Playmates, you might say."

"Leon. He was the male with you when you arrived?" Riza asked curiously.

"Yeah, that's my brother."

"Do you mind my asking does he morph into a leopard the same as you?"

Jenna laughed. "No. He would be insulted. He takes after our father while I favor our mother. His change brings about the Royal Lion."

"A lion. Oh my! The king of the beasts. Is he huge?" Round green eyes stared curiously.

"He's not as huge as a true lion no, but impressive all the same. I suppose it has something to do with the size of the human state. Look at Gio, I've never seen a wolf so large before."

"Hmm, speaking of Gionne, he'll be back in about twenty minutes to fetch you for dinner. Did you want to change?"

"My clothes haven't arrived yet so I guess it's go as I am." Jenna was not pleased at the thought of letting anyone including this female see her in this state but she had little choice in the matter. No more choice than it appeared she had in any other matter.

"You're about my size. Let's go to my room and find you something. Contrary to what Gio might say, I do have more than jeans."

"I've never worn pants," Jenna stated.

"I hadn't either until I started training with the guard. It takes some getting used to."

"Hmm."

"Don't bother thinking about it. Gio wouldn't like it. Jeans aren't as easily accessible as the shift most females wear."

"You don't think the males are that controlling, do you?"

"Let me see, most females wear tight, clingy shifts with slits up both sides and no underclothes."

"It is comfortable."

"Yes it is, but you should read some of the history books in the library. They explain much about all the feral breeds. You will find that evolution has not changed the male of the species — much."

An instant rapport developed between the two females. They continued their discussion of dominant males as they headed for Riza's room in another wing of the palace.

\* \* \* \* \*

After Gionne left Jenna in Riza's care, he called an impromptu meeting of his council and guard. Gionne sat at the head of the boardroom table as each of the males filed into the room. Several would not meet his eye. Gionne stood and paced the room. As he walked, he stretched his neck from side to side and rolled his massive shoulders.

He turned his troubled gaze to Emil, his advisor. He had refused to discuss the topic of this meeting with him in advance. Emil appeared nervous so he supposed he had heard about the earlier altercation.

Gionne cleared his throat before speaking. "I have led this pack for two years now. I believe I can say in all honesty that I have sacrificed much to be a good leader. The pack has been my life, my family." As he spoke, he tried to look as many of his males in the eye as possible. "Now, it is time that I begin a life that is still part of the pack but separate as well."

"Gionne—" Emil attempted to speak but one slicing glance from his alpha silenced him.

"It is time for me to take a mate." Gionne's gaze now rested on the young guards in the back of the room. Several heads hung in shame. He felt their pain and remorse at their actions. Strolling to the back of the room, he placed a hand on Dirk's shoulder. The young blond male raised his head to meet Gionne's eyes, a thin scratch apparent on his cheek. "I have taken Jenna the young feline as my mate." The words seemed innocent enough but the warning was clear.

No one uttered a word.

"I am sure in time you will all come to know and accept her as my mate and the alpha female of our pack. Until then I expect—no, demand—that she is treated with all the respect and honor she deserves."

"Gionne, the felines—" Emil began to speak again.

"This is not up for debate. The right to choose a mate is a private matter not a pack concern. It is done."

Emil bowed his head. "Yes, Your Highness."

"Now, I must exit to prepare myself for dinner. Jenna will be there and I hope you will all make her feel welcome."

He hesitated a moment. "Dirk, I need a word with you in private."


Gionne turned the corner leading to his private rooms, the corner of his mouth turned up in a smile. They were no longer his private rooms. Surprised not to find Riza waiting there, he opened his door expecting to find her inside. The room was empty. "Riza, Jenna," he roared.

There was no answer and he tried the door adjoining the rooms to find it locked. Pounding on the door, he called their names once again. Receiving no answer, he gave the door a mighty kick with his bare foot. Wood splintered as the door slammed open against the inside wall. The room was empty.

\* \* \* \* \*

Jenna and Riza were coming down the hall when they heard the commotion. Riza pulled her gun from her small clutch bag. "Stay here," Riza, ordered as she charged into the room prepared to help defend her brother.

Jenna did not listen to the other female, instead followed close on Riza's heels prepared to lend her small might to the defense of Gionne.

Hearing a noise behind him, Gio turned to find the two females. Both were dressed to kill in tight, clingy shifts, but they looked as ferocious as he felt.

"What is going on?" Riza demanded. "We thought you were being attacked."

"Where the hell were you? I thought something had happened to the two of you." The whole time he spoke his eyes devoured Jenna looking for any sign of injury. "Are you okay?"

"I'm as well as can be expected, can't say the same for this door. So much for a lock."

"Do you think a locked door would keep me from your side? You should have learned earlier that nothing would stop me." He pulled a resistant Jenna into his arms, gently enclosing her in his embrace.

Suddenly, a thought occurred to Gio. "If you thought I was under attack what are you doing charging in here?" He glared at his sister. "Your responsibility is to protect my mate. I can protect myself."

"I told her to stay behind. She does not listen."

Tugging on Jenna's hair, he tilted her face to meet his gaze. "Were you so worried about me that you thought to defend me, my little feline?"

Narrowing her gaze at him, she refused to admit anything. "Of course not, I just wanted a front-row seat if someone was going to kick your ass."

Gio chuckled huskily, hearing the lie in her words. Petting her hair, he leaned forward to place a kiss upon her forehead. "That's my Kitty."

"Well, I think I'll head on out of here," Riza said, looking around curiously, taking note of the room. "You might want to tidy up a bit before Ella comes to clean." Riza eyed the tattered remains of the bed linens.

"Good idea, and thanks," Gio muttered, his gaze returning to Jenna's face.

"I was terrified something had happened to you," he said as his sister left the room, the door clicking shut behind her.

"I didn't have a change of clothes. Since you insisted I dine with you, I didn't want to appear bedraggled in front of your pack. You may have reduced me to the level of concubine but I do not want my appearance to reflect badly upon the Carbonesse."

"You are not a concubine and your appearance is always stunning. If you would have checked your closet, you would have found an assortment of clothing."

"Oh, you keep clothes on hand for your female guests. I should have known."

"They are for you alone," he muttered as his lips brushed hers lightly.

"When did you have time to buy clothing for me?"

"I was prepared for your arrival."

"You were so sure I'd accept your terms." She shook her head. "What would you have done if I had refused?"

He had asked himself that question a million times. The answer was always the same. He would not have accepted no for an answer. She was his, she had always been his. He knew it. Leon knew it. It was time she realized it as well. "Thankfully, we did not have to find out." He evaded a direct answer for the moment.

"I must ready myself for dinner or we will be late."

She walked past the broken rubble that was a door into her room. He hurried to change his clothes, not wanting to leave her side for long.

"Are you ready?" She jumped at the softly spoken words.

With a deep resigned sigh, she said, "Lead on."

Gio grasped her hand, pulling her into his arms. Lowering his lips, he lightly brushed hers. The time fell away as he held her and kissed her gently, tenderly this time. Hesitantly, her lips parted beneath his and his tongue took advantage, slipping between her lips to explore the depths of her mouth. Their tongues met and dueled. Her rough little tongue had always excited him. Whenever she licked at his mouth, his mind always wondered what it would feel like licking other parts of his anatomy. He intended to have her appease that hunger in the very near future.

He continued devouring the nectar of her mouth. While she was pliable, he intended to take full advantage. Her heart pounded rapidly against his chest and she purred into his mouth.

\* \* \* \* \*

She was reluctant to release him when he raised his head. "As much as I hate to let you go we must leave for dinner."

His words pulled her back into reality. "Gio, I admit we have some unresolved feelings and you are playing on them. But this seems to all be happening too fast."

"Too fast. I have waited years. First you were too young and then—"

"Don't speak of it."

"At some point, we must," he insisted.

"But not tonight."

"Not tonight," he agreed.

For a moment she leaned into him, her nostrils flared as she inhaled his scent. It was musky, tangy—Gio. A scent she had never forgotten. Would never forget.

"We must leave now or I'm going to put you on your knees and slide my cock between these lips." His thumb traced her bottom lip.

Cream instantly gathered between her thighs. She wrapped her lips around his thumb and sucked it into her mouth. She suckled powerfully upon it and watched the flame in his eyes ignite.

"Fuck!" he gasped, jerking free. "You're going to kill me." He grasped her arm and propelled her out of the room ahead of him.

# Chapter Seven

**ဢ**

If she wasn't nervous enough about the upcoming dinner, Gio managed to make it worse. She noticed he kept glancing her way as they strolled down a long hallway. "What do you keep looking at?" she finally asked.

Gio chuckled. "My sister's curves are not as lush and full as yours. That dress along with those perky nipples will have all the males alert, so to speak."

"Gio," she gasped.

"It is a good thing you have the scent of a well fucked female," he stated matter-of-factly.

"What."

"Every male in the room will scent the fact that I have claimed you in the most primal way. They will all be jealous but they will accept the fact you belong to me. It is our way."

"I belong to myself."

"But your body belongs to me. No one touches it unless I allow it. We are here now so stop arguing or I will mount you in front of my pack and leave no doubt in anyone's mind to whom you belong."

Jenna strangled back her reply. Certainly, he was joking but she didn't want to push him. She had heard unbelievable stories of the lupine mating rituals.

Jenna felt the eyes upon them as they entered the dining room fifteen minutes late. She refused to cower, instead stood defiantly at his side. Gio led her to the head of the master table. He was right in the fact that all the males looked at her. Most of their eyes held a mocking awareness, only a couple showed open lust. She held her breath, her body tingling with uncertainty and arousal.

"This exquisite creature at my side is Jenna, my lifemate and alpha female of the pack."

Without a doubt, Jenna was the most surprised by his sudden announcement. She whipped her head around to look at the male at her side. How dare he assume she would accept him without even asking? She told him she didn't want him to dominate all areas of her life. Another thought popped into her head, he considered her his mate. He had not just used her for his gratification.

Masking her surprise and outrage at his sudden announcement, she tried to seat herself regally at his side. Unfortunately, she feared she ruined the haughtiness of the move by the slight groan and flinch she made when her sore backside touched the hardness of the chair. By the curl of Gio's lip, she realized he knew of her discomfort and the reason for it. She hoped it wasn't obvious to everyone.

The declaration met no resistance. Shortly after they took their seats, the meal arrived. Jenna was not surprised to notice that the meal consisted of mostly many different types of meat and nothing else.

While the feline race were certainly meat eaters, they also enjoyed a variety of vegetables in their diet. Not wishing to draw attention to herself, she ate without complaint. Her nervous stomach would not allow her to eat much anyway.

"Is the food not to your liking?" Gio asked.

"It's fine. I'm just not very hungry."

"Are you watching your figure?"

"No. And I don't practice the low-carb meat diet either."

Gio looked confused at her response. She supposed to him that eating almost all meat seemed normal.

Jenna huffed and turned back to her meal, pushing the food around on her plate. Some of the meat was nearly raw and while she did enjoy fresh meat in her feline form, while in human form she preferred her meat fully cooked with a side or two of veggies.

Instead of eating, Jenna found herself studying Gio's pack. The room held several large tables that seated around fifty people. It appeared most of his pack ate together. There were probably a dozen or so guards on duty at all times that were not present but other than that they all dined together. She noticed the females that delivered the food to the tables had taken seats at a table in the corner. She found this custom somewhat odd.

Their table was large with several empty seats. Emil sat on Gio's right and next to him was an older male she didn't recognize. To her right sat two younger males, the one closest had long blond hair. She thought he was the male she had seen this morning returning from the hunt. He looked at her and she gasped. A thin scratch across his cheek identified him as the wolf who had attempted to mate her.

Their eyes met and she saw that he realized she had guessed his identity. His lip curled in a rueful smile.

Her hands shook so badly that when she reached for her glass of water she knocked it over onto the table and the blond male.

"Sorry...I...sorry," the words tumbled from her lips.

"No worries," the male said in a husky voice as he stood, brushing the moisture from the jeans riding low on his slim hips. His actions drew her gaze to the obvious erection molded by skintight pants. To make matters worse he began to remove his wet shirt.

As he undid the second button, she drew her gaze away, covering her flushed cheeks with both hands.

For the first time, she realized the scene was drawing smirks and chuckles from the surrounding males, even Gio laughed at her embarrassment.

"Gio, he is the male wolf from earlier," she whispered the words for him alone.

"I know who he is." Understanding eyes traveled from her to the male that had reseated himself, now shirtless. "You are now his alpha female and he will honor you as such."

In short order, she had a new glass of water and everyone except Jenna resumed eating their meal. Now she knew she wouldn't be able to choke down another bite. She glanced shyly at the blond from beneath her lashes.

His shirtless form was not as impressive as Gio's but it was certainly inspiring in its own way. Corded muscles rippled beneath tanned skin with a chest swathed in a fine golden pelt.

Frowning, she forced her eyes away from what was most certainly very fine eye candy. Her frown deepened. For years she had yearned for no male but Gio and now that he had possessed her and taught her of sensations she hadn't even known existed she feared he had unleashed a darkness within her. She was a slut.

She shut her eyes, trying to force these traitorous thoughts from her head. She loved Gio, she always had. She would overcome these wanton feelings.

Gio's hand brushed against hers and she glanced at him. His dark, soulful eyes studied her. She smiled hesitantly at him and he resumed his conversation with Emil and some of the others about water conservation.

Her gaze landed on a friendly face across the room, Riza. She returned Riza's smile and decided to ask Riza to sit with them next mealtime. If she were to dine with the pack, she would prefer to sit next to a friendly face and one that didn't play havoc with her emotions.

After dinner, the servers delivered pitchers and mugs of ale to each table. Jenna declined a mug of her own but upon Gio's insistence took a sip of his. The taste was slightly bitter but not totally unpleasant. The cold drink warmed her insides. "Not bad." She lifted the mug to her lips once more for another taste of the potent brew. Resting back in her chair, she shut her eyes. A smile tugged at her lips, she felt good.

"Gio," Jenna gasped in surprise when Gio grabbed her up and deposited her on his lap. Looking around she realized the lights were now dim and they were alone at their table. People mingled in groups or lone couples. No one seemed particularly interested in them.

Jenna relaxed against his chest only to shoot up straight in his lap again when she felt his hand slide into the slit of her shift and his fingers brush her pussy.

"What do you think you are doing?" she hissed indignantly.

"Pleasuring my mate."

"You can't do this in public."

"Why? Look around." For the first time, she noticed some of the couples were exceptionally close. In one corner, a male relaxed back in a chair and a female appeared to be riding him. Another group had three males and one female, they were—

"Oh my!" Two thick fingers drove into her sex.

"Gio, not here."

"You agreed I was in control of all things sexual."

"In private."

"It is our custom to mate openly. You must accept your mate and alpha for all to see. This way they know you accept me and them." The want in his dark eyes had her melting.

"I can't be exposed."

"Your body is beautiful. There is no need to hide it. You could ride me." He nodded toward the couple in the corner. "Or you could suck me." He nodded in another direction. She looked over her shoulder. "Nothing would please me more than for you to wrap those gorgeous lips around my cock. Let me feel your raspy tongue licking my shaft."

Mesmerized by his words she slid off his lap to kneel between his parted thighs. He released his cock. It jutted free, huge and intimidating, staring at her with its one eye. She licked her lips nervously, but at least this way she stayed dressed and the table hid her pretty well.

She ran the fingers of one hand over his shaft and was surprised how satiny the skin felt. It hadn't felt at all soft inside her.

Gio wrapped his hand around hers, teaching her how to please him. "Come here, Kitty. Let me feel that feline tongue."

She flicked her tongue across the head of his cock, lapping a drop of moisture from the tip. His taste was salty but pleasant. She licked her lips. "Mmm," she groaned. This time she licked the entire length of his shaft and his hips bucked up off the chair.

"You're killing me," he growled, wrapping a hand in her hair. "Take me in your mouth, suck me."

She took the blunt head into her mouth, sucking powerfully upon it. He thrust and the head went all the way to the back of her throat and then out again. She smacked her lips, enjoying this activity so much she forgot they were not alone.

"Enough," he said.

She was so engrossed, she didn't realize he wanted her to stop until she felt the pain of his hand pulling back on her hair.

"Did I do something wrong?"

"No, but I want to be inside you when I come."

He pulled her up and settled her over his cock. She was very wet but it still wasn't an easy feat for her body to accommodate his substantial erection. Her canal stretched to capacity, he bucked up and pulled down on her, the sensation nearly drove her over the edge.

Finally, he hilted himself in her depths and she sighed deeply.

Without warning, he yanked her shift over her head, exposing her for all to see.

She gasped and tried to cover her breasts.

"No. Ride me proudly. Let them all enjoy your beauty. The beauty of their alpha."

Heat inflamed her body. She could feel the eyes upon her.

"Relax. Look at me, only at me. Keep your eyes on mine. Let me watch you as you come apart atop my cock," Gio crooned soothingly.

He held her hips down and bucked forcefully between her thighs. She arched her back and he rotated her on his cock.

"It's too much, too much," she cried as she leaned forward, pressing her forehead to his. He bucked ferociously again and she shattered, screaming out her release.

After a moment, she gasped. "Oh my god, I forgot where we were."

He chuckled throatily. "You certainly boosted my reputation."

"Your reputation as the resident stud." She tried to slide back off his erection.

"Oh no, we're not finished."

"I am." She pouted. "People are staring. I can feel their eyes."

"They stare because you are so beautiful and your scent too alluring. You are the only female in the room in heat. All the males want you. They are wondering if I'm going to share."

"Share." She gulped.

"If I lean you forward they'll all be eager to mount your ass."

She looked into his eyes, trying to read him.

"Would that excite you?" he asked.

Jenna thought about the girl earlier writhing between the three males, and her vagina clenched.

One large hand in the middle of her back pulled her forward. The other hand shifted enough to plunge one finger knuckle-deep in her rectum.

"Do you want something larger?" The finger drove deeper. "Another thick cock filling your ass. Two cocks plunging in and out of you. Maybe a third to fill your mouth."

The sudden image of the blond's large cock filling her ass while she rode Gio intensified the heat within and her cream flowed thick but she wouldn't admit to such an erotic fantasy. She shook her head.

Gio made a gesture with his hand and a male appeared at their side. A quick glance observed a naked, aroused male with a thick erection jutting out from a nest of golden curls. Jenna gulped as the thing bobbed close to her face. She glanced up surprised to find the blond male with the scratch on his face.

"Don't you owe your alpha female an apology?" Gio's deep voice stated.

"I am sorry, my lady." His hand reached out and stroked her hair, his fingers trailed down her back and across her ass. "I would do anything for your forgiveness."

Gio brought her chest to his, tipping her ass up. The tip of the other male's cock danced just out of reach. Gio's finger probed deeper into her ass.

"Can you think of a way he could make it up to you?" Gio asked.

She turned her gaze back to Gio's chocolate eyes. The way he watched her was unnerving, he knew what she felt, he could feel her dissolving around him.

She whimpered.

He nodded to the male and he stepped closer. "Do you want to taste him?"

She turned toward the male and the damp tip of his cock brushed her lips. She licked her lips, tasting his musky pre-cum. He thrust forward and his immense width filled her mouth. She swallowed deeply, taking him farther.

His hand wrapped in her hair then held her by the back of the head as he pumped slowly in and out of her mouth.

Gio's movements were leisurely, a finger teased her anus, a thumb flicked her nipple and his cock thrust leisurely within her liquid heat just fast enough to keep her simmering.

She wiggled her ass, wanting a more forceful penetration.

"Enough," Gio stated in a voice heavy with desire. Gio stopped all movement and the other male's cock slid from between her lips with a pop.

"I think she's ready for her treat." Gio's mouth curved in a sexy grin. The simple task of breathing took all her energy.

Lowering Jenna's head, Gio took her mouth in a deep kiss as his hands engulfed the globes of her ass, spreading her cheeks. He suckled her tongue within his mouth and she groaned. Something nudged her anus.

She tore her mouth from Gio's, breathing hard. She looked over her shoulder; the blond male was behind her now with cock in hand.

She whimpered. It appeared he didn't need her consent to fuck her, only Gio's. Not that she was complaining.

The blond reached between their bodies, rubbing against her pussy where she joined with Gio.

"I need your cream," the blond groaned close to her ear.

She didn't think he'd have any problem finding some, since it seemed to be gushing from her.

"She is sweet," Gio said.

She closed her eyes, absorbing the touch of both males.

The other male made slurping sounds and murmured approval. She assumed he tasted her juices.

"Just remember she is mine," Gio stated.

A grunt was the only reply, then she felt his thick head probe her anally.

Gio shifted her, tilting her for better access. She stiffened at the feel of the other cock.

"Relax, Kitty. This is my present to you." The other lubed cock began its entrance.

"Enjoy," Gio murmured, and then took her mouth in a deep kiss. The tongue thrusting between her lips much like the two cocks thrusting into her passages.

She felt dizzy, lightheaded, it was almost painful but there was too much pleasure to notice the pain. She was full, stretched to capacity. She burned from belly down. Her breasts swollen with need, the tips peaked tight as each male tugged and pulled at a nipple.

Releasing Jenna's lips, Gio muttered, "Look at me. Let me see your pleasure."

The sight of Gio's heavy-lidded chocolate gaze absorbing every nuance of her pleasure was a sublime experience.

"You are so hot and tight," Gio groaned.

"Come for us, Kitty."

How long they thrust in unison, she was unsure. It seemed like hours but possibly only minutes when the first burst of orgasm hit her.

She cried out, her eyes glazing. Both males slowed their pace as she shuddered around them and then as if on cue resumed their rapid thrusts.

This time when the climax slammed into her, she moaned right before her world went dark. The last thing she remembered was the sound of both males howling as they found their release.

Euphoric bliss engulfed her as she roused herself against Gio's chest. Their eyes met and he smiled gently. The blond stepped to her side. Bending down, he placed a gentle kiss on her lips. "My name is Dirk. From this day forward, I am at your service. You will always be safe with me. I will protect you, my alpha female, with my life." With a nod to Gionne, he turned and walked away.

# Chapter Eight

**ဢ**

Jenna looked at no one as they left the pack and headed for their room. "So, now I am considered your mate and you can loan my body out," she asked after they reached Gio's room.

"That was for your pleasure not mine," he warily answered.

"I did not ask for that."

"No and you never would but you are the alpha female, it is expected occasionally. There has to be at least one male that would protect you as his own. Who would take you as his if something happened to me."

"I don't need anyone to protect me."

"Our world is full of danger. I wish I could tell you everyone accepts you but I fear it's not so. Dirk desires you. He wanted you as his own. He has accepted that cannot be but he will watch over you."

"So, I am to be your mate, willing or not? Do I have any say in who fucks me next? Can I make requests if I find someone I like?" she taunted viciously.

Dark, angry eyes glared at her. "It is your right as alpha to fuck any unmated male you please." The words seemed forced. "None will ever fuck your pussy though, that belongs only to your mate." He slowly moved away. "And hopefully your heart as well."

Jenna was unsure if she heard the softly spoken words correctly and was too unsure of him to ask him to repeat it.

"Am I to fuck you in front of your pack every night?"

"It is not mandatory."

"And will you join in the other groups and fuck the willing females."

"As alpha it is my right but you are my mate, I have no need of another. The Valde mate for life, unlike the Carbonesse."

"What do you mean by that?" Jenna questioned.

"It is a fact that felines mate with multiple partners and take multiple mates."

Jenna couldn't deny the accusation. Some males had more than one mate.

"Just so we are clear, I won't share your pussy or my cock," Gio proclaimed.

"I don't remember asking you to, you're the one that suggested it."

"And it got you hot," he accused.

Jenna threw up her hands and stalked across the room. "The Carbonesse may occasionally have more than one mate but we don't have public orgies," she threw the comment over her shoulder as she pranced into her room, wishing she had a door to slam.

Pacing the room for several minutes relieved some of her agitation. After all, who was she really mad at, Gio or herself? Dirk obviously was no benefit to Gio. Gio tolerated him for her safety and her pleasure. She couldn't imagine sharing Gio. She was surprised that he could or would share her even if it was somewhat unwillingly.

It was late and she was tired. Gio was still in the other room. Opening her closet, she looked for a nightshirt. The shifts were lovely. Whoever had purchased them had considered her preferences. The gowns were in colors of green, gold and black. Her favorite colors, the same colors of this room. It made her wonder. As gorgeous as they were, none were suitable to sleep in.

Nervously, Jenna approached Gio. "I don't have any of my things. Do you think you could loan me something to sleep in?"

"I am sorry, I have stocked your closet with many gowns but did not think to provide you with a sleeping gown. I will loan you a shirt."

She changed into the shirt he provided in the bathroom. Smooth, white silk caressed her curves, gliding sensuously against her already sensitive nipples. She inhaled deeply, drawing in the scent of Gionne. Sleeping in this shirt would be like sleeping with Gio wrapped around her. Well, maybe not quite so tempting but still it would be distracting.

When she exited the bathroom Gio was perched on the side of her bed, wearing only a pair of pajama bottoms that rode low on his narrow hips. She tried not to stare at his powerful chest, rippling abs or the trail of hair that so tantalizingly disappeared beneath his waistband.

"I trust you found everything you needed. I had your bathroom stocked for you as well. I'm sorry I did not think about a nightgown but I suppose I always assumed you slept in the nude as I usually do." His heated gaze ran slowly over her bare legs, up to her chest, stopping for a moment to appreciate the peaked nipples before coming to rest on her face. "You do look lovely in my shirt though."

"Thank you. It carries your scent," Jenna blurted out.

Gio looked taken back for a moment.

"I didn't mean it as an insult. I have an excellent sense of smell."

Gio stalked toward her. "Yes, so do I. Do you want to know what my senses tell me?"

"I—no, probably not."

Gio was behind her now and he moved in close until his breath tickled her neck. He chuckled low. "Ahh, but there's no fun in that. I smell a female. A desirable female in estrus and I believe the female is aroused as well."

"Huh, don't put too much stock in your extraordinary senses."

Gio wrapped an arm around her, hauling her close, rubbing against her.

"Do you intend to hump my leg?" she asked sarcastically.

* * * * *

Gio threw his head back and roared with laughter. He had missed her sharp wit and even sharper tongue. That tongue had often flayed him open. He had learned that when she was nervous she used her arrogant, haughty attitude as a shield to hold him at bay. "If I were the wolf right now I'd do more than hump your leg."

"I thought you said you could control the beast."

"I can if I chose to."

"I think maybe you should return to your room."

"I agree if you will come with me," he coaxed using a dark, velvet voice.

"No. I will sleep in here," she declared.

"No. From this night forward, you will sleep at my side. As human or beast, we will sleep together. I will not force you—unless you ask."

"Gio. No. We need to stop." She shook her head, her blonde hair cascading around her. "I'm not ready to commit."

"It is too late, you are mine. The moment you stepped foot on my land it was too late."

"I don't think I can sleep if you are at my side," she confessed.

Gio chuckled. It would be difficult to sleep next to her but it would be impossible to sleep without her. "You could change to your feline form. If I remember correctly, you enjoy sleeping in that form."

"In my current state I'm too vulnerable as a feline," she replied honestly.

"I will stay in human form," Gio offered.

"You wouldn't mind sharing your bed with a feline?"

"Soon, I want to share more than my bed with a feline," Gio suggested hopefully.

"In human form we are compatible but in feral form we are very different. I'm not sure what kind of relationship we can have."

"We will be mates as humans and beasts."

"You mean that..." Jenna's voiced tapered off as if she was unsure how to continue.

"That I want to mate with you in beast form. Of course I do, the feline is a part of you the same as the wolf is a part of me. I desire all of you."

"So you're saying that when you are in wolf form you find my feline form attractive?" Jenna asked cautiously.

"Yes, the beast in me finds the feline and human sides of you desirable. As does the man find the woman and the feline desirable. Do you not find me desirable as a wolf?"

\* \* \* \* \*

Jenna wasn't sure how they had gotten started on this conversation. Moreover, she was afraid to look too closely at what he was trying to tell her. She had always known that either form of Gionne attracted her but she feared there was something wrong with this. "I, uh, you are an attractive male in any form," she muttered, not meeting his gaze.

"You are safe from the beast tonight but not for long. The beast rages within me to claim you as his mate."

"To claim the feline as his mate," Jenna asked.

"To claim all of you, but you are safe for now. So sleep with me in any form you chose and know that I will not be repulsed and I will control myself." He held his hand out to her. "Understand me when I say, dominating you when you do not wish to be dominated is not my style."

Jenna slowly extended her hand to him and let him lead her to his room. She would stay in human form for she had more control that way.

True to his word, Gio made no demands on her other than her sharing his bed. Even though she protested, Jenna was glad Gio was near. She knew she would never be able to sleep among these lupines tonight if not for her trust in Gio to protect her. Of course, his nearness presented another problem, that being tightened nipples and a throbbing heat between her thighs.

A trait of the feline is superior night vision and she used this ability to watch him as he lay next to her on his back. With his head turned to the side, she wasn't certain if he was asleep. The covers rode low on his hips and his thickly muscled chest moved evenly as he breathed. The thought of rolling over, resting her head upon his chest and feeling his warmth surrounding her was tempting. The soothing rhythm of his heart and breath was enticing.

Turning on her side, she inched closer.

Stopping, waiting, anticipating.

When she received no reaction from him, she inched closer still. He lay undisturbed. She thought he must be asleep. She held her breath as she slowly raised a trembling hand, reaching toward him. Her mouth dried and her eyes dilated with anticipation—fear. She hesitated for a moment but the naked expanse was too tempting to resist. Her hand shot forward but before her fingertips could brush his chest, his head turned and dark eyes captured hers. With a gasp, she jerked her hand back.

"Was there something you needed?" he asked in a husky passion-laden voice.

"I couldn't sleep."

A smile curled his lips. "And you wish for me to help relax you for sleep?"

"I, uh…" Jenna stuttered anxiously.

"Do not be ashamed of your needs." He rolled to his side and hauled her up to him, allowing her to feel the evidence of his arousal pressed against her stomach. "I have needs as well."

"I don't know…I don't understand."

"You are in heat. I have aroused your hungers. Now they must be fed."

"I've been in heat before, it was not like this."

"But now you have been mated, we have forged a bond. Your body has had deep penetration and craves it even more. It is about procreation, the continuation of our species."

"We are not the same species. Have you thought about the fact that a child of our making might be feline not lupine?"

"It matters not to me. My sister is half feline."

"A child of ours will not ascend to rule your pack."

"Who knows what the future holds. Now is not the time to worry over such matters."

With these simple words, he took possession of her lips. His tongue sought hers and she luxuriated in the feel of its caress. A large hand engulfed her breast, massaging the fullness. His thumb tweaked the already extended nipple through her shirt. Reaching down he hooked her top leg over his thigh, leaving her vulnerable to his seeking fingers. "Now is the time to please my mate."

Placing both hands on his chest, she shoved and jerked her mouth from his. "No."

Gio pulled back. Jenna was pleased that he appeared to accept a refusal if she wished.

Shoving him onto his back, she leaned over him. "No, this time I don't want to be dominated. I need to explore your body. I want to taste and feel all of your textures and essences."

With a growl between pleasure and pain, Gio stretched out on his back. "Be my guest. Explore at will."

Jenna's cat eyes gleamed and she licked her lips. She had a taste of him earlier and it only whetted her appetite for more. This male had been the center of her fantasies for most of her life. She was unsure where to start so she let her keen curiosity guide her.

Placing both of his arms over his head, she enjoyed the view of bulging biceps. It reminded her of how he had tied her but she felt no need to restrain him, she wasn't a dominatrix.

Sitting up next to him on the bed, her knees brushed his side and her hands dove into the thick pelt on his chest. Curious fingers found the erect male nipples that topped his massive pecs and playfully circled them. His quick gasp of breath brought a smile to her lips. She was going to enjoy her chance to dominate him. She leaned forward, finding one male nipple with her lips. His chest hair tickled her nose but his taste was salty, delicious and addictive. "Do you like this too?" She nipped the taut flesh.

A guttural groan with his only response.

Shuttered eyes watched her as she shifted her position to straddle him. She felt his erection beneath his pajama bottoms and settled over it. It felt huge against her tender folds. She closed her eyes, savoring the feel of him beneath her. A startled gasp escaped her lips when his hands grasped her thighs and he began to shift her against his length.

"No, Gio, this is my turn."

He removed his hands and threw them back over his head. "Then you must touch me, stroke me," he begged. The Valde as well as the Carbonesse were a male-dominant race. The alpha male was used to taking charge in all matters. This went against his nature and Jenna was pleased he allowed her this.

"How do you want to be touched? Where?"

"Everywhere with your hands, your body, your mouth. I want to feel that rough little tongue of your stroking my flesh, licking at my cock."

She grasped the edge of her shirt and pulled it over her head, flinging it to the floor.

"That's better," he groaned.

Leaning forward she let her breasts rub against his hair-roughened chest. Scissoring her fingers through his long hair, she tugged his mouth to hers. She kissed him deeply then pulled back, nipping at his lips then licking their sensual fullness.

Gio grasped the rails of his bed, his knuckles turning white in his fight not to take control.

The salty taste of his skin was addictive but she needed more.

She craved more.

His gyrations beneath her had her wound tight but she wanted to taste all of him before she surrendered to him. Sliding down his body, she sat on his muscled thighs. She reached for the buttoned opening on his pajamas.

Impatiently, Gio's hands beat her there. Grasping the cloth with both hands, he ripped the material in two and his engorged flesh sprang free. Obviously, he wanted to feel her against him as much as she did.

Jenna purred in delight at the thick length jutting from his body. It was impressive, as large as or larger than the other cocks she had glimpsed tonight.

The tip glistened with moisture and she unconsciously licked her lips, remembering his unique taste. Wrapping her hands around him, she began a slow stroke. His skin was as soft as velvet but underneath he was granite-hard. Thoughts of this engorged organ inside her had her wiggling impatiently on his thighs. She was anxious to feel the thick length stretching her tight once more but first she had other plans.

Her tongue darted out and licked the blunt tip of his shaft, tasting his seed.

"Lick me, suck me," he growled, thrusting his cock upwards toward her lips. The smooth skin pulled tight over his heavy length and the head was red with excess blood.

\* \* \* \* \*

Gionne fought the inner beast, the need to conquer and devour. He couldn't take much more of this form of pleasure. His blood pounded with a roar inside his head. He gripped the rails tighter.

Smacking her lips together, she tasted him. That rough little tongue lapped at his flesh, the feel and sight drove him wild. She lowered her mouth again, rolling her tongue around the head and then down his shaft. Never had another given him such exquisite pleasure. He moaned encouragement.

She didn't complain when he grasped her head. Wrapping her long hair around his palm, he guided her. His other hand closed around one of hers, setting a rhythm to her stroking touch. She opened her mouth over him and he surged inside. She couldn't take all of him but she tried.

His control snapped as he began teaching her how best to please him. Dragging himself out from under her, he knelt on the bed in front of her. She was still on her knees and he positioned her to be able to accept him deeper. Holding her hair back so he could see everything, he angled her head and thrust tentatively within her mouth.

"That's it, baby." As he stroked deeper she began to purr and those vibrations were nearly his undoing.

Pulling his wet member from between her lips, he yanked her up to meet his mouth, his tongue mimicking his cock. He tasted his salty pre-cum on her lips and it drove him wild. Grasping her by the waist, he lifted her. "Wrap your legs around me."

As she complied, he made his first thrust into her wet heat. Palming her smooth generously curved bottom, he guided her as she rode him. He filled her to the max at this angle and the base of his shaft grinded against her clitoris. A furious pace soon had them both singing out their release.

Afterward, he nestled her to his side. As she came down from her high, he felt her trying to withdraw. He held her tight. "No, Jenna, stay here in my arms. What we have is right do not be ashamed of it."

"Will it always be so intense?" she asked on a sigh.

"Only when you are in heat. Otherwise it will still be intense and pleasurable just not so urgent and constant."

"Is it as intense for you?"

"Your alluring scent inflames my senses. I do not believe my cock has been flaccid since you stepped foot in the palace."

"Oh."

"How did you relieve your desires during your heat cycle before?" he asked the question that had often haunted him.

She diverted her eyes as a flush rose up her neck and across her face. "You can tell me."

A toss of her head allowed her hair to shield her face from his view. Jealousy tore at him as he wondered what she hid. "Did you allow males to pleasure you without taking your innocence?"

Her head popped up and wide eyes stared at him.

"Were you pleasured with their tongues?"

Her head shook emphatically in denial. "No." She ducked her head again and whispered, "I sometimes touched myself."

Her words brought more relief than he was entitled to. Grasping her hands, he brought them to his lips, kissing and suckling each finger. These fingers had kept her faithful to him even though he did not deserve it. "You have no reason to be embarrassed. Do you think I never pleasured myself?"

Misty eyes observed him. "You have?"

"I told you about lying on this fur. What did you think I meant?" he asked with a husky chuckle.

She shrugged her shoulders. "I don't know, I thought maybe you took other females on it."

"While I was dreaming of you, how big of a bastard do you think I am?"

Her hair slid forward hiding her from him once again. "Well, you do have the nightly orgies, after dinner."

"I was not mated but still I didn't join in."

"Not all those males are mated to those females."

"No, it is their choice to participate."

"You never stayed before tonight?"

"I cannot say I never watched." His eyes gleamed wickedly.

"Oh, wouldn't that be kind of hard?"

He chuckled. "Oh, yes, at times it was very hard." He settled her back against him, his hard shaft nudging her bottom.

Smiling at her gasp of pleasure, he tweaked a nipple. "You must sleep now, you need your rest. I promise it will still be hard come morning."

# Chapter Nine

Jenna was uneasy about having breakfast with the pack but everyone else seemed unperturbed so she nonchalantly strolled to the seat she had the night before. Emil and another pack member had immediately set upon Gio as soon as he entered the room. "Pack business!" Emil had stated. So now, she sat here alone staring at a sea of unknown faces.

Seeing Riza enter the room, she immediately waved her over. "Good morning," Riza greeted her and dropped into the chair on her right.

"Yes, it is."

"I hear it was a good night too, at least for some of us," Riza teased.

Jenna felt the heat rising up her neck and fanned herself with a napkin.

"I hope they washed this table."

"Riza," Jenna reprimanded.

"Sorry."

"What did you…I mean, where were you last night?"

"I left after dinner as all good unmated females do."

"Nobody warned me."

"Gio would have tortured me if I did. He asked me not to sit at this table last night," Riza hesitantly confessed.

"Why?"

"I guess he thought I might say something or you might want to leave when I did."

"So, he intentionally made a spectacle of me," Jenna fumed.

"I don't know if I'd say that but I think he needed you to show your devotion to him publicly. He wants you to be accepted and you to accept us."

"I guess I can understand that. These dominant males are always staking some sort of claim. I guess I satisfied the pack's curiosity about if we were mated."

"Yeah, I guess so. Of course, you probably didn't have to screech like a feline in heat to do it though," Riza chuckled.

"What?" Jenna squeaked.

"Sorry." Riza chuckled and held up her hands in surrender.

"So, how are my two favorite ladies?" Gio asked as he took his seat.

"Fine, fine," Riza answered.

Jenna glared at him. "Do I screech?"

His dark eyes held amusement until he turned them on his sister. They narrowed with a promise of retribution.

"Well?" Jenna prompted.

"Oh yeah, but it makes me hot," Gio taunted.

"Well, you howl."

"You can make me howl again right now if you want." His eyes dared.

The sound of a chair scraping away from the table drew Jenna's gaze and she wasn't totally surprised to see Dirk take a seat across from her.

She blinked nervously and looked away.

When the food arrived, Jenna was pleased to find not only strips of pork but fried potatoes and fresh bread. It looked delicious. "Ohh, this looks wonderful. I don't usually eat raw meat."

"That's not what you said last night," Gio teased.

Dirk choked back a laugh.

"All right, you two, I'm losing my appetite," Riza complained. "You know some of us have to sleep alone."

"Some of us might be sleeping alone." Jenna glared.

"I don't think so," Gio replied smugly.

"Not likely," Dirk chimed in and the two males held each other's gaze across the table.

"So, what was the big powwow about?" Riza murmured so Emil and the other males at the next table wouldn't overhear.

"It seems there is a band of coyote breeds camped on a lower ridge in the northeast," Gio explained.

"That is not our territory," replied Riza.

"Correct but I would still like to meet with their alpha, explain our boundaries and try to avoid any problems before they occur." He glanced at Jenna. "I may see if Leon would like to accompany us."

"I'm sure he would appreciate that." A smile tugged at Jenna's lips.

"Can I go with?" Riza asked.

"No, until I've met the pack I will take no female near them, especially an unmated one."

"I can fend for myself. Besides you would protect me as well as the guard and Jenna's brother."

Gio narrowed his eyes at his sister. "Nonetheless, you will stay behind in case Jenna needs you."

"I can watch over Jenna," Dirk remarked.

A tic worked in the side of Gio's cheek. Jenna held her breath, awaiting Gio's reply. She knew if Gio left Dirk to guard her he would want to fuck her. She shifted nervously, clamping her damp thighs together.

"I prefer you to accompany me, Riza will guard Jenna." The alpha's tone held no compromise.

"As you wish," Dirk replied, his soulful eyes glancing at Jenna.

\* \* \* \* \*

Jenna couldn't mistake the low growl of a wolf coming from right outside her door. She knew that Gio had left this morning to oversee the problem with an encroaching coyote band but he had assured her that she wouldn't have any problems from anyone in his pack. Silently, she padded to the door trying to scent the wolf but found her senses overpowered by a strong flowery fragrance. It was an obvious attempt by the intruder to mask his scent. Before she could step away from the door, the wolf on the other side hit the door forcefully, startling her, and a gasp escaped her lips. The power of the blow shook the door but did not break it. She remembered how easily Gio had burst through their adjoining door and fear clutched her heart.

Moving as far away from the door as possible, she stripped and altered her form. A feline of her size was no match for a large male wolf but she felt better prepared to face an attack in this form. Pacing nervously, she awaited the attack. What seemed like hours but was probably only a few minutes passed until there was a knock at the door.

"Jenna, it's Riza."

The feline registered the familiar female voice. Was this a trap—could it have been her?

"Jenna, are you in there?" The tone of Riza's voice had risen and she tried the knob. The door rattled as Riza twisted the knob.

Deciding to trust her instincts, the feline transformed and Jenna quickly scooped up the sheet but not before Riza yelled again.

"Jenna." Riza rammed the door with her shoulder.

Jenna yanked the door open, a sheet wrapped around her nakedness. She looked both ways down the hall before pulling Riza into the room and locking the door behind them.

"What's going on? Why didn't you answer the door?"

"That's what I'd like to know," Jenna said, then explained the situation to Riza.

* * * * *

Always the protector Riza insisted on searching the hall for a scent trail but returned, unable to find a trace, due to the perfume. "I don't know but I don't like it. When Gionne returns he's going to fuckin' flip." Riza couldn't believe someone from her pack, someone with obvious access to the palace would betray their alpha in such a way.

"Do you think it was one of the young males again?" Riza asked Jenna.

"I don't know but I don't think he was here looking for a quick romp. The presence seemed evil, ominous. I had the feeling whoever it was meant to do me harm."

"Gionne will return in a few hours and I'll stay with you until then."

A knock at the door put Riza in protect mode, pulling the small pistol she called out. Hearing Emil's voice, she answered the door. He wanted to let Jenna know that the convoy that delivered the goods to her pride was returning and it appeared her brother was among them.

"Leon—Leon is here," Jenna gasped and took off out of the room at a breakneck speed. Riza followed close on her heels, determined that nothing bad would befall her brother's chosen one.

Leon leapt from the horse as soon as he saw Jenna's frantic run. She didn't stop until he enclosed her in his arms. "Jenna, I thought you would be glad to see me but—"

"Oh Leon, I'm so glad you're here. I thought you might be with Gio," Jenna cried.

Riza watched as Jenna greeted her brother. She saw the look upon Leon's face when he realized Gio had mated his sister. It wasn't surprise, more like resolve.

"I haven't seen Gio. What has happened to scare you so much?" Leon asked, a furious look upon his face. Riza could only imagine what he was thinking.

"It's Gio's pack. They don't want me here," Jenna whispered.

"Has Gio not protected you?"

"He has tried but I'm frightened." Jenna explained yesterday's attack and Gio's actions as well as the scare this morning.

"If Gio cannot assure your safety then you must return with me," Leon demanded.

"I don't know, Leon. He has declared me his mate."

"Then he should protect you. Has a binding ritual been performed?"

"No, not yet," Jenna hesitantly replied, casting her gaze to the ground as if she feared her brother's reaction.

"Then you are not yet his mate so I am still your alpha, and you will return with me. If the Dark Beast wants you he will solve his problems and come for you," Leon snarled, enraged at Jenna's treatment. "I entrusted him to guard you."

Riza remained quiet, listening to the siblings until she felt compelled to speak. "Jenna, do not leave. Gionne will be angry. I will protect you until he returns or your brother may stay."

Leon turned angry eyes upon the lupine female. "*You* will protect my sister? You do not look as if you could protect yourself," he snarled.

Before Leon could blink, Riza leveled her gun at his heart. Leon's eyes flashed fire before shuttering to an unreadable expression. Meanwhile, the two guards accompanying him dismounted. Members of the Valde immediately surrounded them. It was a recipe for disaster.

Riza nervously glanced at Jenna and in that second, Leon pounced. Knocking the gun from her hand, he dropped her to the ground, breaking her fall with his body. Then he rolled her until she was pinned beneath him. Helpless.

Riza was infuriated at him but mostly herself. She never let anyone get the better of her. It was a stupid mistake. She growled low in her throat, embarrassed he had so easily bested her.

"So, little doggie, do I need to muzzle you?" Leon taunted.

Riza's fury erupted and she bucked beneath his bulk, trying to break free. The giant male pinning her began to purr and she felt the evidence of his arousal against her stomach. She settled beneath him. She would not give him the pleasure of her struggle even though she longed to arch up against his powerful body.

"Leon, she's my friend, turn her loose," Jenna exclaimed.

Leon didn't immediately respond, instead he leaned closer, sniffing her scent. "Too bad we're not alone or I might teach you a new trick or two," he whispered.

Her only response was in the dilation of her eyes and a low hiss.

Leon released his captive and stood next to his sister. By this time they were surrounded.

Emil stepped forward out of the crowd. "What is going on here?"

"It's all a misunderstanding," Jenna supplied.

"There is no misunderstanding, you are returning with me until such a time that Gio can assure your safety. If he can not control his pack he will have to find another female to take as mate."

Riza began to speak but Emil held up a hand to silence her. With Gionne unavailable, he was the ruling male. "Please explain what has happened to cause this disturbance."

After hearing the explanation, Emil expressed his remorse over the situation. He agreed with Leon that he should take his sister home until they could guarantee her safety. "I would not want anything to happen to our alpha female. After all, she could be carrying our future pack leader."

"Emil, you know Gionne would not want her to leave," Riza argued.

"Silence. What I do is for the female's safety and the sake of the pack. Gionne would want her safety looked to first and foremost."

With one last look at Jenna, Riza stomped off. As soon as she reached the forest, she stripped and transformed. Choosing the shape of the wolf, she set off in search of her brother. She had to let him know that Jenna was leaving.

# Chapter Ten

ℬ

They had been on the trail about an hour when Jenna's nerve endings began to tingle an alert. The forest around them quieted even the wind ceased to blow. Jenna shifted in her saddle. Her chestnut mare's ears had perked up and she whinnied nervously. Jenna glanced at her brother. "They're out there, I can sense them."

"I know."

"I only hope it's Gio and not…"

"Do not be afraid, Gio and that female are among the pack following us. I'd be hard-pressed to miss the perfume the female doused herself in."

"It's not her perfume. My stalker used that perfume and Riza just about rolled through it trying to get the scent of the wolf."

A lone howl sounded over the next hill, Jenna recognized it as Gio's and relief flooded her. Cresting the hill she saw them, twelve wolves in all and at the lead was the salt-and-pepper. He was larger than the rest and even in his wolf form, she could tell he was displeased. The hair along his back stood on end and his lip rose in a snarl. Dirk stood a step behind him and he didn't appear happy either. Gio stepped forward away from the pack until he was only a few feet from them. The horses danced nervously. Jenna gripped her reins tightly, afraid the wolf scent would startle her mount.

Unmindful of the eyes upon him, the beast shifted to take the shape of Gio. In this form, he appeared even more displeased if that was possible. His gaze boldly raked Jenna, and after assuring himself she was well, he turned to her brother.

"Did you think I would let her go so easily, that you could betray my trust?"

"I have no wish to betray you. I only wish to see to my sister's safety."

"It is my responsibility to protect her," Gio exclaimed.

"While you were protecting her she could have been killed."

A pained look crossed Gio's face. "You need not concern yourself further. I will keep her at my side until I discover who is behind this."

"That's not—"

"Excuse me," Jenna yelled, cutting off whatever her brother's reply had been. "I'm right here, you know. I'm capable of making up my own mind."

"Then dismount that horse and come to me," Gio demanded.

"Stay right where you are," Leon ordered.

Both male voices held a ring of command and authority. They were used to having their demands followed without complaint.

"I am not some toy the two of you can play tug-of-war over," Jenna huffed. "I will decide my own fate. It is time I decide my future." With those words, she took her life back. It was her choice now. If she returned to Gio, it would be willingly as his mate. If she left with her brother, she would be closing the door on a future with Gio.

She glanced at her brother. He sat smugly at her side, confident she would chose to return with him. He was a good and caring brother. She loved him very much. Her eyes traveled to Gio. He stood before them all, completely comfortable with his nudity, and why shouldn't he be with a body as rawly masculine as his? His eyes that had glared so fiercely at her brother softened as they rested upon her. For a moment, she read uncertainty and fear in his gaze and it gave her the courage to make the choice that would decide her future, her fate. She made the decision with her heart.

Her gaze locked with Gio. "I'm sorry…" she began and she witnessed Gio's face crumble and his shoulders slump before she turned her eyes to her brother. "My place is with Gio now," she finished boldly, glancing apologetically at her brother before sliding with feline grace from her mount. She ran full tilt on the uneven ground and crashed haphazardly into Gio's powerful frame. The collision met with a low grunt and a powerful hug.

"I see your decision has been made. I hope I do not live to regret it." Turning his gaze to Gionne, he said, "Protect my sister with your life."

A look of understanding passed between the two males. "It will be so."

"You have taken her innocence but not made her your lifemate. I expect this to be remedied."

"She is my lifemate," Gio stated forcefully.

"There has been no binding ritual," Leon said reproachfully.

"The Valde require none but if the Carbonesse do, it will be done as soon as possible."

"You have broken our agreement."

Smiling ruefully, Gionne replied, "You may consider the supplies a gift between families."

Leon nodded. "We are still in your debt."

Gio's eyes traveled over the female in his arms. "No. I am in yours."

With a knowing look and a silent salute to his sister, Leon continued with his guards at his side. In the distance a small black wolf watched him. Leon blew her a kiss before he urged his mount into a trot.

"Did you see that?" Jenna asked with a chuckle.

Gionne's brow furrowed. "I will have to speak with my sister. Felines are a sneaky bunch, you know."

Jenna whacked him in the back of his head and he laughed.

"Come," Gio urged her into the woods. The pine needles crunched under their feet as they made their way into dense coverage. Stopping, Gio pulled her shift over her head.

"Gio," she gasped. "Can you not wait?"

A deep chuckle followed her exclamation. "As much as I'd enjoy staying here, we cannot. You must transform now, we are too far from our homelands. I've sent the others ahead and I don't want to be too far behind." His hand gingerly brushed her cheek. "Thank you for staying. I thought…"

"I know what you thought but I have to give us this chance."

"It is more than I deserve."

"You are right it is. I will expect to be rewarded handsomely for my sacrifice."

His chuckle rumbled in his chest. "What is the reward you wish for? I will grant you anything."

"I can not be too hasty. I will think on it."


In their beast form, they ran through the woods. The rugged terrain was no problem for the duo. Their surefooted gait carried them over the snow-capped ridges and icy slopes of their mountain range. Gio carried her shift in his jaws since Jenna refused to leave it behind. They played once again as they had as children. Gio was larger and more powerful than Jenna, but she was quick and agile.

Gio came to a stop, his nose lifted, his ears perked up. Jenna lifted her head and caught a whiff of fresh game and a long pink tongue came out to lick her lips. Gio dropped her shift over a nearby log and without a word, the two beasts trotted off their separate ways. They had devised this game many years ago.

Jenna stealthily approached the deer from below, careful to stay downwind and out of sight. Studying the herd, she singled out her mark. It was a young female grazing slightly away from the herd. She was within ten feet of the doe when a twig snapped under the weight of her paw. The chase was on. She was right behind the doe, and she could take it down herself but that was not the plan. Gio always made the kill for he feared a flying hoof would hurt her. She herded the doe into a deep gorge where her dark beast awaited. In an instant, he was on the doe, his powerful jaws closing around her throat. The doe's long legs kicked to no avail and then she was limp.

Jenna trotted up and licked at Gio's mouth submissively and he affectionately nipped at her shoulder. They danced around their kill for a moment before diving in and gorging on their feast.

\* \* \* \* \*

A while later, they lay sated side by side. One appetite had been satisfied, the other still burned voraciously. The wolf eyed the feline then began to lick at her face. Blood coated her whiskers and muzzle and he knew if she transformed without properly cleaning, Jenna would be horrified.

As beast or man, Gio thought he was basically the same. The beast was more aggressive but the design of his two sides was similar. Jenna was another story. The feline was aggressive and wild; she enjoyed the kill and the feast. Jenna the human suppressed her untamed urges. She preferred to be cautious and careful. He wondered what would happen if Jenna ever truly accepted her feline side and merged with it. Yesterday in his bed, he thought she came close to merging her two sides. With his help, he thought she would eventually be able accept fully what she was. A Carbonesse, part human, part feline, all female and his mate.

The leopard's fur was soft and sleek as the wolf nuzzled her. She lay purring contently as he manicured her pelt. A true cat that enjoyed preening. The aromatic scent of the feline in heat teased the wolf's nose. He rose to stand over her and slowly trotted behind her. Her estrous scent called to the male wolf and he prodded her with his muzzle, asking her to stand.

The feline leopard languidly raised her head, looking over her shoulder at the male looming over her. The look told him she knew what he wanted. Teasingly, she stretched and arched her back. Her backside tipped up in the air, her long tail swinging side to side in a tempting peep show for the inflamed male.

This slow feminine display intrigued the male but he was impatient. He lunged forward, nudging her tail with his muzzle. Her scent was sweet and hot.

The leopard darted forward, trotting out of his reach, and he trailed dutifully behind. With feline speed, she scurried through the underbrush with the aroused male hot on her trail. She led him on a wild chase. She vaulted over branches and obstacles with ease and grace while the wolf powered his way through the forest. Eventually, she took a path the wolf knew dead-ended into a u-shaped ravine with a sheer rock facing. He was positive she knew this ravine had no way out for they had often used it to corner prey. The rock wall acted as the perfect trap for this willing female.

The wolf padded quickly behind the feline, cornering her against the steep impregnable wall of rock. The leopard turned to face him with wary eyes, her tongue lolling out of her mouth as she breathed in a slow pant. The large wolf scented his prey sensing a nervous, but aroused female in heat.

Closing in, he blocked off any passage of escape with his massive frame. Looming over the feline, he nipped her shoulder. She ducked her head and rubbed submissively against the neck of the large male. Using the strength of his powerful body, he maneuvered her around into the position he required. With a powerful lunge, he covered the female and bit down on her shoulder, holding her in place for his possession. At last, his inner beast could run wild. The cries of the wolf and leopard reverberated off the rock facing, echoing across the valley of the high mountain plateau.

# Chapter Eleven

౬

Waking up from a nap the feline found she was no longer alone with Gio, for the other male Dirk was there. Gio and Dirk were engaged in conversation at the edge of the woods. Noticing her gaze upon them, Gio approached. Her tail thumped the ground in greeting.

"Hey, Kitty." Gio bent forward, petting her head. "I hope you now understand why we need Dirk. Your safety is the most important thing. There is nothing I wouldn't do to protect you." His voice was husky with regret. "I'm going to take a walk, I won't be far."

The feline watched Gio walk away and the other male approached.

A firm, knowing hand caressed her back, then her belly. The feline arched, enjoying the stroking hand.

"Transform for me, Jenna. I need you in human form. You are not my mate and in wolf form, I would fuck your pussy. As delectable as your ass is the beast inside would demand I take all of you."

The feline raised her head, looking at the male. This was another thing she had only shared with Gio. She looked warily into the blue eyes watching her. She felt safe.

Transformation complete, Jenna lay on the ground, naked, next to Dirk.

"You are so beautiful."

She smiled nervously.

A hand enclosed her breast and carnal heat flooded low. "I am going to cherish you. I am going to gorge myself between your thighs until my cock is ready to explode, and then I'll fuck your ass even harder than I did last night."

Jenna whimpered as his mouth lowered to nibble a torrid nipple. His mouth was hot and the feelings he evoked were primal, carnal. She didn't experience the warmth of love as she did with Gio but the heat was still there.

He suckled powerfully on the tip and she bucked against him as sweet fire flooded her pussy. He turned his attention to the other breast and a hand dipped between her thighs.

"Oh, yeah," she gasped and tightened her thighs around his hand. Thick fingers probed her wet folds, finding her clit and strumming it.

He lifted his head from her breast. His eyes gleamed and his smile was feral. "You are so hot and wet for me. I only wish I could fuck your pussy."

Jenna tensed; she knew Gio would not allow it.

"Don't worry, your charms are bountiful and I will enjoy everything else. You'll enjoy it too," he promised as he scooted down her body to lay between thighs that gaped open, offering up their hidden nest.

His mouth joined his hand and he licked the length of her pussy. "Mmmm, a hairless mound. I like that." His breath caressed the heated flesh his tongue had laid bare.

Two fingers speared her swollen pussy and his tongue lapped her clit. Juices flowed and he drank.

She squirmed. It was too much and not enough.

He inserted a third finger and his teeth nipped her clit. "Come for me, baby. Let me taste all your sweetness."

His words hurled her over the edge as she rode his thick digits. As the spasms shook her, he removed his fingers, inserting his tongue into her dewy canal. He licked and suckled long after her last ripple of delight.

As she lay replete, he crawled up her body, lowering his fully aroused frame over her. His hungry mouth closed over hers and although she was temporarily sated, she knew he was far from it. His thick erection scorched her belly and he filled his hands with the globes of her ass.

He ground his cock against her, his heavy sac slapping her mound. With a growl, he tore his mouth from her. His engorged length trailed fire between her thighs. His blunt tip nudged her clit then probed her creamy folds.

His jaw clenched, he arched away. "Hands and knees," he growled.

She knew if she didn't move quickly he would mount her pussy regardless of the consequences. She scampered to her hands and knees, backing up until his cock grazed her bottom.

Hurried hands gathered moisture from between her thighs, coating her anus. "It's going to be a rough ride," he groaned as his distended member prodded her anus. His hands spread her cheeks and he slowly thrust forward.

Her breath expelled from her body in a *whoosh*. Her head came up and she gasped for air. She could swear the thing had grown from last night. It grated her flesh as he sought full possession. One hand reached between them, finding her clit and squeezing.

A jolt shot through her body and her juices gushed. With a lusty grunt, he hilted himself. "Tonight you'll take every inch of me," he whispered in her ear. "I'm going to fuck you until you beg me to stop and then I'm going to fuck you some more."

He pulled out then thrust all the way in. She screamed.

He wrapped his free hand around her jaw, raising her head. "Look there in the trees. He's watching me fuck you. He has been watching us. He's heard every moan, pant and groan I've pulled from your lips. He saw as you climaxed on my mouth, while I ate your pussy."

Jenna saw Gio standing just inside the tree line. He leaned against a thick trunk, his cock in hand. He stroked his thick phallus and she licked her lips, watching him. His beautiful face was so full of hunger she wanted to cry out to him.

Dirk bucked furiously into her and his tongue trailed her spine. "Come for me and let him watch."

Two fingers probed her pussy. "You're so hot and wet. You're ready. You want two cocks, don't you?" He thrust harder. "Come for me and I'll call him over. You can suck his cock as I pound your ass."

Jenna shattered, she closed her eyes. She couldn't watch Gio as she came apart on another male's cock.

When she could breathe again, she opened her eyes and Gio was there, kneeling before her.

She parted her lips and he was inside her. She took him deep, deeper than she thought possible. She wanted to eat him whole, devour him.

The two males pumped inside her and tears of bliss streamed down her face. If this wasn't nirvana, she didn't know what was. She thrust back against Dirk and suckled down on Gio.

Dirk's release hit first and his hot, spurting seed sent her over the edge. Her gasping release fired Gio's and she drank his tangy cum down her throat.

Gio gathered her sated form to him and settled down upon the moss-covered ground. She was almost asleep when she felt Dirk snuggle up to her backside.

Arriving back at the palace the next morning Jenna was pleased to find the debris from the broken door removed from the room.

"I had the door taken away. I see no sense in replacing it. You may still have your bedroom retreat to nap in since I designed it especially for you, but I will allow no locked doors between us."

Jenna ignored his dominant attitude since she had no preference for locks between them, instead her mind keyed on the fact that he had designed this room for her.

"You designed this for me?" She turned wide, questioning eyes to Gio.

"Yes. I see this as the perfect setting for your untamed beauty."

"Thank you. From the first time I saw the room I felt at home. It is something I would design for myself. When did you do it?"

Gio hesitated for a minute. "I decorated it a couple years ago," he answered honestly, his dark eyes searching hers for a response.

"Oh," Jenna muttered, her mind churning with possibilities. She surmised that he must have designed this room before their disagreement years ago. She was surprised he had not changed it since then.

"Well, it is very nice. I appreciate it."

* * * * *

Gio was surprised she hadn't gloated that he was obsessed with her. That he had designed this room hoping against hope that one day she would belong to him and that the only way he had ever managed to have her was through force. Gio hung his head as he realized that even though she had chosen to stay with him she had not yet proclaimed her love. Possibly, the love she had once had for him was gone but the desire still burned within her. With time and patience, he hoped that one day she would love him half as much as he loved her. Until then, he would use her desires to bind them.

"I must meet with my guards. I have a stalker to find." Lifting her face to meet his gaze, he said, "Do not be afraid. I will protect you. I will have Riza stay with you and I will be back shortly."

He called Riza from his room, asking her to stay with and protect his mate. She was the only one he knew he could trust fully. Someone close to him, possibly very close was a traitor and he intended to find out who it was and put an end to these threats today.

Shortly after Riza arrived, Gionne left the room, making sure they locked both doors behind him. He would have another guard outside their rooms within minutes.

* * * * *

"How have you been?" Riza asked.

"Fine."

"That brother of yours is something else," Riza said lightly, too lightly.

"Indeed he is," Jenna said, smiling at the other female.

"What did you think of him?" Jenna asked, suspicious that the other female was interested in her brother.

"He's arrogant, domineering and entirely all too cocky."

"He's rather handsome, though, don't you think?" Jenna asked innocently.

"Huh, I didn't really notice," Riza lied not very successfully.

"Yeah, I can understand how you didn't get a good look at him since he was lying on top of you." Jenna tried to keep the amusement from her voice but failed.

"I suppose he is attractive in a feline way."

A knock at the door interrupted the females' conversation. Riza reached for her gun as she asked, "Who is it?"

"It's Emil, Gionne has sent me."

Riza crossed to the door cursing. "Will Gio never trust me?"

Jenna watched the other female open the door. She was surprised when Riza gasped, turned for a second to look at her then crumpled to the floor in a heap. Terror rose in Jenna but before she could react, Emil stepped over the prone female and into the room. He held a dart gun in his hand, aimed at her.

Emil was shaking his head. "The son is prone to make the father's mistakes. I advised them both but neither would listen to me. The Royal Valde bloodline must remain pure. I thought I had put an end to the two of you before but I did not make it final. This time there will be no mistakes."

"You put an end to us?"

"Yes. Gionne thought it was his father's wish but it was mine." Emil stepped closer. "He thought his dying father was opposed to the two of you but in truth he was pleased. He thought the joining of the two royal families would benefit the Valde and the Carbonesse. It was because of that feline mate of his. He had never forgotten her and she colored his view. If I had not intervened he probably would have taken her as his lifemate after Gionne's mother passed away."

"You lied to Gio about his father's wishes, and you stopped Riza's parents from taking a life bond."

"I did what was best for the Valde. It is my responsibility to protect the ruler even from himself. The welfare of the pack must come first." He waved the gun around as he spoke.

Jenna considered her options. Her only hope of overcoming him was in feline form. She had never seen Emil in his wolf form. By the size of the man, he would not be extremely large, she hoped, and he was older. Possibly, she could take him.

"Do not even think about it, a small feline is no match for a male wolf," Emil said, his voice sounded agitated. Obviously, he had read her intentions in her eyes.

"What do you intend to do with me?"

"I will rid Gionne of you just as I rid his father of the other feline bitch."

"You killed Riza's mother?"

"It was the only way. I hid her away until the offspring was born then I eliminated her. If I had known that one day Gionne would find his sister I would have killed the whelp as well." He shook his head before continuing his frantic rant. "That could have been a fatal mistake."

"Riza saw you, now she knows."

"Yes. So, she will have to be taken care of as well."

"You don't think you can get away with this." The longer Jenna listened, the more horrified she became. Emil was obviously very disturbed, she wondered how he had managed to hide it all these years. Possibly the strain had finally snapped his demented mind.

"It matters little what happens to me, it is what is best for the pack."

Out of the corner of her eye, Jenna saw Riza begin to stir on the floor and she hoped to distract Emil long enough for the sleep agent to wear off. "How did you convince Gio that his father was against him mating with a feline?"

"It was easy, too easy. He was afraid his father would be against the match so he came to me for advice. He did not know of his father's previous relationship with a feline. I suggested that I broach the subject with his father since he had been unwell." Emil paced the floor, his eyes had taken on a glazed look as he remembered. "I had not expected his father to be so receptive to the idea. I had no choice. He forced me to take action." He was shaking his head, a bewildered look upon his face. "You understand, don't you, I did not wish to hurt him. I had to. I poisoned his drink and he slipped into a coma."

An evil smile curled his lip. "It worked better than I thought possible. I told Gionne that his father had a stroke while we were discussing his love of a feline."

Jenna gasped, she couldn't believe anyone could be so cruel. She thought back to that day in the woods. Gio had been so upset but he never mentioned his father's illness. She thought of the way she had acted. She felt horrible that she had turned her back on him when he needed her more than ever. "How could you possibly let Gio think he was responsible for his father's illness? He was your alpha and you poisoned him," Jenna screamed.

"The end justifies the means. The Valde are strong. Gionne is strong. Of course, I told him he was not responsible for his father's illness and subsequent death but the idea lingered. The guilt made him a strong leader, putting the welfare of his pack first, until you came here uninvited."

"Gio insisted I stay. He forced me to stay," Jenna retorted.

"You came here as a bitch in heat, sashaying under his nose. He thought with his cock not his mind. In time, he will tire of you but I will not wait. You are bad for the pack. I will not have the next alpha to succeed carry feline blood in his veins."

Chaos broke loose all at once. A low groan escaped from Riza as she began to rouse, spurring Emil into action. He fired the dart gun, nearly hitting Jenna as she dove to one side.

Off balance, Jenna fell to the floor, expecting any moment to feel the sting of the dart. Instead, she heard the door shatter and a menacing growl. She turned just in time to see Dirk burst through the door accompanied by a lupine Gio. The large salt-and-pepper wolf lunged at Emil. He had the older male pinned to the ground in a split second. His massive jaws closed around Emil's neck.

"No, Gio…no," Jenna yelled.

Emil was sick and deserved punishment but she didn't want Gio to rip him to shreds. That was something that could haunt him the rest of his life.

By now, several of Gio's guards had filed into the room. Dirk helped a disoriented Riza to her feet. Gio released his hold upon Emil as one of the guards hauled the terrified man to his feet.

Dirk crossed the room to Jenna's side, lifting her up. "Are you all right?" Concerned eyes ran over her.

"I'm fine." She turned her eyes to Gio as he approached in wolf form.

Gio growled at Dirk and he released Jenna, stepping away. The large salt-and-pepper wolf turned worried eyes to her. He padded to her side, running his eyes and nose over her, checking for any sign of injury. Finding none, he sat next to her and licked her face affectionately.

Jenna sighed deeply. It appeared her ordeal was over but there was so much to tell Gio. She wrapped her arm around the large beast, burying her face in his thick coat. Even in this form, he was a great comfort to her. She hugged her dark beast closer, crying into his fur coat. She cried for herself, for his father and sister but mostly for Gio and the years they had lost. She had much to tell him but for now, she just wanted to be near him in any form.

# Chapter Twelve

**୨୭**

The next few hours passed in a blur. Jenna explained all that Emil had told her to an angry, disbelieving Gio.

Tear-filled eyes watched Gio as he tried to come to terms with the truth. "At least it is over, Gio; he cannot harm any of us further."

Drawing her into a tight embrace, he rested his chin on her head. He absorbed her strength. "I blame myself. I should have sensed the evilness that resides within Emil."

"Why? No one else did. Not your father, any of your guards or I. So, why blame yourself?"

Gionne had no words to respond to this, but he knew it was his responsibility to protect his pack and his mate from harm and he had almost failed them all.

"Gio, I owe you an apology."

"You owe me an apology for what?" he asked in disbelief.

"I should have been more understanding when you asked me to wait. I didn't let you explain. I was rash and jumped to conclusions and my actions hurt us both."

"You have nothing to apologize for. My guilt separated us. I should have told you the truth. If not for Riza, I don't know if I'd have ever gotten over my guilt enough to be with you. After finding Riza, I knew my father couldn't have been appalled at the thought of my mating with a feline." He sighed. "It is a relief to at last know the truth."

His mind replayed that long-ago day. He remembered how excited she was to come of age. The plans they had made to talk to their families. On the last day together, she had snuck away, intentionally leaving Leon behind. The hunger he felt for her that day was fierce. Her estrus had been strong upon her. Never before had he been around her at this time of her cycle and her scent intrigued him even more than usual. Just two days before he had been exuberantly planning for this day. However, when he had seen her, guilt riddled him. He had thought she would understand. She had refused to wait to mate and had even accused him of having someone else on the side. He couldn't imagine how she had thought he would seek another. She was all he ever wanted.

Gionne had been shocked, he couldn't believe the words that spilled from between her lips. The lips he had been the first and last to kiss.

When she had refused to listen, the beast within had clouded his rational thinking. He had come close to taking her that day but at the last minute, reason had prevailed and he let her go. As soon as he released her, she ran off out of his sight. Knowing all he knew now, he wondered if it wouldn't have been better if he had just taken her then, planted his seed and to hell with everything else.

Instead, the wolf had run to the summit of the mountain. Throwing back his head, he cried out in despair for all of both breeds to hear. He cried for his mate even though at that time he thought she would never be his again. He had returned home that night to find his father dead and he now held the role of alpha male of the pack.

"I have never apologized for that day. I am sorry," he said sincerely.

"I am only sorry that we lost so much time. I loved you then and I love you now. I always will," she confessed.

His mouth dropped to hers, taking it in a deep powerful kiss that spoke of his love and a promise of a lifetime together. "I never thought I would hear those words. Although, I have lived these last couple of years hoping and praying that someday you would forgive me and love me. I never stopped loving you." Stroking her hair, he continued, "I designed your room and spent hours sitting in it thinking of you. The only way I kept my sanity was a promise I had from your brother."

"Leon made you a promise. About what?"

"You. He promised me that if you ever became interested in a male he would let me know before you took a mate."

"He did."

"Yes, he did. I think he knew all along what we were too stubborn to admit. We belong together."

"Well, I guess I will have to thank him." After a moment, she asked, "Was this some elaborate ruse from the very beginning? Did Leon know you were going to demand to hold me as collateral?"

"No, but I am sure he knew you would influence me. He probably thought I needed to see you again to give me a shove in the right direction. You don't think he would have left you here if he didn't think it was for your own good." He chuckled. "After all, you were in danger of becoming an old maid."

Jenna bit down hard on his male nipple through his shirt.

He yelped. "All right, all right, I was teasing. I am so pleased you waited for me."

"If I had only known of the promise, I would have become involved with a male just to force your hand."

"Kitty, my Kitty, you never really believed I loved another, did you?"

"I don't know. I was so insecure."

"There wasn't anyone else. Not from the first time we kissed all those years ago."

"You never loved another."

"No. I had sex with willing females when I was younger but after I fell in love with you, I couldn't. In my heart, all these years you have been my mate."

"Oh, Gio. You don't know what that means to me." Tears pooled in her eyes. "No wonder you were so—"

"Hungry, ravenous, insatiable?"

"Yeah."

"I'll always be that way for you," he promised.

"I have decided what I want for my reward for staying with you."

Gio hesitated only a moment as he thought of all the things she could ask for. "Your wish is my command." He prayed her wish did not involve another male but regardless, he would grant it.

Jenna leaned forward and whispered in his ear. Gio blinked his eyes in surprise. It appeared his little feline had accepted her two sides and his. "Damn. Your wish is definitely my pleasure."

"I was thinking—"

"I like the way you think," he said, nuzzling her neck.

"I bet you do. Anyway, I thought we could begin in human form, and then I could change first."

Oh yeah, her feline form licking his thigh the other day had given him definite ideas. "That will be a great start." There were several interesting combinations he wished to try out. The beast within began to come to life in the most primal of ways. He looked into her eyes and smiled. "Is now too soon to begin?"

"One other thing."

"Anything," he promised.

"Dirk…"

Gio shut his eyes so not to reveal his pain. He did not want to share this—her—but it was his fault. He had been the one to introduce her to Dirk and to the pleasure of a ménage.

Jenna softly caressed his cheek and he opened his eyes. Her golden eyes gleamed and a wicked smile tugged at her lips.

"I don't think I need his protection anymore. Do you?"

Elation unlike anything he felt before engulfed him. "I believe you are safe now. I'll have a talk with him. He'll always watch out for you but from a distance." His lips closed on hers. From a far, far distance.

\* \* \* \* \*

Much later, Gio left to interrogate the prisoner, hoping to gain some insight into all that had transpired. There was a guard posted outside her door but Jenna didn't think she needed it.

She shifted and the satin sheets deliciously caressed her tender flesh. Tugging the top sheet over her nakedness, a smile curled a corner of her lips. Life was good. She finally felt safe and loved. She felt as if she belonged here. She was Gio's lifemate, his chosen one and the alpha female of the pack. Gio had told her to plan the binding ritual of the Carbonesse and she knew just where to have it. Their spot in the forest. She hadn't been to their special place since that day. Now, with all the ghosts and miseries behind them their spot would be special again. She pictured the area with a fine sheen of frost, and the snow-capped trees, the clearing full of Carbonesse and Valde celebrating together as one pack. It would be perfect.

She giggled with glee. She loved Gio with all her heart; he was all she truly needed. She cared for Dirk, he appealed to something dark and forbidden within her. She enjoyed her time with him but he needed to find a mate of his own.

Gio fulfilled her body and soul. Her hand dropped to cover her stomach. She was almost positive she carried Gio's baby. She couldn't wait to tell him; he would be a perfect father.

# FERAL LUST

஧

# Chapter One

**ຄວ**

Riza Valde stood at the window of the library overlooking the courtyard brimming with guests. She had come up here to get away, to have a moment to collect her thoughts. The last few months had been a whirl of activity leading up to the joining ceremony between her brother Gio and his chosen mate Jenna. The ceremony would bring together two species of shapeshifters. Gio was alpha male of the Valde lupine pack and Jenna was the sister of Leon Muldrew, the alpha of the feline pride. Of course, her birth was proof of the fact that the breeds had come together before. She was a half-breed but it wasn't something she discussed. It was hard growing up as a half-breed in an orphanage. It would be different for Gio's children—they would be accepted and loved.

She huffed as she scanned the crowd below looking for Leon. The big feline was the reason was hiding in the library. Since she'd first seen him, he'd been on her mind and in her dreams. He disturbed her in a way no other male had ever managed. It wasn't purely physical, though tall, muscular blonds were on her to-do list, or would be, if she had a to-do list. No, it was something else, something primal, elemental that drew her to the feline. Breeds believed that the first time you scented your mate, you knew them for what they were. While the thought crossed her mind when Leon was near, she knew it couldn't be. Even though Leon liked her and appeared to be attracted to her, he didn't react as if he thought she was his mate.

No, Leon was a player and he treated her like any other available bitch. She needed to get a grip on her wayward hormones. Leon was a sexy, attractive male and she was just reacting to him as any normal unmated female would. Lusting after him was as far as she could allow it to go. It wouldn't do to have an affair with Jenna's brother. It might make things uncomfortable. Besides, Gio would go through the roof if he found out. He expected her to be a virgin for her mate. If that was going to happen, she needed to find a mate and quickly. It was getting harder and harder to seek her solitary bed. Especially when she knew what was going on most nights in the community hall. The sounds and scents of the couplings nearly drove her up the wall. More than once she'd considered joining the fun. If she did, she'd be marked for life and considered a pack bitch, fucked by one and all.

At twenty-one, she wasn't over the hill but most lupines her age had a mate to ease the ache of a heat cycle. She was tired of being alone but, with her heat cycle drawing near, she thought it best if she steered clear of Leon, at least for now.

As if her thoughts had conjured him, Leon appeared. As it was to the lion within him, stealth was part and parcel to his nature and he'd entered the room without a sound. He had a natural athleticism and grace, no matter what he wore. Today, he was dressed for the occasion and his elegantly tailored clothes emphasized his broad shoulders and lean hips. His sheer presence stole her breath. His size overshadowed everything. "Hiding, Riza?" he purred as he stalked across the room.

"No. Just taking a break." She smiled hesitantly, the hair on the back of her neck bristled in awareness. "What are you doing up here?"

"Looking for you." The whiskey-rough timbre of his voice shivered along her spine, settling in a quake between her thighs.

Riza laughed, knowing better than to take Leon seriously. Her brother had already warned her about the "randy feline", as he called him. Gio had sensed her interest in the other male and told her that he liked and respected Leon. He was, after all, Jenna's brother and they had been friends for years but…

Riza shivered as she remembered what Gio had said about Leon. *Leon's a great guy but he has a way with the ladies, if you know what I mean. There's always one around and sometimes two or three. He wouldn't set out to hurt you, but he would.*

Leon's quick stride carried him around the big oak desk to within inches of her. His warm, musky scent hung in the air. A predatory air followed him, his deep-set eyes and high cheekbones reminded her of his feral nature. "Are you going to rejoin the party or do you want to stay here?" His hand trailed a heated path across her cheek into her hair. "Personally I'm all for staying right here," he murmured as he tilted her head and poised his lips just over hers. His breath, with just a trace of bourbon, fanned her face. Her senses reeled at his proximity. She needed to remember not to take him seriously. Her pulse pounded and she was sure he could feel it—feel the way his potent, masculine air stirred her blood.

A wayward moan escaped her lips. Leon didn't need any more encouragement and his lips brushed hers in a whispery caress. Gleaming golden eyes watched her reaction from beneath thick, blond lashes.

As much as she wanted to, she couldn't let this get out of control. "Leon I…"

His tongue glided over her bottom lip—the raspy caress of a feline tongue. In her adult life, she'd kissed only one male and it was nothing compared to this. She didn't know if it was the difference in texture or the difference in the male but this kiss was spine tingling. She could only imagine what that coarse tongue was capable of on other, more tender parts of her anatomy. Her pussy slicked with lust. It was best she not imagine it.

"Riza, open your lips for me, baby. Let me come inside." That voice, those words… If he only knew what he was doing to her. Ahh but it was Leon, he probably already knew. Hell, the lust was so thick in the room even a human could scent it.

Of their own volition, her lips parted and waited to be penetrated. Their tongues met—his rough, hers smooth—and they danced to the music that floated up from below. Now she knew what Gio meant when he said an experienced male could bypass her defenses in no time.

She had to grasp his shoulders as her legs weakened. Riza prided herself on always standing on her own two feet. She might be small in statue but she made up for it in might. She trained with the Valde guard but just now, she felt weak as a babe.

The strong band of Leon's arms gathered her close and lifted her up to snuggle against the brute strength of his chest. She felt secure and protected. She didn't want to enjoy it but she did.

When he changed tactics and began to lick the inside of her mouth, she wiggled, trying to alleviate the growing ache burning low in her belly. A large hand settled on her ass, binding her tightly and she felt his thick erection straining against her thigh.

Heart-pounding, thigh-quivering arousal surged through Riza and she knew it was time to stop. "Leon," she gasped as she pulled her lips from his.

Their eyes met and he appeared as dazed with arousal as she felt.

"Riza," his tone coaxed as he lowered his head, trying to recapture her lips.

A well-placed shove to his chest took him by surprise and she was able to regain her feet.

"What's wrong?" Leon questioned. He knew she was as into the kiss as he had been. Even though his usually keen senses were off, he knew she was far from immune to his touch. He had felt her heart pound and the tips of her breasts harden as she turned to liquid in his arms. He only wished he could have smelled her arousal as well. A nagging sinus infection had eliminated his sense of smell and to a feline that was similar to losing sight. As alpha of his pride, it was important not to show any weakness, so he hadn't told anyone of his condition. If he didn't recover soon, he would have to seek medical advice.

"Nothing's wrong. I just don't think this is the time or the place." Her hand nervously brushed back an errant curl that had come loose from her elegant coiffure. The silky texture had felt wonderful and he longed to unwind the stylish twist and allow her long, dark hair to swing freely down her back. He imagined wrapping his hands in it as she knelt before him accepting his cock into her mouth. Damn, just the thought alone made him ache.

He cleared his throat. "You're probably right about that but you could come home with me." Emerald eyes flared with wary need as she took a step back. "Or we could take a run tomorrow," he amended.

"Look, Leon, I like you but I don't want to be another conquest in a long line of conquests. So thanks, but no thanks."

He blinked rapidly, startled by the quick and total blow-off. He was used to getting his way and refusal didn't sit well. "Riza, it's not like that."

"No. What's it like?" Her flippant tone grated his nerves.

"I like you too."

"You like all women. Gio warned me."

His hands drew into fists, his nails extending just enough to dig into his palms. "Gio warned you about me? He fucked my sister the first chance he got and he warned you about me?"

"Hey, Gio loves Jenna, they joined today," Riza reminded him in a chiding tone.

"I helped him with Jenna." Anger burned that Gionne would betray him.

"So? Does that mean he's supposed to sacrifice me? You get to trade sisters, except you just want me temporarily?"

"Damn it! You aren't giving me a chance," he snarled his displeasure, though he wasn't sure he could deny her words.

"A chance to what? You've already fucked your way through the feline females. I guess now you want to start on the lupine females. Can't have enough bitches spreading their thighs for you."

Taken aback at the acid-toned tirade, his eyes narrowed. "I thought you might be different, but obviously, I was wrong." Leon stormed across the room. "Don't worry, you're safe from me." He slammed the heavy wooden door behind him. He had to get out of there. It wouldn't do to run into Gio and Jenna while in such a mood, but soon he'd have a word with his new brother-in-law.

Frustrated, Riza slammed her hand on the desk, and with an angry swipe, sent papers flying. Why did she have to act like a shrewish bitch? Gio had mentioned Leon's reputation but he hadn't painted the picture as dark as she'd suggested. The truth was simple. She was scared. She wasn't used to losing control and she didn't like it, so she'd pushed him away. She worked hard to be in control of her life. She didn't want to lose it but did she want to lose him? Was that what she wanted? If he left now, she might not see him for a long time. He could find someone else—then where would she be? She didn't expect anything permanent with the big feline but she wanted a chance. She'd never know unless she tried. From the first moment she'd seen him, she'd known he was different. She would go after him. As angry as he was, he'd leave a scent trail a mile wide. He shouldn't be too hard to find.

As Riza stepped onto the patio, the party was winding down. There were very few felines left and Leon was nowhere in the vicinity. Gionne and Jenna were saying their goodbyes to a few guests. Thankful they were distracted, Riza took the opportunity to sneak away. Circling the perimeter of the property, she found Leon's trail. He'd left alone, in feral form, his discarded silk shirt left on the ground. She picked it up, inhaling the scent of musky male with just a trace of bourbon, and her pussy dampened. His scent acted as an aphrodisiac and her spine tingled in want of the change. Pulling off her gown, she rolled it up with his shirt. Shifting to lupine form with her gown and his shirt in her mouth, she started after him.

It was a cool evening, great for a run in the woods. His trail followed the stream and about a mile down, she found him. He had shifted back to human form and was bathing in a pooled area. The deep water hid his form from her eyes.

In wolf form, she curled up in the brush and watched the male. Leon's long hair was unbound and streamed across his shoulders in wet, rebellious waves. It was spring in the Faldron Mountains and there was a little ice left at the edge of the stream. The cold didn't seem to faze him. In fact, he still looked angry and she was surprised steam didn't rise from the frigid water.

The evening breeze carried his scent to her and her eyes landed on his pants. He'd discarded them at the edge of the water. With inborn stealth, she edged forward and grabbed the material and pulled it back into the brush. His scent was heavy on the cloth and she had to squelch her urge to roll on the material.

She peeked from cover as she waited for him to emerge. She might be in wolf form but she still had her mischievous, playful feline side.

Changing into human form, she donned her slightly wrinkled gown. She wanted to apologize and she couldn't do that while in feral form. A splash drew her gaze as he turned toward shore. Shaking his head, his wild golden mane fell about his shoulders. Her head spun.

A tawny, muscular chest with just a smattering of hair was first to come into view above the water. His next step revealed rippling abs with a trail of hair leading downward. The next step revealed his crowning glory hanging long and thick down his thigh. If the frigid water had any effect on his cock, it was hard to tell.

Riza swallowed nervously at the sight. Her hands trembled as she wiped their dampness on her gown. What was she thinking? She should leave before it was too late. Her eyes darted up to his face, met his glowing golden eyes, and she realized the time to run had passed.

She held his gaze, refusing to cower before him, as he sauntered closer, unconcerned with his nakedness.

*Don't look down. Don't look down.* Her gaze flickered briefly. "Oh my god." Her hand flew to cover her mouth, to stop the flow of words, but nothing could stop the imprint of his perfect body in her mind. His image was engraved forever on her eyelids and her thighs quivered. She locked her knees to stay upright.

"I wanted to apologize for earlier," she said quickly as he approached.

"Is this the traditional lupine way of apologizing?" His gaze lowered to his clothes in a crumpled pile of leaves under her feet. "If it is, take off your gown and I'll apologize to you." Dark humor laced his words but his eyes were serious.

She glanced down but her eyes lost their way as they encountered his considerable erection, now fully jutting from a nest of golden hair. Nervously, she shuffled and squatted to pick up his clothes. Finding herself on eye level with his groin, she froze. The long, thick, vein-riddled length jerked beneath her gaze.

A gentle hand closed around her jaw, shutting her mouth and tilting her face to meet humor-filled eyes. "You shouldn't leave your mouth hanging open like that or I might think you're waiting for me to fill it."

Riza shut her eyes as heat bloomed across her checks. She had never been in such a predicament.

Leon lightly grasped her upper arms and guided her to her feet. "You are an innocent."

His words fueled the blush that spread across her face and chest but she didn't reply.

"Why didn't you just tell me earlier that I was moving too fast for you?"

"I don't know," she whispered.

"I should have known except..." He hesitated. "I guess you throw me off-kilter."

She tried to smile and a nervous laugh escaped her lips. She didn't know where to look. She couldn't meet his eyes and she wasn't about to look below his waist again so she settled on his chest. It was a nice chest—heavily muscled, tight dusky male nipples, lightly furred.

"Contrary to what you were told, I was raised to respect innocence. And for your information, we don't have pack bitches. Not to say there aren't available females in my pack," he said matter-of-factly. She supposed he saw nothing wrong with it. As an alpha male it was his right to mount the willing females. By nature, males were dominant. It was a lesson she'd learned early in life.

"So, now you won't try to seduce me." It wasn't a question.

Leon laughed. "I didn't say that but I won't rush you into anything you don't want."

"If I do want it?" Her eyes fluttered up to meet his ardent stare.

"Oh, baby, don't say that right now. You don't realize how dangerous those words are." He pulled her closer as his hands slid down her arms to loop around her waist. She could feel the heat radiating off his body.

"I don't understand," she muttered, her mind in turmoil.

"I know. Give it time. There's no hurry."

"Okay." She swallowed nervously. She should be happy for the reprieve. Happy he seemed willing to wait, but deep inside she wasn't. A part of her wanted the dominant male to pursue her ardently. She wanted him to bend her to his will—to take her, mount her and mate her. A low moan escaped her lips.

The sound seemed to rouse Leon and he released her. "If you're done with your anatomy lesson, I should probably get dressed."

"Leon," she reproached as her eyes took another quick jaunt over naked flesh.

He inched closer. "Unless you want to take your gown off so I can show you how we are meant to fit together."

Nervously, she scooped up his clothes and threw them at him. "It's a shame to cover such perfection," she muttered as her fascinated eyes were drawn to his hair. She'd never seen it loose before. As it dried, it lay in waves around his shoulders. It reminded her of the beast she knew lurked within him.

"Thank you."

"What?"

"I said, thank you," Leon purred as he stepped into his pants, pulling them over his sinewy thighs. Her lashes fluttered as she watched him stuff his erection beneath the cloth and force the zipper closed.

"Please tell me I didn't say that out loud?" She shut her eyes to stem her humiliation and even the coolness of the breeze could not stop the heat on her cheeks.

"That I was perfect. Yeah, you did."

"How embarrassing." She turned away as he finished dressing. She should just leave. She'd embarrassed herself enough for one night.

"Don't be embarrassed. I think you're perfect and it doesn't embarrass me to say so." His arms came around her, holding her tightly. Her head fell back against his chest and his lowered his head as he brushed a kiss against her temple. "Thanks for bringing my shirt."

"You're welcome."

"It's getting late. I should walk you home," Leon said but made no move to release her. The musk of male lust saturated the air and her pussy grew slick in reaction.

"I know the way." Riza didn't attempt to move out of his arms. Instead, she sighed as she leaned against the big male. The press of his erection against her ass roused her inner beast and she longed to turn in his arms. To taste and touch every inch of the skin her eyes had so recently discovered.

"I'll walk you just the same." It was several minutes before either of them moved.

* * * * *

The compound was quiet as Riza hurried through the dim halls. Even the community hall was empty as she crept by. The door stood open and only a trace of stale lust remained. She was sure Gionne and Jenna had long retired as had most of the pack. It had been a long day of celebrating and imbibing of spirits. She should probably check with Dirk to see if he needed an extra guard for tonight. She wouldn't sleep anyway.

Entering her room, she tugged her gown over her head and flopped on her bed. Her velveteen comforter rasped her swollen nipples. Rolling to the side, she covered a tight-tipped breast with her hand. It was obvious she was going into heat and Dirk wouldn't let her work guard duty in her condition. You'd think it was a disease and the males were afraid to catch it. It was rather amusing to watch them scurry away from a bitch in heat. As much as the scent drew them, it scared them away. They all were afraid of *the trap*. As if she'd want to trap any of them.

She huffed and rolled over on the bed, staring at the pink canopy hanging overhead. She needed to redecorate. This was the room of a girl, not a woman. No wonder no one took her seriously. It'd be a waste of her time to report for guard duty. She barely guarded anything in the best of times. Gionne and Dirk insisted on treating her like a defenseless girl. Standing in the middle of her bed, she ripped the pink material from the rails. She'd never been overly fond of the canopy anyway. Gionne'd had the room decorated for his little sister, when he'd found her at the orphanage. It had been a thoughtful gesture and at the time, she had loved it just because it had shown he cared. At eighteen, pink lace hadn't been her style but she hadn't complained. Anything was better than the off-white linens of the orphanage. Now though, it was time for a change. It was time Gionne acknowledged she was an adult and a guard.

She wasn't defenseless. *"Too bad we're not alone or I might teach you a new trick or two."* Her cheeks still heated as she remembered her humiliation at Leon's hands. She had pulled a dart gun on him when he had accused her of being unable to defend Jenna. It had only taken him a moment to disarm her and pin her beneath him. The most humiliating part was how her body had responded to him lying upon her. That was when she'd first known he was different. Much different from any other male she'd met.

Unfortunately, he probably saw her as just another female. He wanted her. That was a fact. But Leon liked females—all females. At least they were on speaking terms and she'd had her anatomy lesson. And what a lesson. Just the sight of him set her senses ablaze. She could only imagine touching and tasting such forbidden delights. Even the scent of lust from the community hall wouldn't tempt her tonight. No, there was nothing in there half as tempting as what she'd glimpsed today.

A smile curled her lip at the thought of his goodbye kiss. Since discovering her innocence, he'd been a perfect gentleman. He had insisted on walking her home but had stopped at the courtyard, declining to come farther. The kiss had been gentle, born of tenderness and caring, not of passion and desire as the earlier ones.

Leon had left with a promise to see her very soon. Gionne wouldn't like it but it was time he let her grow up. Her eyes closed, Leon's name on her lips.

\* \* \* \* \*

A nearly full moon lit Leon's way to his stronghold and his steps were lighter than they had been in years. Jenna was finally settled and happy with her mate and his future seemed brighter. The merger of the Muldrew and Valde families was a positive step. The lupines were powerful allies in a sometimes uncertain world.

The mountain was flourishing from the spring rains and game was once again plentiful. It was the time of the seed moon—the time for planting—and his people busily worked their fields. If the coyote band would just stay on their lands, everything would be perfect.

As he neared his home, the call of a female seeking a mate filled the air. His ears pricked. At one time, he would have stopped and serviced the female but tonight he had no interest. Entering his stronghold through a side door, he hoped to reach the peacefulness of his rooms undisturbed.

"Leon." He turned to find Tomas, the head of his guard, awaiting him.

"Hello, Tomas."

"It was a good day. Your sister seemed quite happy."

"Yes, it was a good day," Leon agreed.

"The lupines will be fine allies."

"I've known Gio for years. I trust him."

"I was thinking there might be more joinings between the felines and the lupines."

Leon wondered at his suggestion—did he know about Riza? He didn't think any of his pride saw them together but he could be wrong. He wasn't ready to discuss his feelings for the little lupine. "I suppose it's possible," he replied. "It's been a long day. If you don't need me, I think I'll retire for the night.

"Of course, don't let me detain you."

Closing the door behind him, he stripped off his shirt and stretched. It *had* been a long day and his tense muscles ached. A long soak in the hot tub would be just the cure.

Unfortunately, it wouldn't alleviate the dull ache that had filled his balls since he'd had to leave the innocent Riza. He wasn't used to innocent females or denying himself.

Steam rose around him as he relaxed back in the hot water and his mind turned to thoughts of Riza. He inhaled the heated vapor, hoping to clear his sinuses. Until his sense of smell returned, he couldn't enjoy the full flavor of Riza. The sense of smell was a powerful aphrodisiac. The scent of a hot female sent his lust into overdrive, and a female in heat... He avoided those. Their scent could drive an unmated male crazy but it was a trap. Fucking a female in heat was a sure way to find yourself committed, with a bunch of kids.

The click of a door drew his attention. Jaylyn, a sometimes bedmate, sauntered into the room. Her choice of clothes revealed her intent. A gown—the hem cut high, revealing lots of thigh, the neckline low, showing off bountiful breasts—graced her curves. Ordinarily, he would have risen to the occasion but he found himself curiously unaffected by her overt display.

"Hey, lover, do you want your back scrubbed?" Jaylyn purred while leaning over the tub. Her breasts nearly fell out of their miniscule covering. He could see the edges of her brown puckered nipples. But all he could think of was smaller, firmer breasts that had never been touched or suckled. His lip curled at the thought. He wondered what color Riza's nipples would be, a variation of brown or pink. Soon, he intended to find out.

A splash of water brought him back to the present. "No, thanks."

"What did you say?" Jaylyn blinked. She sounded incredulous at his refusal.

"Not tonight." He had never turned her away before. Hell, he'd never turned any female away until recently, but tonight she left him cold. The ache in his balls was not one she could alleviate. Not one he wanted to alleviate with her.

"You're refusing me? Are you feeling okay or…?"

Leon pursed his lips. He wanted to be honest. It was time he became more than just a playboy. He might not be ready for happily-ever-after but he was beginning to think it might have some merit. "There's someone else."

"That's never stopped you before. Maybe she'd want to join us?" Jaylyn's hand dipped under the water and brushed against his flaccid cock.

"This time it's different." The words surprised him almost as much as his hand wrapping around her wrist, stopping her exploration.

"Different?" Her brow arched. "Okay. Well, I'll be around when you get tired of having just one female." Jaylyn flounced out of the room. If she'd been in feline form, he was sure her tail would have been twitching in annoyance. His lip curled as he wondered which male of his pack would benefit from the rejection.

With a sigh, he sank back into the water. Thoughts of a little lupine filled his mind. She was ripe and ready for the taking. Her innocence surprised him. His taste didn't usually run to virgins but Riza was different. His lips curled upward as he imagined splitting open her tight, virgin cunt. Teaching her to suck his cock and enjoy his thick shaft dominating her ass were experiences he hoped to enjoy soon. He wasn't sure where they were headed but he was sure he would make her his…at least for a little while.

# Chapter Two

ॐ

"I didn't expect to see you so early on the day after your joining," Riza said as Jenna took a seat across from her at the breakfast table.

"Gionne has some business to attend to. Besides, I'm hungry. Eating for two you know." Jenna rubbed her round stomach and smiled happily. "So, tell me what were you talking about with Leon yesterday?"

Riza choked on her sip of coffee. "The ceremony, the weather and such."

"I guess there wasn't a lot of time to talk."

"No." Riza shook her head and busied herself filling her plate. The smell of crisp bacon and scrambled eggs had her stomach growling. She hadn't eaten much yesterday with all the excitement.

"It's hard to talk and kiss at the same time."

"What?" Riza's fork clattered to the table.

"I came upstairs to freshen up and heard voices. I just peeked. You looked cozy." Jenna grinned around a piece of toast.

"It was just a kiss."

"It's never just a kiss with Leon."

"What do you mean?" Riza asked. Jenna was Leon's sister. She knew him better than anyone. Riza wanted to question her but was leery of revealing too much in the process.

"Nothing. I just don't want you to get hurt. I would be ecstatic if you two joined but I know Leon. When he falls, he'll

146

fall like a ton of bricks and no other female will stand a chance. I don't want you crushed."

"There's no need to worry. I can handle Leon." Riza tried to portray a confidence she didn't feel.

"That's what I told Gionne."

"You told Gionne." Riza sighed and closed her eyes. "Did you have to tell *him*?"

"He is my mate and your brother. He only wants what's best for you."

"He's already warned me about Leon." Riza stared into her coffee. "The last thing I need is another lecture."

"We care about you, Riza."

"I know. I have to get to the training field." She shoved back her chair and turned from the table, leaving her full plate untouched. She guessed she should thank her lucky star they didn't know she'd left the compound to go after Leon last night. She could only imagine the lecture she'd get for that.


Riza landed on her ass with a heavy thud. A grimace contorted her face as she raised her head to glare at her blond sparing partner.

"Where's your head today?" Dirk asked.

"Where's your head, asshole?" She rubbed a hand over her bruised derriere. Not only was her ass bruised but her favorite pair of jeans was ruined.

"Testy." He smirked.

"Shut up and practice." Riza gained her feet and poised to attack. If she wanted to be taken seriously, she needed to be serious.

"Not in the mood to talk. What's wrong, cat got your tongue?"

"What the fuck do you mean by that?" Riza charged, sending a flying kick at Dirk's head that nearly connected. At the last minute, his arm blocked the blow, knocking her away but she landed on her feet.

"It means yesterday your tongue was down Leon's throat and I wondered if you got it back."

"What are you, a Peeping Tom? You have to get your kicks watching others now that Gionne won't let you fuck his mate anymore." Delivering a verbal blow that was sure to sting, she spun around and kicked out. This time, her kick landed in the middle of his chest but he managed to catch her foot, shoving her backward to land on her sore ass again.

"Who I fuck isn't any of your business," Dirk growled, standing over her with his hands planted on his hips.

"And who I fuck isn't yours." Riza stomped off the training ground, struggling not to limp. Did everyone know about her and Leon? Maybe it was on the bulletin board.

# Chapter Three

ஐ

"Leon, I didn't expect to see you today. Is everything all right at the stronghold?" Jenna asked her brother.

"Hey, Sis." Leon leaned down to place a kiss on Jenna's cheek and a pat on her rounded, obviously pregnant stomach. "Everything's good. Actually, I stopped by to see Riza." He flopped into a chair across from his sister and eyed the ball of yarn she was using to knit.

"Riza. Hmm, I wondered how long that would take."

"What?" Leon asked, spreading his hands and grinning.

"For you to come sniffing around."

"Jenna!" he tried to sound shocked.

"Look, Leon, don't play games with me or with Riza. She's my sister-in-law now and I like her. I don't want you breaking her heart." Jenna injected a serious tone into the conversation.

"Do you think I could?" he questioned, hoping he didn't sound like an anxious adolescent.

"I don't know. Do you care?" Jenna drilled him with a direct gaze that made him want to squirm. Jenna had long been after him about his playboy ways. She thought it was his duty to settle down and produce an heir. He intended to someday. He was just waiting to find the right woman. He was beginning to think he'd found her.

"Maybe. What'd she say about me?"

"Suspiciously, very little, and usually when Riza's quiet it means trouble."

"I'm just here to join her on an afternoon run."

"Gio won't like it."

"Why?" Leon could understand Gio's defensive attitude but he didn't like it.

"Gio's protective of Riza. She grew up in an orphanage and in some ways, she's street smart, strong and savvy, but she's still an innocent. He won't want her used and discarded."

"I know. I don't intend to use her. We're friends and we'll see from there." Leon lowered his voice. "Just don't warn her away from me." He was not used to asking for favors. He didn't want to plead but this was important to him. His relationship with Riza was on shaky ground at best and any interference from Jenna could tumble it before he had a chance to cement the union.

Jenna cocked her head and narrowed her eyes. "Okay, but don't make me sorry."

His eyes darted around. Several females were tending a flowerbed. A blonde tossed him a come-hither look over her shoulder but he felt no interest in the shapely female. "So, where is Riza, or Gionne, for that matter?"

"Riza's on the training grounds and Gionne's in his office, I believe. I just came out for some fresh air. It's good for the babe." She rubbed her stomach.

"Don't you think Riza's a little small to train with the guard? I don't want her hurt." He didn't like the picture in his mind of Riza wrestling with a male. He was the only male she should wrestle.

"She's fine. It's good exercise and Gionne won't let her do anything really dangerous."

"I still don't like it," Leon grumbled.

"You do care." Jenna patted his cheek. "I knew there was a heart in there somewhere."

"I love you, Jenna." He grinned.

"I know. I love you too, brother. Now let's go find Riza for you."

*  *  *  *  *

Riza trotted to keep up with Leon as he hiked up North Trail Peak. She hadn't traveled this trail since the recent forest fires had claimed much of the woods. She was glad to see the land recovering. Scurrying over the remains of a burnt tree, she asked for the second time, "How much farther?" It wasn't that she was tired, though her ass was still a little sore. She was in great shape. She trained hard almost every day but Leon said he had a surprise for her and she was curious.

"We're almost there." Leo stopped in front of her. "Shut your eyes and give me your hand."

Without her eyes, her other senses compensated and she detected a sweet aroma. Leon hesitated in front of her and she stumbled into him. His woodsy scent filled her lungs.

"Be careful here, the ground's not level and there are some sharp stones," Leon told her as he led her around an outcrop of rocks. Her feet were bare—like most breeds, she rarely wore shoes.

"Are you ready?" Leon asked, his breath a whisper at her ear.

"Yes," she replied, suddenly breathless with excitement. No one had ever surprised her like this.

"Open your eyes."

"Leon," Riza gasped as her eyes settled on a large blanket spread in the middle of the clearing. "A picnic." A basket sat on one corner of the blanket but what truly amazed her were the flowers. Aromatic, cut flowers littered the clearing. She turned, grabbed his hand and squeezed. "Where did you get all the flowers?" She saw roses, daisies, daffodils and many others she didn't recognize.

L.A. Day

"A friend of mine has a hothouse. I had to promise to bring him a fresh kill once a week for a month. I didn't know your favorite flower."

"So you brought them all." She blinked rapidly, refusing to cry. "They're beautiful."

"You're worth it. Wait until you see what's in the basket."

Giggling, she dropped to her knees and flipped open the lid, inhaling deeply. "It smells delicious." Leon pulled out a bottle of wine and an insulated container.

"Seasoned rib tips, baked potatoes, fresh bread and wine." Riza's stomach growled and they both laughed.

"I guess you're hungry. If you want to fill our plates, I'll pour us some wine."

"Okay." Riza filled plates for each of them and settled cross-legged in the middle of the blanket. "Mmm, this is delicious." Riza closed her eyes, savoring the rich flavor of the rib tips.

"Have some wine." Leon handed her a wine goblet, the red liquid swirling in the crystal.

Tentatively, Riza took a sip. She wasn't used to drinking. The wine was sweet with just a little bite to it. Licking her lips, she lifted the glass to her mouth again. "This is good."

By the time she'd finished eating, she'd polished off her third glass of wine. "I'm stuffed." She laughed, rolling over on the blanket and patting her flat stomach. "My jeans are too tight."

"Take 'em off." Leon flashed a feral grin. "If it'd make you feel better, I'll take mine off too."

"Ha, real funny." Scooping up a handful of cut flowers, she buried her heated cheeks in the array, sniffing the fragrant blossoms.

"Don't you trust me?" Leon purred.

"Maybe I don't trust myself." Her eyes fluttered up to meet his lust-filled gaze.

Leon's grin vanished as he silently watched her. Golden eyes gleamed as he rolled to her side. "Leon," she gasped breathlessly. His nearness played havoc with her nerves.

"Shh, I won't do anything you don't want." Thick fingers rubbed her belly in slow but tight circles.

"But…"

"Riza, I know you're innocent. Trust me."

Biting her bottom lip, she studied him. He hovered over her, the feral predator waiting to pounce. An involuntary shiver rocked her frame. Her pussy quivered from just the brush of his big body as he settled close to her and she clenched her damp thighs together. Her arousal fragranced the air and she knew he could smell her ripe scent. The scent that proclaimed she was nearing her heat cycle. Honorable males didn't dally with females in heat unless they had serious intentions and she held that thought dearly as she made her decision. Throwing caution to the wind, she nodded. "Okay."

A grin split his handsome face and her heart turned over. *Oh lord, she would probably regret this.*

His head lowered until his lips brushed her cheek. "Your skin is so soft," he whispered at her ear. "I want to taste you." His tongue dipped into her ear and she gasped as tingling sensations rode her spine.

"Leon."

"Relax," he purred, his hand sliding from her hip to just below her left breast. "I won't take you but I need to touch you, taste you. I need to see if you're real, if what I feel is real." His ardent plea stirred her deeply.

His tongue parted her lips at the same time his hand closed on a cotton-covered breast. Riza whimpered, arched and then shuddered as delicious sensations unfurled low in her belly. Her hands fluttered, unsure what to do. They landed on his shoulders—his warm, heavily muscled shoulders. The silk shirt slid easy across his skin as she learned the contours of his back. Long, golden hair bound at his neck drew her fingers and they tangled in the silken strands before tugging loose the tie. A curtain of hair fell around them, enveloping them in his musky, male scent.

He growled low in his throat as she writhed beneath him. Petite in stature, she truly felt diminutive as he blanketed her body. His mouth devoured hers as his tongue thrust repetitively between her lips. With every breath, she inhaled his scent, his musk. She breathed him, tasted him and absorbed him into her pores. Her heart pounded and her senses tingled as her pussy ached with need. She arched upward as her hands tore at his shirt. Her inner beast surged to life and his shirt ripped beneath her extending nails as she fought to hold off the shift to feral form.

"Riza," he growled, as their lips broke apart. "Breathe." His own voice was breathless as he gently stroked her body.

"Help me, Leon." She felt tears pool in her eyes. She hated feeling helpless and out of control. Never before had the beast within tried to wrench control from her.

"It'll be okay, baby. It's my fault. I took you too far too fast. I didn't expect you to react with such need."

"I'm sorry." Tears began to roll and she sniffled. She'd done nothing but embarrass herself since their first meeting. It was a wonder he wanted anything to do with her.

"Sorry! Don't be sorry. Riza, you were burning me alive. It's never been this good. When we make love, we'll set the world on fire." His arms wrapped around her, holding her tight, rocking her in his arms.

Harshly, she inhaled as her body trembled, still trying to come down from such dizzying heights. "Leon, I can't…"

"I know. Let me make it better for you." His warm hand slid under her T-shirt raising it over her chest. Her stomach muscles twitched as he exposed her unbound breasts. "I'll bring you down nice and easy. Next time you won't be so overwhelmed."

Riza whimpered under his knowing touch. She should stop him before she lost control again.

"Close your eyes and breathe." His big warm hand palmed her breast and a thumb gently strummed her nipple. "Relax and concentrate on my touch."

Her nipples tingled and little jolts of energy shot straight to her clit. She licked her lips and sighed. Heat filled her veins and bloomed on her skin.

"Do you feel good?" Leon purred, his lips brushing her ear.

Riza nodded. Good didn't begin to describe the way he made her feel.

"This is going to feel even better." His warm breath fluttered across her chest. Startled, her eyes popped open and watched as his mouth closed over one tight-tipped breast. Her breath lodged in her throat. His mouth was hot, wet as he suckled gently and light exploded behind her eyes. His raspy tongue flicked her nipple and something burst. She groaned and arched upward. "Leon."

"That's right, baby. Enjoy it, revel in it."

She mewled unintelligibly as he rolled her nipple between thumb and finger. All these years she'd been exposed to the scents and sounds of mating but she'd never realized the true joy of it.

"What are you feeling?"

"I don't know. I tingle and I ache," her voice vibrated with need. She had no words to describe the sensations.

"Here?" he asked laying his hand low on her belly. At her nod, he slid his hand lower until his fingers cupped her denim-covered mound. She gasped and arched up as white-hot sensation burned. His fingers pressed down tightly over her aching center.

"Leon." Oh lord, she should stop this.

"You need this, baby. You're so hot and wet. I can feel it through your jeans. You need to come."

He began working her jeans over her hips and she panicked, grabbing at his hands, but he refused to give way. "No..."

"It's okay. I'm just going to touch you." She didn't protest further as he striped her pants down her legs. Cool air settled over her heated flesh and she shivered.

Lying nearly naked next to him, a blush heated her skin and she clenched her thighs together.

"Relax," he purred as he stroked her thighs. She unclenched her legs and one hand dipped between them. His fingers parted her slit, finding her clit and she lost her will to protest. "That's it, bend your knees." Her thighs trembled and she tried to press them back together. "No. I want you open." His breath fanned her tender folds. "You look so delicious drenched with sweet cream." The words had no more than left his lips when the heat of his wicked tongue flicked her nub.

"You shouldn't...you shouldn't," she pleaded as her back arched and she writhed beneath his touch.

His raspy tongue took one slow lick through her folds. "Ahh, fuck." Her heels slammed the ground as she bucked against him. "No...no," she begged. The sensations he ignited frightened her.

His thumb worked her clit as his tongue dragged a merciless path along her pussy lips. Her body vibrated, her heart pounded and she couldn't breathe. The sensations built and tormented but release lurked just out of reach. "Leon, please..."

"Okay, baby, come for me." He pinched her clit as his tongue scrapped her folds and something—a finger?—thrust into her pussy. In and out, it drove deep and that was all it took for the sensations to boil and burst. She screamed as her hands wrapped in his hair. Her legs closed on his head as she rocked and groaned. Her pussy clenched and pulsed as he continued to lap up the cream that poured from her body.

Leon's mind spun dizzily as he slurped the most delicious cream he'd ever tasted. He hadn't tasted a virgin's cream in years but he didn't think that was the difference. No, it was something else. He had his suspicions but…he wasn't ready to jump to conclusions. If only he had all his senses functioning properly.

Lifting his head, he met misty green eyes. "Riza." She looked like a well-loved woman. Tousled hair, flushed cheeks and swollen lips drew a grin to his face. "It's okay." He stretched to lie alongside her. "Damn, that was sweet." He licked his lips, savoring her taste as he willed the ache in his cock to subside. He wanted her but he wanted it to be right for her. She wasn't ready for him to take her, not yet. His cock throbbed as he thought of burrowing into her virgin flesh. Sweat dotted his brow as he thought of parting her. He wanted to break her open and be her first—her only man. Closing his eyes, he shook his head, trying to clear his thoughts.

"Is everything okay?" she asked.

Her voice drew his gaze. A rosy blush feathered her cheeks and her eyes darted away. "There's no need to be shy," he assured her.

"I never…"

"I know and that makes it all the sweeter." She was tight on his finger. He could only imagine what it would feel like to fill her with his cock. *Shit!* He couldn't think of *that*. Not now.

"I guess I'm a novelty." She tugged her shirt down covering her small, beautiful, upturned breasts.

"Hey. You're more than that. Much more." He tilted her chin up to mesh their gazes. "I told you I've never felt anything like what I feel with you."

"I thought…"

"You thought it was just a line so I could get in your pants? I don't lie, Riza. I admit I've had my share of conquests but I don't seduce virgins. The females I'm with know the score." That was true, usually Leon plied his charms on the experienced females who knew what to expect and enjoyed a good fuck with their alpha male.

"Oh. So, what are you saying?" Wide, misty eyes watched him and his chest swelled.

"I don't know. I've never... Hell, Riza I'm out of my depths but I know what we have is special." He hesitated, wishing, not for the first time, that he had all his senses so he could be sure of what his heart and body were telling him. "I know when I see you, I ache. I kiss you and my heart pounds. I touch you and I'm instantly hard."

"Leon..."

"Why try to hide it? You've seen it and felt it." He shifted against her, letting her feel how hard he was for her right now. "Baby, I see you and I want to carry you off to the nearest bed." He grinned and rubbed his cheek to hers. "Or, blanket."

"Leon, I feel funny when I'm with you too. It's just lust though, that's why I tried to avoid you." Her shy confession hurt. Leon was surprised to feel a pang in his chest at her words—*just lust*. There was certainly lust involved but just lust? He wasn't sure.

"Avoiding me didn't work, did it?"

"No."

"It only made you want me more—made me want you more." He shifted his hips against her, emphasizing the point.

"Yes but I don't want to be just another on a long list of conquests."

"You could never be just another anything. Not to me. We'd better get you dressed before I do something we'll regret."

"But you didn't..." Her eyes lowered and he felt his cock grow impossibly longer behind the tight denim.

"That's okay. I'll manage." He'd take her home and then find a secluded place and yank until he went blind.

"I could…" She gulped and her eyes fluttered nervously.

His heart pounded at just the thought of her touching him intimately. "That's probably not a good idea." His engorged cock throbbed angrily, reminding him that he didn't have to be noble. She had offered.

"But Leon I don't want…" She met his gaze, her eyes overly bright. "I don't want another woman to…"

"Riza, I won't."

Her small hands settled on his zipper. "Let me, please."

"Fuck, Riza." His cock pressed against the denim from the inside, helping her to lower the zipper.

"I can touch you and kiss you." She parted his pants and his eager cock sprang free into the warmth of her hands.

"Riza, I won't last long. Baby, I'm too hot. You're not ready for this," his mouth muttered protests as his cock stretched in her warm grasp. It was too late to stop now.

"I am." Her determined eyes met his and she licked her lips. "I am."

Her hand was small but strong as she gripped his shaft and his hips bucked. He clenched his jaw. He didn't want to embarrass himself. Known for control and stamina, in her hands he melted. "Take it slow."

"Show me. Teach me," she begged and his will to resist crumbled.

A growl escaped his lips as he enclosed her hand. Her fingers didn't reach all the way around his girth but he settled her fingertips along the vein on the underneath side of his cock. Shuffling her hand up and down, he taught her the rhythm that was sure to send him over the edge. "I'm close," he panted, "but I don't want it to end." Blistering heat suffused his cock and he gritted his teeth as he held his release at bay.

"I want to taste you."

"Oh shit." He'd never survive sliding through her luscious lips.

Her lips hovered over his cock and he was positive his shaft stretched another inch. He strained toward her mouth. "Lick me," he gasped, his hand tangling in her dark, silky hair. "Riza, suck it."

Her hot little tongue darted out, flicking the head of his cock and pre-cum trailed in its wake. "Damn, that's sweet." He fought to control his lust, his desire to thrust deep.

Her lips stretched around his cock head as she lowered her mouth. He sucked in a strangled breath as she took him deep. Her teeth lightly scraped his rigid flesh as she drew back. He panted. She was a fuckin' natural at sucking cock.

She circled his cock head and slammed down his length and he nearly lost it as most of his shaft disappeared into her mouth and throat. "Fuck." He grasped her head, wrapping his fingers in her luxurious hair and holding it back as he began to pump his hips. There was no way he was going to spill on the ground after being that far down her throat.

"Suck it—use your tongue," he encouraged as he thrust deeper into her warm, welcoming mouth. His sac tightened as lust rode him hard. She looked so hot with her mouth stretched wide for his cock. He gritted his teeth but he couldn't hold back any longer. His release surged up his shaft.

"I'm coming," he warned as he pumped faster. His balls burned with release. He held her head still as his seed washed down her throat. Slowly he pumped the last of his cum into her mouth and collapsed back on the blanket.

If he hadn't been so replete, he would have laughed at the look on her face. "Did you get a little more than you bargained for?"

She smacked her lips. "I...mmm." She ran the back of her hand across her swollen lips. "I think I liked it." She grinned and light danced in her emerald eyes.

His heart thumped. What more could he ask for. "Wait until I stretch your tight little cunt with my cock."

"Leon, I never…"

"You want it. You want my cock filling your pussy…filling your ass. You want to be my bitch," Leon purred. Adrenaline surged as he watched her eyes flare with hot, aching need. "I can't wait to part your virgin cunt."

Riza's eyes widened and she swallowed deeply.

"I want you to hunt with me tomorrow," he whispered.

"What? Hunt?" Her brows drew together as if she wondered if she'd heard him correctly.

"Yeah, we owe my friend a fresh kill as payment for our feast."

"Is that all you want—to hunt?" Riza stuttered over the words, bringing a smile to his face.

"No. I want you spread eagle and willing beneath me. I want your ass tipped up in the air begging for my cock but tomorrow we hunt."

"Only hunting?" she asked in a breathy voice as her eyes lowered to his semi-erect cock.

"I won't take your virginity—not yet. But I won't promise not to taste you again. I won't promise not to strip you down and lick you from head to toe." He felt his cock harden. If he wanted to keep his control, he had to get them out of this situation.

"Oh my god."

# Chapter Four

❧

Riza couldn't help but grin as she looked at one of the three beautiful bouquets she'd made with the flowers Leon had given her. She'd heard Gionne's comment to Jenna about the flowers. *Leon's in hot pursuit. I'd better remind him Riza is innocent and had better stay that way.*

She could only imagine Leon's reaction to that. She wasn't as innocent as she had been and who knew what tomorrow would bring. She only hoped Gionne didn't interfere with their relationship. She was twenty-one, old enough to know her mind and take a mate or lover if she chose.

Riza twirled about the room to imaginary music as she inhaled the scent of a deep-red rose. Tomorrow, she would hunt with Leon in feral form. She'd get to see him as a powerful, predatory lion. She couldn't wait. She tried to picture him with a tawny mane and rippling muscles under golden fur. The fur kept melting away and she saw him as he looked stepping from the water. His bare rippling muscles covered with a smattering of hair.

Riza stumbled and fanned herself with her hand. It was getting hot! She was getting hot as her heat cycle came upon her.

Her lip curled as she wondered what the lion's reaction would be to a wolf in heat. A picture of a lion mounting a wolf flashed in her mind. It would be dangerous to go to him in her condition but she did not intend to stay away.

\* \* \* \* \*

Riza reclined in the lounge chair on her balcony. The cloud-laden sky was dark without a trace of the seed moon.

Only an odd star or two twinkled here and there, reminding her of the wink of Leon's golden eyes. The sounds of feral mating had long since died off and only an occasional howl filled the cool night air. Her eyes had yet to close as she waited for dawn to light the eastern sky. At sunrise, she was going on a hunt with Leon and she couldn't wait. The taste of paradise he'd given her only made her hungry for more. His talk of possessing her pussy and her ass was scary, exciting. Growing up in an orphanage, she'd seen it all. She'd never participated but she'd witnessed females being taken in a multitude of ways by one, sometimes two or three, males.

She remembered one hot day when she'd been sneaking back from a dip in the pond and had stumbled across a young couple. Shocked and yet aroused, she'd stopped and watched. Jake, an older boy from the orphanage, knelt behind Ella, his hips furiously thrusting as he fucked her. Wet skin-slapping sounds filled Riza's ears. Riza remembered gasping, and Jake's eyes had risen, meeting hers. He'd smiled ferally as he'd withdrawn from Ella's cunt. He'd wanted Riza to see his long, wet cock. With their eyes still locked, he'd thrust forward and Ella had screamed as he'd breeched her ass. Riza had broken eye contact as he worked more and more of his cock into Ella's body. She could still hear Ella's cries of tormented bliss as the large cock had taken her ass.

Holly, Riza's roommate at the orphanage, had told her that males fucked their female's asses as a way of dominating them. It was total submission to offer your man your ass. She'd said ass-fucking hurt in a good way and that once taken that way she would crave it. Riza had always thought Holly was crazy to think such a thing.

Riza stretched her tense muscles. Now she was beginning to understand. She certainly craved the feel of his tongue. Her pussy quivered just thinking about stretching for his thick cock. Her stomach fluttered and her ass puckered as she thought of Leon breeching her sphincter. Oh lord, she was in trouble. Her heat cycle was nearly upon her and she ached to have him possess her in every way possible. The roar of a powerful animal filled the air and her ears pricked. Was it Leon? Her body hummed as she stared into the darkness. She was barely able to contain the urge to change under the darkened sky.

* * * * *

Long before the sun was up Leon arrived at their agreed upon meeting place. It was a small meadow not far from the lupine stronghold. He didn't want Riza traveling far without him. Riza might think of herself as a guard but to him she was a female and he would treat her as such. He'd wanted to meet her at the stronghold but Riza had refused. She feared Gionne would not allow her to leave with him. Soon, he would have to speak with Gionne about Riza but today was for them alone.

Leon scouted the area and saw nothing amiss but he did spot a herd of does bedded down with their young. Fawns were a tasty treat but he had no heart for killing them. He preferred a buck or a doe without offspring. They could scout some more when Riza arrived.

Striping off his shirt, Leon recited a prayer for the hunt. A prayer for safety and one of thanks for the animal that would give up its life to them. A slight sound alerted him to a presence moving closer. He knew it was Riza. He could sense her nearness. His spine tingled as she neared.

* * * * *

Riza had left the stronghold as the sun was rising. She couldn't risk coming across Gionne. He would immediately realize how close she was to the full bloom of heat and he would forbid her to leave the safety of pack. He would forbid her to see Leon. As her alpha and brother, he had the right.

The brisk morning air invigorated her step as she neared the clearing. Surprisingly, Leon was already at the pre-arraigned meeting spot and Riza's heart thumped at her first sight of him in the morning light. She stopped, not wanting to interrupt as he stood stripped to the waist, his arms raised in what she knew was a prayer. The muscles in his back and shoulders flexed as he lowered his arms and her heat burned feverishly.

Without turning, he called her name. "Riza." She stepped over a fallen log and into the filtered light of the clearing. "I was praying for a safe and successful hunt."

"I saw." The smile on her lips trembled as he turned and reached for the snap on his jeans. They'd agreed to hunt in feral form and Riza avidly watched as Leon began to disrobe.

"I've never seen you in feral form. Jenna said you morph into a lion." Riza nervously licked her lips.

"Does that scare you?" His thumb rode the thick ridge visible beneath the denim.

"No, w-why would it?" The stutter of her words belied her denial.

"It shouldn't. I just know your experience with felines is limited. I've seen you at a distance. The day you held the dart gun on me."

Riza arched a brow. She wouldn't say her experience with felines was limited. She had assumed Leon knew she was half-feline. Jenna had scented it immediately. She started to tell him and then stopped. It might be fun to keep her secret for a little while. "Hey, don't remind me of that day."

"Why? I rather enjoyed taking you down. Having you beneath me, except for that horrible cologne you bathed in." He flashed a cocky grin in her direction.

"That wasn't my cologne. Emil used it to cover his scent when he was trying to get rid of Jenna. I was trying to save your sister."

"I know. Thank you. Not many females would risk their lives that way. Now I'm thinking I don't want you doing it again," he purred as he lowered his zipper.

"I can handle myself. Next time, it won't be so easy to take me d-down." She stuttered and blinked rapidly as his cock sprang free.

Leon's golden gaze trailed over her. "You think so? I bet I could take you down."

"You're b-bigger."

"Yeah." His fingers caressed the length of his cock and her eyes followed in fascination. "I am bigger."

She licked her lips. Her pussy quaked as she watched his hand. She remembered the feel of his distended flesh and her fingers itched to reach for him.

"Do you want to take me down? I might let you if you promise to get on top," Leon teased as his hand caressed the burgeoning flesh.

"I…"

"You need to undress before you change." Leon took a step closer.

"I know." Nervously, she twisted her hands.

"You shouldn't be shy. I've seen and touched every inch of you. You've seen, touched and sucked several inches of me too."

"Leon…" She took a step backward.

A feral grin split his face and she knew she was in trouble. *Oh lord. This was a bad idea.* "Leon, I've never changed in front of anyone."

"Change in the privacy of the woods if that makes you more comfortable."

She nodded her head but her feet refused to budge. Leon's pants dropped. "Okay." She darted for cover.

"When you return, I'll be in feral form. Don't be afraid, I won't hurt you," he called to her retreating form.

\* \* \* \* \*

166

The lion stalked the clearing waiting for the lupine female to join him. The sinus infection affected him even in feline form and he could barely scent his little lupine but he heard the rustle of leaves as she approached. The hair on his neck rose as she neared. The small dark wolf stopped at the tree line and a growl rumbled low in his chest as he licked his lips.

The lupine approached, head up, ears twitching. She was sleek, shiny, beautiful, and he wanted her. She stopped in front of him and her emerald eyes met his. He shook his mane, fluffing his hair as he padded in a tight circle around her. He was over twice her size. Her tail twitched nervously and he buried his nose in her backside, trying to get as much of her scent as possible.

She trembled but her tail rose slightly, granting him access. She was wet and he licked at the building moisture. Her sweet, ripe taste fired his blood. His cock was heavy and dripping with pre-cum. The beast was ready to take her—to make her his bitch.

The lupine whimpered as he lapped at her backside and a part of him knew he was too large and too heavy to take her but another part didn't care. Lust rode the lion hard and he growled. With a roar, he postured and his chest pumped out. His tail twitched as he prepared to mount his bitch.

The lupine shivered and he hesitated. Turning his head to one side, he blinked rapidly. The female was scared. He could sense her fear. With a growl, he shook his mane and stretched as he morphed back into human form. Kneeling at her side, he stroked the lupine and she turned wary eyes his way.

"Riza, transform for me."

The lupine tossed her head as her nostrils flared. Her back arched as transformation began.

"Leon." Riza curled her legs up and covered her breasts with her hands. Wide, dazed eyes stared at him as her skin flushed. He knew she was aghast to have changed forms under his eyes.

Lifting her, he sat her on his lap and rocked her back and forth. "I'm sorry, babe. I thought I could handle it. I've never had trouble controlling my instincts like that. I would have hurt you if I'd taken you for the first time in feral form. Fuck! It's hard enough to keep my hands off you as it is. The beast in me only knows how much I want you."

"I don't think I would have minded." Her face nuzzled his neck, burrowing beneath his unbound hair.

"You would have minded when I tried to force my cock into your virgin cunt." He could imagine the lupine scream of horror as his feral half mercilessly breeched her tight canal.

"Leon!" She shifted on his lap and her small, hard-tipped breasts scraped his chest.

"It's true, as a lion I'm even bigger." Wide eyes lowered to the erect cock straining between their bodies. "And rougher. I wouldn't want to hurt you but in the grip of such powerful lust I would have mounted you with little care."

"Oh."

His hand glided along her thigh and hip. "But as a man, I'll take all the time in the world preparing you. I'll stretch you, so there'll be little pain when I penetrate you." His fingers parted her slit, finding her wet and needy center. Gathering moisture, he worked a finger into her tight canal. A gasp escaped her lips and her eyes rolled back as she arched, offering her peaked breasts up for his mouth. It was an offer he couldn't refuse and his mouth engulfed the pebbled tip. The touch, the taste of her filled his mind and senses. If he could scent her, the moment would be perfect.

She writhed as his finger worked deeper into her soft, wet heat. "I want you so much," he whispered against her soft skin. "I'm starving for you, hungrier than I've ever been." Pressing her clit with his thumb, his finger butted against her maidenhead and stopped.

"Don't stop." She twisted on his lap as her hip rode his aching erection.

"Settle down, you'll push me too far." His finger pumped slowly in and out of her tight depths.

"I need you." Her hands buried in his hair and lifted his head to meet her mouth.

"Riza. I want you...need you too." Their lips brushed and his tongue slid along her full bottom lip. "You're so wet...so tight...and the heat..." He inserted another finger in her scorching canal. She would burn him alive.

Riza accepted his tongue, welcomed it in a suckling caress. Heat-driven lust urged her on. She'd been unsure of mating with Leon until he had acknowledged her condition. There was no doubt he knew she was in heat. He knew if they mated, she'd most likely conceive his child. If he was willing, she was too. She wanted him and his child.

Another thick finger joined the first, stretching her tight confines and she gasped. Panting for breath, she rode his fingers.

"Riza, are you sure? Once I start...I don't know... It's never been like this." Leon's voice quaked with need and fired her lust.

"Yes, Leon. I don't want to stop. It feels too good." She ached for him. His fingers weren't enough. She wanted more. She wanted all of him buried deep inside her body. She needed his cock to stretch her and fill her with his cum. It was the time of the seed moon. The time for planting and she wanted his seed. She wanted it to take root in her body.

Rolling, he stretched her out, pining her beneath him and she didn't even notice the coolness of the ground. "I'm going to make this so good for you...so good for us." His hands gathered her breasts to his mouth as his leg parted her thighs. She bucked against his thickly muscled leg. Her hands glided down his smooth back, finding and squeezing his tight backside. Liquid heat pooled low in her belly as she ached for his total possession. She arched up. His hands, mouth and thigh weren't enough. She needed more.

"Leon, please." Her drenched pussy pulsed. The rich, thick aroma of her cream scented the air.

"I know, baby." His lips trailed a scorching path down her stomach and her belly trembled. "I want to taste you, drink your cream as you come for me." His head dipped and her insides twisted as his rough tongue lapped her clit.

"Oh sweet heavens," Riza cried at the heady torment of his feline tongue on her tender flesh. "I can't..." her words lodged in her throat when his thumb pierced the tight hole of her pussy, pushing deep.

"Leon!"

"Come for me," he purred against her quivering pussy. "Feed me your cream."

Sharply, he nipped her clit and purred as her pussy pulsed. Thigh-quaking pleasure let loose and she cried out as liquid heat poured from her body. Growling, he fed voraciously between her thighs.

Feral lust gleamed in his eyes as he raised his head. "Mine."

Blind lust tore through his body. His cock throbbed in want of his little lupine. The taste of her rich cream ignited his blood and he sucked in a deep breath and tried to control his desire. His need to possess her ravaged his mind. He wanted to part her thighs and thrust deep into her virgin cunt but he didn't want to hurry Riza. This was an experience to enjoy. It was a time to treasure together.

His eyes traveled from her breasts, across her small waist to the splay of her thighs. Damp curls covered her mound, obscuring his view of swollen pussy lips. He inhaled deeply, bemoaning the loss of his sense of smell. He knew her scent would be ripe with arousal as she lay spread and waiting for him.

"Riza, I'm going to prepare you for my cock." His hand shook with the force of his control as his fingers found her slick folds.

She nodded as her eyes widened and she gulped. She was so beautiful, innocent and trusting and he was about to make her his. His spine arched as he fought his inner beast.

With their eyes locked, he inserted his finger into her tight depths and enjoyed the flare of the flames in her eyes. Adding two more cream-covered fingers, he parted tight inner flesh and stretched her slick canal. She gasped. Gleaming teeth worried her bottom lip and he hesitated.

"Are you okay?" Slowly, he worked his fingers deeper.

She nodded her dark head. "Yes." Her breath hissed out.

"There will be some pain." He wished he didn't have to hurt her but there was no other way to make her his.

"I know."

"After the pain, I'll give you ecstasy," Leon promised.


Riza bit her lip nervously as she watched the looming male. The call of her heat was building again but a nagging voice warned of wrongdoing. No words of joining or love had passed his lips and she feared mentioning them. Leon was a player. A seducer, and unless she stopped him, he would take her innocence. She licked her lips, the words stuck in her throat.

"Riza, you're so beautiful, this is so beautiful. Together, we will find paradise." A fingertip circled an especially sensitive spot deep inside her, bringing a howl to her lips. "That's it, baby. Relax, accept me."

He adjusted his position and his thick shaft brushed her folds. The blunt tip prodded her clit and she whimpered at the budding sensations.

"Tell me you want me." His deep baritone shivered her spine.

"Leon."

The thick head of his cock lodged in her opening. "You're so hot. You're killing me. Are you ready? Can you take me?" Leon's husky voice tore her last defense.

She nodded. "Take me, love me," she gasped as the primal urge to mate filled her.

"God, yes," he groaned. Grasping her hips, he held her steady as he leaned forward. His cock burrowed deep and she struggled to breathe but the sensations of fullness, rightness, continued to build. Wrapping her legs around his waist, she urged him deeper.

Tugging at his hair, she pulled him down and met his mouth, biting his full lower lip. Leon roared and thrust deeper piercing what was left of her hymen. Pain tore through her but it only fired her lust—her heat—and she clawed at his back. Growling into his open mouth her beast surged to life.

"Riza," he gasped as his hips fired in rapid succession.

"Harder, Leon. Oh my god." She tasted blood on her lips but it didn't faze her as heat spiraled from her belly outward. She gasped for breath as her extremities trembled. "Now," she begged as color exploded behind her eyes.

Leon's sweat-covered body blanketed hers as he unlocked her legs. Pushing her thighs to her chest, his cock burrowed deep and hard. He threw back his head and roared as he released his seed. A wild mane framed feral eyes and a blood-smeared chin. He looked more beast than man.

"Riza," his voice rasped as he tried to speak. Drawing back, his semi-erect cock slid from her ravaged body. Pain tore at his heart to see the traces of blood mixed with their joint release. "Are you okay?"

Over-bright eyes met his and she nodded as he lowered her legs. He gathered her close as she trembled with aftershock. "Baby, I didn't mean to be so rough." He picked pieces of leaves from her hair. He'd taken her like an animal in rut. She deserved better. She deserved silk sheets and tender loving.

"I'm okay."

"You're bleeding." His thumb rode her bottom lip, wiping away a smear of blood.

"I think that's your blood."

Raising fingers to his lip, he grinned. For a wolf, she certainly was a wild cat. "Nevertheless, I should have been gentler."

"I didn't want gentle. I wanted you."

"You had me and now you're mine," Leon proclaimed. He wasn't about to let his little lupine get away. He shouldn't have taken her innocence, not in a rush on the forest floor, but he couldn't resist her. Even now, he was ready to take her again.

"Are you sore?"

"I don't think so. Why?"

He moved against her, allowing her to fill his burgeoning cock. "I want you again. This time I'll take you slow and easy." His hand lowered to her slit, finding her clit. He worked the little nub in slow circles. She clenched her thighs around his hand as she panted for breath.

"What about the hunt?"

"I caught my prey and now I'm going to heat it up and eat it."

A strangled gasp escaped her throat. "I think it's already hot."

"It's going to get hotter and wetter." He reached for his discarded clothes, pulling them under her. This time he would give her a cushion between her and the cold, hard ground.

Meshing their lips, he stretched out next to her. Groaning as she suckled his tender lower lip. Riza was passionate, fiery and he liked it. His lips trailed down her jaw and neck to her breasts and he dragged his tongue across tight-tipped peaks.

Her hot little tongue trailed his shoulder and neck. Sharp teeth scraped his skin then began to suckle. He shuddered with need. He hadn't had a love mark on his neck in years but he would allow her to mark him. He'd marked her with his scent. Marked her as his woman.

Leon's taste filled her mouth and nose as she suckled his flesh. She longed to suckle him deep into her mouth. Her blood simmered as his mouth and hands devoured her flesh.

Adjusting her legs, she pressed them together, trying to ease the ache. "Leon." She parted her thighs, begging for his touch. Leon grasped her hand and brought her fingers between her damp thighs.

"Touch yourself. Feel how hot you are." Lacing their fingers, he slid them through her folds. "Feel this tiny nub." He pressed her fingertips to her clit and she gasped at the sensation. It felt nothing like the times she'd touched herself.

"Have you ever masturbated?"

Riza coughed as she tried to swallow. She couldn't talk to him about *that*.

"Don't be embarrassed. It's okay to touch yourself." He tipped her chin up. "Let me see your eyes as we pleasure you."

"Leon, I can't…"

"I let you watch me stroke my cock earlier. You liked it, didn't you? You were jealous. You wanted to touch me…suck me." A spark flared in his eyes as he spoke and she wondered if he could read her mind.

"God, yes." She wanted to touch him, stroke him, suck him and devour him.

"Let me see you make yourself come," Leon urged.

She shook her head. "I've never… I tried but it didn't work. I don't know how." She was embarrassed to admit she'd never brought herself to climax.

"I'll help you. I'll teach you. Don't you have any toys?"

Riza snorted. "I can just imagine. Gionne would kill me."

"He's such a prude when it comes to you. I'll get you toys and teach you to use them." He thrust two of their joined fingers into her pussy and she sucked in a deep breath. "You need a plug to stretch your ass."

"Leon."

"You know you want me to take it. You want me to dominate you. You want my cock to own your ass." His fingers left her pussy to rim her anal hole. "This bud wants to be stretched, to know the pleasure of my finger, my tongue and my cock.

"I don't…" She shook her head. She didn't think she was ready for that.

"Someday you'll beg me to fuck your ass."

She moaned, "Right now, I need…"

"You need more than your fingers in this hungry little cunt." He spread her knees wide as his eyes lowered. Raising her hand, he sucked each of her cream-covered fingers. "You taste so delicious. I want more of your sweetness before I give you my cock."

His head lowered and he lapped her already-sensitized skin. The first swipe of his tongue nearly put her over the edge and she arched up, meeting his mouth. "You are hungry," he murmured against her folds. "So am I." His tongue dipped into her vagina and licked the inside of her canal. She screamed.

"Fuck me, Leon." Her hips arched and bucked under his mouth as she sought a deeper, fuller penetration. His thumb buffeted her clit as his tongue burrowed deeper and she climaxed hard. Her pussy pulsed around his tongue. His vibrating purr as he feasted set off another minor quake.

"Damn it. I wanted to take you slow and easy but you're killing me." Wrapping his fingers around the base of his cock and squeezing, he stemmed the flow of release. He was ready to erupt just from watching and tasting her. The pressure pulled him back from the edge as he sprawled between her thighs.

"Fuck me, Leon. I don't care about slow and easy."

"I want you on your hands and knees."

"What?"

"I want you doggie style, my little lupine."

With a whimper, Riza swung her leg around so she could do his bidding. She presented him with a beautiful picture of her ass. Firm, lean thighs supported two rounded cheeks and he resisted the urge to bite her tender flesh.

"I only wish I had something to tie your hands. I'd like to have you completely helpless and at my mercy. Would you like being helpless? I could force you to suck my cock or I could fuck your pussy. I could even fuck that virgin ass and you couldn't do a thing about it."

"Leon!" She gasped in horror. A flush colored her body as she shifted restlessly. He suspected that secretly the thought appealed to her.

His fingers found her wet, aching center. "It makes you hot doesn't it? The thought of being mastered and dominated? Does it make you want to come?" He shoved three fingers deep into her pussy.

"Yes," the word hissed from her lips as she thrust back against his hand.

"I'll remember that. Sometime, when you're being pissy and don't want to spread like a good female, I'll tie you up. First, I'll spank this nice, rounded ass." His hand squeezed her right cheek. "Then, I'll fuck your pussy long and hard. When I'm coated with your cream, I'll make you suck me clean and swallow my cum."

"Leon, please…I need you." The words engorged his cock even further.

"You belong to me." His cock brushed her folds as he slid his fingers free. "I'm going to ride you hard, baby." His blunt head pierced her pussy and pushed deep. "So wet...so hot, you make me want to spill my seed like a boy mounting his first girl."

He pulled back and thrust deep, pushing the breath from her body. Her inner muscles rippled, trying to hold him in place as he slowly withdrew again. He spread her legs wider as he thrust forward. Her head came up as she arched into the exquisite sensation.

Cream soaked fingers circled her anal opening. "I'm going to pierce you with my finger while you take my cock."

A startled cry passed her lips as the blunt tip of his finger rimmed her ass. His cock slid back and his finger slid forward. Her head turned to the side and he watched her bite down on her lip as he stretched her sphincter muscle.

"Relax, I'm in now." Once he'd cleared the opening, his finger slid smoothly into her hole. He thrust his cock forward and the penetration was even tighter than before. "Now it's going to get real interesting."

Riza cried out as he set a fast-paced rhythm with his finger and cock. Her back arched and her skin rippled. "Leon, I'm going to change," she panted as a fierce spasm squeezed his cock.

"Go ahead but I won't stop."

Her teeth gnashed and little tufts of fur sprouted. Her claws began to extend and she shook, fighting the change to feral form.

Leon reached down with his free hand and pinched her clit. "Don't fight it. Let me fuck you."

Her spine contorted as her tail began to sprout. "Leon," she growled as her jaw extended. He continued to thrust relentlessly as she threw back her head with a howling shudder. She climaxed, her cunt rippled around his cock and the change stopped. She reverted to full human form. If he hadn't been holding her hips, she would have collapsed. Leon shouted as he paused, allowing her inner muscles to milk the seed from his shaft.

"Fuck, Riza." His finger pulled from her ass as his head hung and his hair brushed her back. "Baby, I'll never get enough of you.

# Chapter Five

ℰℷ

Riza tossed as an onslaught of thoughts filled her mind. *I'm not a virgin anymore. He didn't ask me to join with him. Gionne will kill me. He'll kill Leon. What if I'm pregnant? What have I done?*

She shifted her legs. Her muscles ached. Sliding a hand between her thighs her fingers slid between slick folds. The damp flesh was tender, sensitive. Her clit was swollen and achy. Circling the nub, she shuddered at the burst of sensation. Her pussy and sphincter clenched. A moan escaped her lips and her fingers explored her flesh as never before. Now that she knew the glory of climaxing, she wanted it. Confidently, she touched herself as hunger burned in her belly. She was in heat and she needed a mate. She needed Leon. Pinching her clit, she rolled to her side, arching under the intense torment. Thrusting two fingers deep into her pussy, she cried out as pleasure descended.

Panting, she stretched on her bed. Temporarily sated, her mind turned back to her worries. Throwing the covers off, her feet hit the cool tile floor. There was only one thing to do. She had to confront Leon before Gionne discovered her secret.

\* \* \* \* \*

Leon was up early for a meeting with his guard. He intended to see Riza and Gionne that afternoon. He planned to ask Riza to join with him today. His chest expanded with warmth at the thought. He should have asked her yesterday. He hoped she knew how much she meant to him. He couldn't imagine a life without her in it. His eyes flickered to his bed. Soon, she would share it with him nightly. He would fill her with his seed and his child. He pictured her with a swollen stomach and smiled. Turning, he headed for his bath.

Whistling, Leon stepped out of the shower, his mind on his earlier meeting with Tomas. They had discussed an upcoming meeting with the new alpha of the coyote band. So far, the coyotes had respected the boundaries but it appeared a few of the young pups were pushing the bounds. Leon planned to discuss the meeting with Gionne and to ask him to join him and present a united front. It was the second thing he would speak to Gionne about. The first was Riza. He intended to ask her to join with him and he would honor Gionne by asking him for his sister's hand.

Entering his room, he stopped. A small, black leopard lounged on his bed. It wasn't very surprising to find a female waiting in his bed. Lately, he'd turned several away. What was surprising was the fact that he didn't recognize her. By sight, she was no one he knew. His senses were beginning to return and, though there was something familiar about her, he couldn't determine her identity. It didn't matter. He would ask her to leave.

Leon cleared his throat and the leopard raised its head. Emerald eyes gleamed as they trailed his naked form. The cat arched lazily, stretching its back and raising its hips. Leon found himself in the uncomfortable position of growing rapidly hard while standing nude in front of an unknown female. Usually, it wouldn't have bothered him in the least. Today, it made him uncomfortable.

*Fuck!* He hadn't grown hard for a woman other than Riza since getting to know her. He thought his desire for other females had vanished. He was ready to settle down and make a commitment to Riza. She deserved it.

The feline leapt from the bed and stalked closer. Circling, she brushed against his legs and the breath hissed from his body. Clenching his fists, he drew a shaky breath. Her shiny coat was soft against his naked flesh. His spine began to tingle and he clenched his jaw. He couldn't change, not now. The beast within would be more susceptible to the lusty feline.

The leopard nuzzled his backside and a rough tongue licked a torrid path down his cheek. He found himself involuntarily spreading his thighs. The scorch of her tongue contacted his sac and he roared. Hunching forward, hair began to sprout and he knew it was too late to stop the beast within him. Dropping to the floor, his feral side emerged.

The lion circled the willing feline and her tail rose temptingly. Burying his nose between her legs, he sniffed. She was wet and his returning sense of smell gauged her as ripe and ready. Using a paw, he pressed her shoulders down and her hips arched. The lion mounted the feline, forcefully taking possession.

The feline whimpered at the tight, powerful possession but she submitted to the lion. Her thighs trembled but she accommodated the larger male, accepting his domination. With a shriek, the feline found release. The male roared as he spilled his seed.

In human form, Leon silently cursed himself as he stretched on the bed next to the feline. *Damn it, he'd fucked up.* He couldn't blame the feline or even the beast within. He should have demanded she leave before the beast had a chance to respond. As soon as he saw her, he should have escorted her out of his room. He didn't know why he hadn't. There was no excuse for his actions. Recently, he'd gotten good at refusing sexual favors. There was something about the feline lying next to him that had gotten beneath his defenses. Now he needed to find out who she was. It was imperative Riza never discover this transgression. It would never happen again.

The sated feline opened drowsy, emerald eyes as he scratched her head. "Hey, why don't you change so we can talk?"

The feline rolled over, exposing her belly, an obvious submissive move. Her scent wafted to his nostrils and his eyes narrowed. It couldn't be! He closed his eyes. His senses weren't back to normal and he had to be mistaken. She couldn't be in heat.

His heart hurt as if a hand wrapped around it and squeezed. If she was in heat, she was fertile and he might have gotten her pregnant. *Riza,* his heart cried out. He broke out in a cold sweat. His heart pounding as he struggled to breathe. The future he hadn't known he wanted until recently suddenly seemed out of reach.

"Change for me, now. I need to know who you are." He didn't try to sound civil. He couldn't lay all the blame at her feet but, potentially, they had just ruined his life. He couldn't loose Riza now. If he'd impregnated the feline, he'd acknowledge the child but he wouldn't join with her. He might lose Riza anyway but he'd never give up trying to get her back.

The feline arched away. Emerald eyes flared with shock and anger as he spoke. She hissed and bared her fangs. With an angry swipe, she filleted his thigh with two deep gorges.

"Fuck!" Leon roared, grasping his thigh, stemming the flow of blood.

The leopard sprang from his bed to the windowsill and with a raged-filled glance in his direction disappeared. Unfortunately, he doubted it was the last he'd see of her.

He lay back, his head throbbing and his leg pouring blood onto his silken sheets. He had to think. His future depended on it. All of his adult life he'd played the field but he'd always been careful of the trap. As much as he was tempted, he'd always drawn away from a female in heat. Even the beast had warily avoided entrapment. Why was this female different? Was it because of his decreased sense of smell? He'd thought the scent of a female in heat was what drew him. With his senses still off slightly, the lion within had not realized she was in heat. So why had he responded as he had? He had to admit he had enjoyed mounting the feline but not at the cost of losing Riza. Nothing was worth that price.

He had to find out who she was! Her eyes had seemed familiar. And her scent... It lingered in the air. There was something about it. He wondered what had enraged the female to the point of attack. He probed his injured thigh with his fingers. The bleeding had slowed.

She must have thought he knew who he was fucking. Therefore, they must have met before. She wasn't of his pride. He was sure of that. He didn't know of anyone visiting from another.

Those emerald eyes, they reminded him of Riza but she wasn't feline. He sniffed the fragrant air. Aroused female in heat with a hint of... Leon shot straight up in the bed. "Oh fuck!" The scent had a trace of lupine. *What had he done?* Why hadn't he paid more attention when Jenna had chatted to him? She had mentioned something about Gionne's sister being a half-breed. Was she half-feline? At the time she'd told him he hadn't known Riza, so it hadn't mattered to him. A feeling of doom settled over him.

He had to trail the feline and see where she went. Shifting forms, he scooped up his pants and jumped from the second story window to land on the frost-covered ground below. With his nose to the ground, he managed to pick up her scent. Her trail was easy enough to follow and dread filled his heart as he neared the lupine stronghold. Part of him was glad. He hadn't cheated on Riza. The reason the feline had affected him was because it was she. Riza was his true mate and he desired no other. Unfortunately, she now realized he hadn't known her identity when he mounted her. She would think he was still fucking every willing female. Would she forgive him for what she would see as a transgression on his part? He dreaded the confrontation but there was no avoiding it. Riza most likely carried his offspring. That thought brought a smile to his lips. She wouldn't be able to deny him when she was heavy with his child. If need be, he would pressure Gionne to force her hand.

\* \* \* \* \*

The feline stopped in the woods where she'd left her clothes and shifted to human form. Her hands trembled as she tugged on her jeans. She had to get herself under control. She needed to get to her room and shower Leon's scent off her body. What had she done? Single-handedly, she was going to destroy the peace between the lupines and the felines. Gionne would to be furious. Jenna would be caught in the middle. She was Leon's sister. Jenna was pregnant with Gionne's offspring and Riza didn't want her upset. If Jenna and Gionne found out Leon had used her, they'd be furious. She couldn't let them know. Her hand lowered to her flat stomach. She had wanted Leon's child. Truth be known, she still did but what would she do if she were pregnant. She wouldn't tell Leon. She wouldn't join with him out of duty. She wouldn't be the mate of a male who'd fuck any available woman.

Entering the stronghold from the less-traveled east path, she flipped a wave at the guard on duty as she hurried past. Sneaking through the private courtyard, she hastily skirted the opening to the main patio. Hearing approaching footfalls, she ducked behind a stand of pine trees and held her breath, waiting for the steps to fade.

She didn't hear a sound and dared to peek around the heavy brush. She came face to face with Dirk. Damn it, she had all the luck.

"What are you doing?"

"Trying to avoid you, obviously." Riza tried to skirt him.

"Why?" Dirk moved closer blocking her exit.

"It doesn't matter. I have to go."

"Not yet. Why have you been crying?" His eyes narrowed on her face.

"You're mistaken." Riza lowered her head, allowing her hair to fall forward.

Dirk grabbed her arm as she attempted to scoot by. "No, I'm not." He shook his head, his nostrils flaring. "You didn't listen did you? His scent is all over you and you're in heat."

"It's none of your business," Riza hissed.

"It's my business when your mistake is going to destroy this pack." The words angrily burst from his lips.

"Don't exaggerate." She'd thought the same thing earlier but she wasn't up to discussing it with Dirk. She needed time to think before she talked to anyone.

"Gionne will fight Leon. One of them could die and where will that leave Jenna?"

A sob escaped Riza's lips. "I thought he loved me but I was wrong. I don't know what to do." Her mind whirled. Her thoughts were chaotic.

"Are you pregnant?"

"I don't know...probably," she sniffed.

"I can help you." Dirk's voice was calm, resolved.

"How?" How could anyone help her now?

"Join with me. I'll raise your child as mine."

"Why? You don't love me." Riza raised her eyes to meet his.

"I care about you. I care about our pack and I could come to love you. You're beautiful...desirable." His hand brushed her cheek. His touch was warm, soothing.

"Gionne wouldn't have to know, would he?" she asked.

"No, but I would have to mate you. You'd have to carry my scent."

She knew that was the only way to convince Gionne that Dirk was her mate. Nervously, Riza stroked her arms as goose bumps riddled her flesh. She'd never thought of Dirk that way. He was attractive, considerate, a good friend but he wasn't Leon. She wouldn't lose herself in him the way she did with Leon but that might be a good thing. The heartwrenching desire she had for Leon was wonderful but what was passion without love? In time, her yearning for the alpha feline would fade. Her affection for Dirk would grow. "Okay." She nodded her head.

"Do you want to shower first?" Dirk asked.

Oh god, he wanted to do it immediately. "Do you want me to?" He probably didn't want to touch her with the scent of another male so heavy upon her.

"It doesn't matter."

"I don't want to get cold feet." If she went to her room, she was afraid she'd chicken out. She'd start thinking about Leon. She'd want to give him another chance. No, she wouldn't grovel for the alpha male's attention.

"If I take you, Riza, there's no going back. It's a commitment. I could get you pregnant." Dirk's voice was serious as he regarded her with a steady gaze.

"I know." She nodded her head.

His fingers brushed her cheek. "Okay."

His head lowered and his lips parted over hers. He tasted of coffee and she sighed as his tongue gently stroked hers. His hands trailed down over her ass, lifting her to his hard frame. She could feel the thickness of his arousal even through their clothes. His kiss and touch were pleasant but not earth shattering.

"Your scent is killing me." He ground her against his erection. She was in heat and she knew a female in heat stirred the blood of any male.

He carried her to a lounge and sat down straddling her across his lap. "You're hot and wet." His fingers snapped open his jeans. "I'm going to give you a nice long fuck to ease that heat. Then we'll go back to my room and clean up. I want to see those lips wrapped around my cock." Dirk lifted her chin to meet his lust-filled gaze. "This is how it's going to be. I won't have a cold, unfeeling mate. Can you accept and return my passion?"

Riza whimpered. Her heat was heavy upon her and his touch was obviously skilled. She needed a male but she wanted Leon. After everything, she still wanted him but she would accept Dirk for the sake of her pack. Dirk did not make her blood sing but his touch was arousing. She closed her eyes, silently calling Leon's name. She nodded her head in acceptance and she felt Dirk's hand on her inner thigh.

\* \* \* \* \*

"What the fuck is going on here?" Leon roared when he saw Riza straddling Dirk's lap. "Get your hands off my woman."

Riza scrambled from Dirk's lap as he stood. "She's not your woman. She just agreed to join with me."

Leon glared at Riza. "Is that true? Just because we had a misunderstanding you agreed to join with him." Leon jerked his thumb in Dirk's direction. "You were going to fuck him?"

"Why not! You fuck any female you come across." Her emerald eyes flashed fire. He didn't know how he couldn't have recognized her.

"It wasn't like that and you know it."

"Do I? All I know is that I thought we had something special but you can't even recognize me. But hey, that didn't matter. You gave me a good fuck anyway."

"We do have something special." Leon sighed. He knew it was going to be difficult but he hadn't expected this. "I have a sinus infection. It's been throwing my senses off and you never bothered to tell me you were half-feline." Leon tried to explain. He should have told her of his condition sooner.

"That doesn't explain why you'd fuck someone else." Hurt-filled eyes shimmered with unshed tears. "It all comes down to I'm not a purebred feline. You can't accept I'm half-lupine."

"What? Where is that coming from? I admit what I did was wrong but I didn't cheat. It was you. I think some part of me knew it was you."

"Which part was that—your cock? Does it recognize every cunt it enters? That cock head must have one hell of a memory, much better than the one on your shoulders."

"Calm down. We need to talk." Leon threw a glance in Dirk's direction to find him curiously watching them but seemingly unruffled. "In private."

"I don't think I want to talk to you," Riza huffed with a toss of her head.

"At least I didn't cold-bloodedly fuck someone else."

"I didn't fuck him…yet," she threw the words back in his face.

Grabbing her arm, Leon hauled her to him. "You're not going to fuck him. You're mine. You're in heat, which means you're probably expecting my offspring." His lip curled up. "You'll have to join with me."

"I won't join with you just because I might be expecting. You don't really want me. You want the child. You want a good relationship with Gionne. You don't want a half-breed."

"I had a good relationship with Gionne but I threw it away for you."

"Dirk asked me to join with him. He'll accept any child I carry as his."

Leon growled, "He won't raise my child and he won't have you." He snarled at the other male.

"I will if Riza chooses me," Dirk challenged.

A muscle in Leon's cheek twitched as he gritted his teeth, holding off the beast that wanted to roar to life inside him. His beast had claimed its mate and he wouldn't let her go. Unfortunately, ripping one of her pack members to shreds probably wouldn't endear him to her pack. "She won't choose you. She already chose me when she gave me her virginity and I planted my seed."

Dirk shrugged his shoulders and replied calmly, "And yet, she was just straddling my lap. If you'd been a few minutes later I'd have my cock in her right now."

Leon's mind reeled at the thought. "In my pride, fucking someone's mate is punishable by banishment."

"She's not your mate."

Leon's lip curled as he snarled, "Yet."

"That's enough you two." Riza stepped between them. "Leon, you should leave."

"Not without you." There was no way he'd leave her behind with this male. Obviously, Dirk had tried to guilt her into accepting him for the sake of the pack.

"I'm not going anywhere with you."

"You have to let me explain." Leon pulled her close.

"I don't have to do anything."

Leon lowered his head as he whispered, "It's not like you think. I don't want other females. I only want you and not just for the sake of the child." He didn't want to do this here with an audience but he couldn't take the chance on waiting. His voice broke as he continued. "I love you, Riza."

She sucked in a startled breath and raised her eyes to meet his. Her lips trembled as she started to speak.

"Leon, Dirk, what's going on?" The hair on the nape of Leon's neck bristled at Gionne's untimely interruption.

Leon turned to meet Gionne's dark gaze and he noticed the other male's nose flare with anger as he scented his sister. "You have something to tell me, I presume?"

"I asked your sister to join with me."

"Before or after you fucked her?"

# Chapter Six

ରେ

Leon lifted the mug of ale to his lips. How had everything gone so wrong? In one moment, he'd had it all and he'd thrown it away. What if Riza didn't forgive him? What if she chose Dirk? Jealousy was a foreign emotion but it burned deeply in his gut. Because of his foolishness, she'd agreed to join with Dirk. His scent had been all over her and seeing her spread across his lap had infuriated him. Would Dirk convince her to join with him? Were they right now making love? He felt ill.

"Enjoying the show?" Gionne asked as he settled into a seat next to him.

Leon's gaze flickered to his brother-in-law, then back to the room at large. The activities in the room could best be described as an orgy. Men and women came together in couples and groups. Some in human form and some in feral form. The scene was enough to make a dead man come but Leon's cock didn't even twitch. He shrugged his shoulders in answer to Gionne's question. "When can I talk to Riza?"

"When she's ready."

"When will that be? I can't wait much longer."

"No. You're not very good at waiting." Leon understood the sarcasm in Gionne's tone. He knew he should have joined with Riza before he mated her. He had intended to but in the heat of the moment things had gotten out of hand and now look where he was.

Gionne could not say much though, since he had mated Jenna without benefit of a ceremony. "Neither were you if I remember correctly."

Gionne raised his glass. "Touché."

"What's Riza doing? Who's she with?" If Gionne said Dirk, he would lose his mind.

"She's with Jenna."

"Oh." That was good, he hoped. Jenna would try to calm Riza and plead his case. Wouldn't she?

"Can I talk to Jenna?" Leon asked.

"I don't think you'd want to at the moment."

"She's angry." He knew his sister. She was probably furious right now but if he talked to her, he could calm her down.

"She's a pregnant, hormonal female trying to calm another hormonal female and they're both considering neutering you."

Gionne's words didn't paint a pretty picture and Leon grimaced. "You've calmed down."

"The way I see it, I either get you or Dirk for a brother-in-law. Either way, I'm okay with it," Gionne replied.

"Riza wouldn't be happy with Dirk. She doesn't love him. If she's pregnant, it's my child." If need be he would plead his case to Gionne.

"Would she be happy with you? Could she trust you?"

"You've known me most of my life. You know what I was like but I have changed. I haven't been with another female. I won't lie. I didn't consciously know the feline was Riza but I think a part of me did. The beast within knew. You're a male. Certainly, you understand where I'm coming from. My senses were off but somehow I knew it was Riza. I reacted to her, not a nameless female," Leon exclaimed. Damn it, he was getting choked up. It wasn't like him to show emotion, especially in front of another male.

Gionne nodded his head. "That's what I told her."

"You defended me?" Leon was shocked. His friendship with Gionne was longstanding but he'd thought that, if given a choice, Gionne would prefer Riza to mate with Dirk. To stay within his pack.

"You helped me with Jenna. I owed you but if I didn't see the change in you and if I didn't believe you were right for Riza, I wouldn't help you.

"Thank you." Gionne's words rang true. He only hoped Riza had listened to him.

Gionne inclined his head in acknowledgment and Leon turned his gaze away. His heart stuttered as his eyes encountered Dirk at a far table. The other male leaned back in a chair with a look of contentment on his face. A female knelt between his legs, obviously servicing his cock. Leon could see little of the female, only her hair — her dark hair. His blood ran cold, then hot.

Gionne grasped his arm. "Don't do anything stupid."

He yanked his arm from Gionne's grasp, all thoughts of friendship and brotherhood past. If killing Dirk declared war between the breeds, then so be it, but Riza was his. He wouldn't allow another male to claim her.

"Leon, that's not Riza."

"What!" Leon snarled.

"The bitch with Dirk isn't Riza," Gionne told him.

"Are you sure?"

"Yeah, Riza just walked in the door."

Leon's head whipped to the side and his breath left his body. Riza sauntered toward him wrapped in a traditional feline offering robe. She stopped a foot from him with her head held high. She unwrapped the blanket, letting it fall to her feet. She posed nude for all to see. Leon resisted the urge to cover her and shield her from the admiring male gazes. He reminded himself she was a mixed breed and if she could accept the feline customs, he would accept the lupine ones as well.

"I accept your offer and offer my complete submission." Turning she knelt in front of him, her head lowered and her ass tilted upward. Offering her ass for his domination, he could take it and claim her in the most primal of ways. If he refused her publicly, other males would take her and mark her as a pack bitch.

A low growl rumbled in his chest. His cock, which had refused to acknowledge the carnal show still playing out around them suddenly surged to full length. Ripping his shirt open, he reached for the fastening of his jeans. In seconds, he was fully unclothed and kneeling behind his mate. There was no thought of refusal. No other male would touch her.

Parting her cheeks, the tight rosebud winked at him and he licked the full length of her crack. Her heat fired his senses. Finally, he was able to appreciate the full flavor of his mate. Her aromatic scent overwhelmed him. He knew the other males in the room scented her heat and hungered for her, but she was his.

His fingers dove into the liquid heat of her pussy. It was going to be a rough ride but he would prepare her as much as possible. He tongued her hole as he stroked his cock, covering it with her cream. He wished he could stretch her but she'd offered total submission of her virgin ass and he would take it. He remembered how tight she'd been on his finger. His cock was much larger and he didn't want to cause her pain but he couldn't refuse her offer. His cock would be the first—the only—to pierce her rectum. It would be painful at first but she must know that.

The head of his cock perched at her opening. "I accept your offer and claim you as my mate," he growled as he forced his cock head through the rim of her sphincter. Her back arched and her breath left her body in a hiss but she didn't scream.

Grasping her hips, he surged deeper. Her ass parted, swallowing his cock as he forced more of his length into the hot, virgin canal. He growled as his spine tingled. The beast wanted out, wanted to possess his mate. He ground his teeth, holding it at bay. He wouldn't do that to Riza. Mounting her virgin ass in front of half her pack was one thing. To shift to feral form and fuck her ass was another.

"You're killing me," he gasped as he eased back.

She released a strangled groan that was probably meant as an agreement. Part of him wanted to stop, to accept breeching her ass as summation of claiming her but another part urged him on and he pressed farther.

Withdrawing, he plunged his cock, parting the tight, virgin territory. He growled as her wet heat surrounded him. His muscles vibrated with restraint as he held still within her depths. Lifting his head, his eyes met Dirk's across the room. The other male watched with an unreadable expression on his face. Leon snarled and his incisors elongated. Hair prickled along his flesh. The lupine male inclined his head in acknowledgement and Leon roared. His hips bucking as he drove home to complete possession.

"Mine," he snarled. "Mine!"

His balls tightened as release neared. His blood burned and he threw back his head and roared as his mate mewled in tormented bliss. Her tight canal rippled around him, milking his cock as she found release. Pulling free of her body, he gathered her in his arms. "You're mine now. Mine," he whispered as he brushed her sweat-dampened hair from her face. Lifting Riza, he wrapped her in her robe.

"I love you," she replied as he carried her from the room.

\* \* \* \* \*

"Say it again," Leon, urged her as he placed her on her feet just inside her room.

Riza dropped the robe and stepped out of it. The heat of his gaze followed her. "Say what?"

Leon stalked closer and a sexy grin split his face. "You know what. Tell me you love me."

"I do."

"Say it," he demanded as he grasped her arm, dragging her to his side.

"I love you," Riza confessed.

"Thank god. I was terrified when I realized why I was attracted to that feline. I swear I haven't been with anyone else recently."

"I believe you."

"I knew how you felt though, when I saw you with Dirk." Leon shook his head and raised his face to meet her gaze. His golden eyes gleamed with powerful emotion. "I would have killed him to have you."

"Leon!" Riza huffed but secretly she was pleased his desire for her was so great.

"I love you." Leon chuckled. "I've never told another female that, except Jenna."

"I'll allow that one." Riza licked his chest, tasting his salty flesh. She shifted her breasts against his chest.

"I need to clean up, baby."

"Mmm, we can shower together."

She felt the rumble of a growl in his chest. "Lead the way."

Steam billowed from the tiled cubicle as they stepped in. "Nice. There's plenty of room in here."

"Room for what?" Riza panted breathlessly.

Leon chuckled. "I'm sure we can find a number of things to occupy our time in here." Soaping his hands Leon lathered her breasts.

"That feels good."

His hands moved lower over her abs, between her thighs. "Are you sore?"

Riza shuddered at his caressing touch. "No. I don't think so."

"I haven't forgotten about that plug. I'll get you one. I want you to stay ready for me."

"Leon."

"You're mine now. Your pussy and your ass." Two fingers entered her pussy. "It's all about pleasure. Yours and mine. You enjoy it and so do I." His fingers pumped deep and hard.

"Yes," she gasped leaning forward, resting her cheek against the cool tile.

"Nothing is taboo if we both enjoy it." Kneeling before her, he dipped his head, his tongue found her clit in a raspy caress.

Bending her knees she pumped against his fingers and his teeth latched on to her clit. "Oh lord." His fingers pumped hard enough to lift her to her toes. "Jesus," she gasped.

Pulling free, he slapped her bottom and ordered, "Sit on the bench." Her thighs quaked. Her knees were weak and she readily complied. Reaching for the liquid soap, Leon lathered his cock. Riza whimpered as he soaped his shaft and balls. "Are you hungry, baby?"

Riza nodded, unable to speak.

Turning into the stream of water, he rinsed. He stepped in front of her, his cock gleaming. "Open up and I'll feed that hunger."

Pushing her damp hair back, she licked her lips. The wide, fleshy tip looked delicious. Her lips parted and he thrust forward, filling her mouth. He tasted of vanilla soap.

"Suck it. Let me feel that tongue on my cock."

"Mmm," she moaned taking him deeper. With voracious hunger, she laved his cock. Nibbling the tip, she pumped her head. Pre-cum dotted the eye of his cock and she lapped the savory liquid. His taste fired her arousal and she growled with feral intensity. Reaching between his thighs, she grasped his balls and Leon's legs quaked.

"Enough," he gasped, ripping away from her grasp.

"But…"

He turned off the water and reached for her. "We have all night." He chuckled. "Hell, we have the rest of our lives."

* * * * *

"Morning, Leon."

"Hey, Sis. I swear you get rounder every time I see you."

Jenna glared at her brother. "I thought you were supposed to have a way with women."

"I think from now on I only have a way with one woman."

"Glad to hear it. I wouldn't advise you to mention Riza's roundness as she starts to show."

"She'll be beautifully round." Leon laughed.

"It's wonderful to see you so happy."

"It feels pretty good too."

"She gave you a great honor last night."

He couldn't hide the grin that split his face. "Yes, she did."

"Are you going to honor her the lupine way?"

His brow arched. "What do you mean?"

"Riza didn't tell you?" Leon knew his sister well. Right now, he knew she was struggling with telling him something she thought he should know. He had the feeling though, that he didn't want to hear what she had to say.

"No."

"Oh." She furrowed her brow and glanced away.

"What is it?"

"Maybe you should speak to Gionne."

"Gionne! Why?" If there was something he needed to know, he wanted Jenna to tell him.

"Did I hear my name?" Gionne appeared at his mate's side.

"Leon wanted to know how to honor Riza the lupine way." For a woman with a round stomach, Jenna gained her feet quickly and darted around the wall leading to the main terrace. Leon had an urge to follow her.

Turning his gaze back to his brother-in-law, he was surprised to find a guarded expression on Gionne's face. "I have a feeling I'm not going to like this."

Gionne explained to Leon the custom of providing your mate with a protector. It was the custom of all lupine males to provide their mate with another male who would protect and provide for them if need be. It honored the female to know that her mate was willing to share her in order to keep her safe.

"You're kidding," Leon said.

"No."

Leon shook his head. He couldn't offer Riza to another. It was unthinkable. He had shared females before, but he did not want to share Riza. The thought chilled his blood.

"You... Jenna?"

Gionne inclined his head. "Yes, I honored Jenna by providing a protector for her."

"Who?" It was impossible to imagine Gionne sharing Jenna. He knew how possessive he was of his mate.

A grin tugged at Gionne's lip as he replied, "Dirk."

"That bastard...and Jenna." *Fuck! That prick thought he was some kind of stud.*

"He's not that bad. He was willing to protect Riza when he thought you had turned your back on her. He would have joined with her and raised your child."

"Seeing him touch her..." Leon shook his head. "I don't think I can do it." His blood still burned when he pictured Riza straddling Dirk's lap.

198

"You do not have to but Riza will have to live with the talk that you do not love her enough to protect her." Gionne chided him.

"It's not that…hell, I love her too much."

Gionne nodded. "I understand. It was very difficult but I put Jenna's wellbeing first."

"She didn't mind?" It was hard to picture Jenna willingly fucking another male.

Gionne grinned. "Although she would never admit it, I believe she enjoyed having two males. The trick is preparing them and controlling the other male. Vaginal penetration is not allowed."

A cold resolve settled in Leon's stomach.

# Chapter Seven

Dinner was over and Riza reached for Leon's hand. "Let's go back to my room for dessert before we leave for your stronghold."

Leon fought the urge to agree and return with her to her room. Snagging her hand, he pulled her close. "I thought we'd stay here awhile."

"Oh…do you enjoy the floor show?" Riza raised her brows suggestively.

"I guess we'll see." His instincts told him to take her and leave. He was not obligated to share his mate. She knew he loved her. He'd told her that he didn't mind that she was a half-breed and he didn't. Actually, he was glad that she was half feline, though he did find her lupine form sexy too. He thought she believed him. Hell, he'd even agreed to let her train with his guard when she wasn't pregnant. Of course, he did not intend to allow her to do anything dangerous and he planned to keep her pregnant, nursing and caring for their young as much as possible.

"Are you expecting a repeat performance of the other night?"

A rumbling growl rose in his throat at the memory of her total submission. Pulling her onto his lap, his hand slid along her smooth thigh. "I thought we might try something different."

"Different?"

"Hmm."

"How different?" Riza asked as her gaze rested on a male in human form mounting a female wolf.

Leon laughed, "We'll try that later. The combinations, the pleasure are endless but tonight I plan to prove my love, my devotion and acceptance to you and to your pack."

"Leon." She swallowed nervously.

"I love you," he reminded her. Everything he was about to do was to show her how much he loved her. That he accepted her as she was—a half-breed.

"I love you too."

"Then accept my offering as an honor to you." Leon nodded his head and Dirk stepped forward, followed by Cyrus. "I love you enough to share you not with one but two males. They will protect and honor you if ever I cannot."

"Leon, you don't have…"

"It is important that you know, that your pack knows that I place you first above all else—my woman, my mate…my life."

Riza sniffled, her eyes growing watery.

"Don't cry. Accept my love."

Slowly, Leon raised her gown over her head, revealing her gently rounded curves for all to see. Leon heard Dirk catch his breath at the sight she made. Leon had come to terms with Dirk. He knew that Dirk had done what was best for the pack. He had only wanted to protect Riza and her pack. That was why he chose to honor Dirk in this fashion. He knew Dirk would protect Riza with his life if it came to that. The other male, Cyrus, was quite a young man who Leon had befriended during his stay. He trusted that he would care for Riza as well.

"She is beautiful, is she not?"

"Very much so," Dirk spoke.

Leon glanced up at Dirk. "Do you want my female?"

Dirk licked his lips, his eyes never leaving Riza. "Yeah."

"On your hands and knees, Riza. You need to show these males what they are protecting."

"I…uh…"

"I'll be right here," Leon promised. "We will share this together."

She nodded as she dropped to her knees.

Dirk stepped forward his cock already dripping pre-cum. "Open those lips for me, Riza."

Leon clenched his jaw as Dirk slid his cock into Riza's mouth. He breathed deeply to control the beast rising within. His woman's mouth spread wide around Dirk's cock. Riza swallowed and her nose flared as she accepted more of Dirk's thick cock.

Dirk thrust and a strangled cry escaped his lips as Riza took most of his length. "Fuck," Dirk muttered as his hand wrapped in Riza's dark hair. Leon was proud his mate would bring this male to his knees. He remembered the first time she'd wrapped those lips around his cock.

Leon watched uncomfortably as Cyrus knelt behind Riza. Her back arched and a startled moan escaped around Dirk's cock as Cyrus licked her folds. Leon could hear Cyrus slurping Riza's sweet, heady cream and jealousy burned in his chest. Even hearing another male enjoy her cream was torture.

Leon had spoken with both males and prearranged this sharing. He had made it clear that Riza belonged to him. She was his mate but he would offer the sharing this one time only. They both knew and accepted that her cunt was not to be penetrated.

Cyrus leaned back, his face wet with Riza's dew and licked his lips. His gleaming eyes met Leon's as he parted Riza's cheeks. Cyrus worked a cream-covered finger into her ass and Leon nearly jumped to his feet. The beast within roared but the man controlled his rage. He shut his eyes but the sounds were worse. He could detect and identify every noise. Dirk released a rumbling growl as his cock pumped in and out of Riza's wet mouth. Riza puffed around the thick organ and sounds of Cyrus's finger stretching Riza's tight hole were too much.

Leon released an impatient roar and both males looked at him. He shook his head grumbling to himself. The scent of Riza's heat hung heavy in the air and it didn't appear either male was doing much to ease her suffering.

Pushing his chair to the side, Leon stood and began to disrobe. He didn't miss Riza's eyes darting in his direction. "My mate's pussy needs a good fucking."

Leon stretched out on the cool, tile floor. Understanding what he wanted, Dirk slid from her mouth and lowered Riza over his cock. He growled as her hot, wet heat engulfed him. Their eyes met and Riza's were over-bright and dilated. "Ride me, baby. You need to come."

Riza whimpered as he guided her up and down his length. "It's all right, babe. Come for me and we'll give you another treat."

Dirk knelt at their side, his mouth lowered to an upturned breast and his fingers parted Riza's slit. Riza threw back her head, her long hair whipping around her as she arched her back.

Cyrus slid between Leon's parted legs as he once again worked at stretching Riza's back entrance. Leon leaned Riza forward, allowing Cyrus more maneuverability.

"Leon," Riza cried out as her cunt tightened on his cock and her inner muscles milked his shaft as she began to cream. Leon received the shock of his life when Cyrus's tongue began to lap her cream from the length of his cock as he rolled Leon's balls in his hand. Leon tensed but was too far gone and couldn't stop his roar of release.

Cyrus sat up grinning like a Cheshire cat and Leon glared but didn't comment, not wanting to draw attention to the act. Dirk smirked and Leon had the feeling he knew exactly what Cyrus had been doing.

Riza stretched full length on top of Leon, relaxing tense muscles. She'd had no idea Leon even knew of the act of sharing. Therefore, he'd caught her totally off guard at the suggestion. As for his choice in males, she couldn't have been more surprised. After Leon's confrontation with Dirk, she wouldn't have thought he'd ever consider him. As far as Cyrus, she barely knew him. He was quiet, kept mostly to himself. She didn't think of him as much of a ladies man. In fact, she couldn't remember him ever being involved with anyone. Maybe, that was why Leon chose him. He didn't want competition but that wouldn't explain Dirk.

"Ready for round two?" Dirk purred close to her ear.

Riza groaned but her pussy clenched at the thought of two cocks penetrating her.

"You're penetrating her ass," Leon said to Dirk and she wondered about the strange look that passed between the two males. Cyrus quietly moved to the side and Riza wondered if he'd done something to upset Leon but her mind quickly wrenched from that thought to other matters.

Four male hands lifted her and positioned her over Leon's thick erection. She sighed as she straddled his cock once again. This time, she knew Dirk intended to mount her ass as she rode Leon's cock. Dirk's hot, hard body pressed close to her back and she struggled to breathe. Long ago, she'd forgotten they were in a room full of people and a howl from a nearby male as he found release startled her.

Her eyes widened as she took in the scene around them. For years, she had heard the sounds and smelled the scents of mating coming from this room but never had she imagined such a carnal scene. The other night she'd been too nervous and intent on Leon to give the others much thought. Several males stood around watching. As much as she enjoyed the adoring eyes upon her and the touch of ardent male hands, she enjoyed time alone with Leon more. Blinking, she furrowed her brow as she began to withdraw.

"Riza."

Her eyes flew to meet her mate's heated gaze.

"Don't worry about everyone else, concentrate on us."

Licking her lips, her eyes trailed over the male beneath her. He was perfection. He was hers and nothing else mattered.

"Are you ready for me?" Dirk asked as she felt his hands spreading the globes of her ass. "You're so tiny. I don't want to hurt you."

Riza smirked. "You never minded hurting my ass when you tossed me on it on the training field."

"If I'd known how sweet it was I'd never have bruised it." His hands squeezed as the head of his cock nudged her opening. She tensed, expecting pain.

"Relax, Riza. Accept him," Leon commanded.

Exhaling a deep breath, she arched her back, allowing Dirk better access to his target.

"That's right, babe. Enjoy what we're going to give you." Leon tugged her mouth to his, parting her lips and inserting his tongue as Dirk breeched her opening. Riza shuddered at the full sensation of two cocks filling her body.

Her eyes closed as the breath hissed from her body. Her fingers dug into Leon's muscled chest as they slowly began to move. Leon lifted her up his cock as Dirk slid deeper and as she lowered on Leon's shaft, Dirk withdrew. A slow agonizing process set her nerves on edge. She tried to push down and back but the male hands held her immobile.

"Please…harder, faster…something," Riza urged.

As if unspoken words passed between the males, they changed their rhythm. Dirk's hands slid from her hips to enclose her breasts as his cock lodged deep in her ass. Leon increased his pace, bucking fast and deep. Each time Leon's cock plunged into her alongside Dirk's it stole her breath. Her body trembled as her insides quaked.

Dirk's fingers tweaked her nipples as he began to move. His powerful thrusts pushed her up Leon's cock and as he withdrew, her wet canal would slide down Leon's shaft.

"You're so tight, I'm not going to last," Dirk's hoarse voice whispered.

A deep growl erupted from Leon. "I'm not going to last either if you keep riding her up and down my cock like that."

Riza tried to speak but only a strangled gasp emerged as her body began to vibrate uncontrollably. She panted and shrieked as the world tilted sideways on its axis and she toppled into an abyss. The joint sounds of roaring and howling roused her momentarily from the bed she'd found upon Leon's chest.

"Did I survive?" Riza muttered.


Dirk rolled to the side his eyes heavy lidded. "You're a lucky man," he told Leon.

"I know."

"If ever she needs me, I'll be there." Dirk held out his hand.

Leon grasped the other male's hand and shook vigorously. The evening was not one he was likely to repeat but he had found joy in it. It pleased him to give Riza such complete and utter bliss. It had not been as bad as he'd anticipated. Leon's gaze flickered to Cyrus. Parts of it had been better than other parts, he thought. He narrowed his eyes at the male.

Dirk stood and grabbed a blanket. Wrapping it around Riza, he lifted her. "Let me help you."

As Leon stood, Dirk placed the slight burden back in his arms. "Be good to her."

"I will," Leon promised. He turned his gaze to Cyrus. "Thank you. It was an experience," Leon narrowed his gaze on the other male, "I'm sure Riza will never forget."

Cyrus nodded, his lip curling upward at the corner. "If ever you need me, I will be there." With a nod of acknowledgement, Leon carried Riza from the room.

Placing a sleeping Riza on her bed, Leon stepped onto the balcony and uncovered the heated whirlpool tub. Steam rose into the night sky. He added a drop or two of lavender body oil as he adjusted the temperature. Riza would be sore unless he cleansed her now. If he was honest with himself, he knew he wanted to wash the scent of the other males off her.

A flash of Riza on her knees before Dirk filled his mind. Exhaling a harsh breath, Leon turned his face skyward. He wanted to prove his love to Riza and her pack. He had done that. Never again though, would another male touch his mate.

His mind turned to her gift to him, her total submission. He could still fill the tremble of her small, round hips as he'd parted her and claimed her as his mate. Even though he'd made a huge mistake, she'd forgiven him. To the point of humbling herself before him and her pack. It was far more than he deserved. Riza was far more than he deserved.

His heart ached as he glanced at his small mate dozing on the bed. Riza murmured sleepily and snuggled against his chest as he carried her to the tub. The cool night air roused her and as he stepped into the tub and lowered her into the water, she gasped.

"Leon."

"Shh, baby, I don't want you to be sore tomorrow."

"I bet." Riza chuckled and sharp teeth nipped at his nipple.

"Hey. Do that again and I'll do more than wash your luscious body."

"Promises, promises." Riza's head rolled back and she watched him from beneath heavy-lidded eyes.

"You're too tired."

A small hand slid down his chest and across his abs, wrapping around his cock, pinned between their bodies. His sac tightened. "I'm never too tired for you."

"You're too good to me." Trailing his lips along her neck, he promised, "I'll do all the work. You relax. I'll love you long and sweet and then you'll sleep like a baby."

Lowering his head, he suckled a nipple as his fingers found her pussy. Slowly sliding in and out, long and deep, his fingers pleasured her.

"Just a minute." Leon lowered her to a bench seat and hopped from the tub, grabbing the padded cushion from a lounge chair. Hopping back into the tub, he placed the padding at the edge and lifted her onto it.

Riza's nipples puckered tightly in the cool night air. "Is it too cold for you?"

Leon had placed her with her ass on the edge of the tub and her legs spread wide. She raised her head and her lip curled upward. "Somehow, I don't think I'll have a chance to get cold."

Leon growled at the feast spread before him. "Are you sore?"

He raked her folds with his raspy tongue and she bucked upward. "No, I...no," Riza answered shakily.

Chuckling, Leon lowered his head again and inhaled deeply. Her warm, womanly musk inflamed him. He couldn't get enough of her scent. Burying his face in her folds his tongue pierced her tight, wet hole. Her body went rigid and he had to hold her hips in place. Deeply, his tongue stroked her tasty confines and her inner walls quaked around it.

"Leon," Riza cried out as sweet cream poured onto his tongue and waiting mouth.

Laving her folds, he feasted on the tasty treat. "That's right, baby, feed me." He continued to stroke her long after the last tremor ceased to rock her body. Raising his head, he stroked her inner thighs as he met her heated gaze. His cock throbbed and arched up against his stomach but he wanted to make sure it wouldn't cause her discomfort. Slowly inserting three fingers into her tight wet hole, he watched her eyes explode in flames. "Are you sure there's no pain?"

Her pink tongue snaked out, licking her lips as she nodded and he growled in need. Sliding his fingers free, he grasped her hips, anchoring her in place for his cock. He wanted to explode just watching her part for his shaft. Pushing forward he heard a deep moan but wasn't sure if it was him or her.

"God, Riza," Leon panted. "It gets better every time." Gently, he pushed forward and back, his cock urged him to ride her hard but he wouldn't, not tonight.

"I love you," Riza gasped in a breathy voice and he had to struggle not to erupt.

Grabbing her up, he took a step back and sat down, settling her over him. Nuzzling her breasts to his face he whispered, "I love you too. You're my life…my everything. You bring color to my world." He rubbed his damp eyes against her chest as he struggled to breathe.

Her fingers tilted his chin up and their gazes met under the silvery glow of the moon. Watery, emerald eyes stared at him and her lips trembled as she spoke, "To have the love of a man such as you humbles me." Grasping his shoulders, she slid up his cock and dropped back down and his breath caught in his throat.

"It's my turn to show you my love and my total commitment," Riza whispered. As she leaned forward, her dark hair fell around him. A pert nipple brushed his cheek and he turned, latching on to the offering. Enclosing the rounded mounds of her ass, he guided her as her liquid heat rode his cock. Sucking fiercely on her nipple, he bucked his hips and she screamed.

"Leon!"

"Take me. Take all of me and give me all you have," Leon pleaded.

Her sharp nails dug into his shoulders and she ground against his cock. He had to grit his teeth to stop his beast from rising as exquisite pleasure shivered his spine and tightened his sac.

Throwing back her head, Riza howled as her inner muscles clamped and released his tortured shaft. "Yes. Yes," Leon shouted as he furiously pumped his hips, shooting his seed deep into her body.

She collapsed on him and their hearts pounded in frantic harmony. "My love, my mate," he murmured as he brushed her cheek with a kiss.

"Take me to bed," Riza demanded.

"Riza!"

She shifted against him, her hip brushing his semi-erect cock and miraculously he hardened again. "I know you're capable. Take me to bed and love me until neither of us can move."

"Fuck!"

She squealed as he threw her over his shoulder and hopped from the tub, streaming water in his wake. Throwing her into the middle of the bed, he landed next to her.

"You want me to fuck until I can't move. It might be tomorrow by the time I'm through." Her skin was pinkish from the warm water and he slapped her bottom and then rubbed the handprint.

Snarling, she allowed a little fang to show. "Do your best, almighty king of the beasts," Riza challenged.

"You'll be bowing and calling me master before I'm finished," Leon predicted smugly as he grasped her thigh and dragged her closer.

"You think so?" She arched a dark brow.

"I know so. When I've earned your complete submission and my cock is buried deep in your ass, you'll beg me to fuck you hard."

Riza's chest rose and fell rapidly as she panted for breath and his cock ached just watching his sexy mate. Shaking her head, her dark locks fell around her and she grinned wickedly. "Maybe I'll make you beg." Her voice was a husky purr.

His brow shot up as she licked her full, pouty lips. If she only knew how close he was to begging now. "Come on, make me beg."

With a growl, she pounced and he landed on his back in the middle of the satin-covered bed. He shook his head. "Play with fire and you might get burned."

Riza ran her index finger from the middle of his chest across his abs. His stomach flinched. "Burn me."

Leon's heart pumped wildly as her sleekly muscled frame leaned over him. The muted light didn't dim her radiant beauty. Crawling up his body, she straddled his lower stomach and wiggled as she settled over him. The full swell of the underside of her small breasts tipped her nipples up, as if they waited for his mouth. Her hands sifted through the hair on his chest, finding his erect male nipples. She grinned as she pinched the hardened tips. Leon's breath hissed from between his lips.

Riza stifled a moan as she gazed at her gorgeous mate. One muscled arm thrown over his head and his long blond mane spread across her black satin sheets. It was a good thing she'd redecorated, though he was masculine enough to look hot stretched out on pink lace.

Keeping their eyes locked, she leaned forward, meeting his lips. Tracing his full bottom lip, she nipped it before dipping into the moist cavern of his mouth. Their tongues swirled together. He tasted of an exotic musk that must be her own flavor. Wildly, she suckled his tongue and ravished his mouth. His cock pinned beneath her pussy, thumped against her aching core.

Ripping their lips apart she panted, "It's getting hotter by the minute."

"Ignite me."

She shifted on his thick length and knew her liquid heat bathed his groin. Writhing over him, she groaned. She'd never felt voracious longing. She was a glutton—the more he gave the more she wanted. Furiously, she lunged against him. "Leon, I…" She moaned as a shiver of heat ripped through her lower belly. "I need you. Deep, hard…now."

"Take me."

She rose up and his cock unerringly sought her entrance. She dropped over him. "Oh god." Strong hands grasped her hips, raising and lowering her at a thunderous pace.

"You're killing me."

Bucking his hips, he lowered her down his shaft until he filled her completely. She screamed as brutal elation washed over her. "Yes. Oh god, yes."

Leaning forward until her forehead rested against his chest, she gasped for breath. He was still buried deep and hard inside her. Lifting her head, she met his molten gaze. "You didn't?"

Lifting a sardonic brow he purred, "No. I didn't…not yet." He flexed inside her and she shivered. "Who's going to beg?"

"Leon."

"Who?"

She shook her head.

"Get on your hands and knees," Leon commanded in a darkly sensual voice.

"Leon," she pouted.

"Now."

Inner muscles contracted as she pulled away from his turgid flesh. Kneeling at his side, she hesitated and he said, "Hands and knees."

Bending forward, he rose behind her. Warm hands ran over her rounded cheeks. "Nice. Very nice." A finger dipped between her dripping folds then spread moisture up her crack. "Spread your thighs wider."

Her legs quaked as she complied. Nervous excitement bubbled in her stomach. Strong fingers grasped her neck and pushed her head to the bed. Gulping, she shivered as smooth satin brushed her cheek and silken steel prodded her pussy. Her breath burst from her body and he drove deep. His free hand dipped between her thighs. Finding her engorged clit, he pinched and she rocked forward.

"Hold still." He plunged and withdrew his cock. His fingers circled and prodded her clit before slipping away.

She shuddered as wet fingers pressed against her anal opening. Flinching, she tightened the hole.

"Relax. You know you want it. My finger and my cock deep inside you, dominating you."

His finger circled tighter and tighter before impaling her. Her back arched at the double penetration. "You're mine. Mine. Never again will I allow another male to touch you." His voice was husky and anguished.

With sudden clarity, Riza realized he was remembering the other males he'd allowed to touch her. He had honored her in the way of her pack but she knew it haunted him. For a feline, it was unheard of to share your mate. She had not expected him to honor the lupine custom. Never would she have asked it of him. The fact that he had shared her with not only one male but two was astonishing. No one would ever doubt his commitment to her and she didn't want him to ever doubt her love or commitment to him. "I'm yours. Only yours. Take me, Leon." She rocked with him, encouraging him. "Dominate me, make me yours."

A tortured groan escaped his lips as his finger and cock slid free. Taking a deep breath, she relaxed, knowing what was coming. His thick cock head lodged at her anal opening, spreading her wide.

"You're mine."

"Yes."

Still grasping her neck in a gentle but dominant hold, he drove deep. "So hot...so tight."

Riza was near exhaustion but her love for him drove her on. She clenched her buttock muscles and he growled. "I won't survive."

"Fuck me hard, Leon. I'm yours, only yours."

"Fuck!" he yelled releasing her neck. Grasping her hips, he heaved, impaling her hard and fast. He thrust repetitively and she gasped to draw breath.

"Now. Yes, now." She cried, as burning lava filled her veins, exploding in merciless bliss.

"Mine," he declared once more as hot fluid filled her canal.

Collapsing, they lay entwined and quivering with euphoric exaltation. Riza's heart pounded until she thought it would explode. His semi-erect cock slid from her body but still he held her close.

"I've never," he gasped, "*never*, felt like *that*."

"It was sublime."

He snuggled, kissing her neck. "It all started because I didn't want you to be sore."

"Humph. I'm sure I won't be sore now!"

"I'll clean us so we can sleep in peace."

"Mmm, just don't wake me." She yawned as her eyes drooped. "Love you." Her eyes closed.

\* \* \* \* \*

*The moon was full as the lion silently stalked his prey. Lifting his head, he sniffed the air, finding a familiar scent. His eyes glowed as he neared the waters edge. The dark-haired female splashed at the shallow water. Lunging, he grabbed her by the arm. His mouth closed tight enough to hold but not to damage the skin as he pulled her from the water.*

*The naked woman shrieked and trembled on the ground as he stood over her licking his chops. Lowering his snout to the female's mound, he inhaled her fragrant scent. Fear laced the woman's natural scent, giving her a heady flavor.*

*"Please don't hurt me. I'll do anything," the female begged.*

*His nose bumped her downy curls and she whimpered. His tongue darted out and lapped her heated folds. A startled gasp escaped her lips and he growled, pinning her with his heated gaze.*

*The lion's cock dripped with pre-cum as it extended long and heavy from his body. He took a step forward allowing the lubricant to drip onto her. He padded slowly up her body, his paws on each side of her, and his liquid streamed over her belly, her breasts… He stopped and watched the female, wondering if she'd really do anything.*

"Fuck," Leon gasped as a warm, wet mouth closed around his cock jerking him from his slumber. Riza looked up from her position between his thighs.

"It about time you woke up," Riza said, her hot breath blowing across his wet cock.

"Mmm, I was dreaming." He eyed his pretty little mate with her mouth stretched around his cock. This was even better than his dream.

His cock popped from her mouth. "About me?"

"Oh yeah and you were just about to suck my cock."

"That can be arranged." She nipped his fleshy cock head and he arched up to meet her mouth.

"Glad to hear it. It's about time we had a talk about how many different ways we can fit together."

"Oh really." Her dark brows arched. "I'm much better at action than talk." Riza shifted to feral form and a long tongue swiped his naked thigh.

"Fuck, this is definitely better than my dream."

# FERAL INTENSITY

ॐ

# Dedication

❧

*From their lips to my ears.*
*This book is dedicated to a special group of friends.*
*They know who they are and how important their support*
*is to me.*

# Prologue
*Faldron Mountains*

ೞ

Trotting behind his alpha and two other guards, Dirk was ever watchful as they neared the prearranged meeting place. Gionne, the alpha of the Valde wolf pack had agreed to meet with Rian, the alpha of a newly formed coyote pack, in a clearing just ahead. From what they knew, the coyote pack was small, an offshoot of the larger Aden Pack from the other side of the mountain. They were no match for the Valde pack but Dirk couldn't shake an unsettled feeling as they neared the meeting place. The coyotes had settled on the northeast ridge of the mountain. The land was just off the Valde homelands and they needed to ensure that the coyotes would respect the boundary. Forest fires and droughts had taken their toll on the once-abundant wildlife. There was still plenty for all as long as everyone took only what was needed.

Gionne stopped on the boundary of their land. Still hidden in heavy underbrush the small group formed a semicircle, peering out into the clearing. The open area was quiet, nothing moved but Dirk sensed the presence of the coyotes. The alpha emitted a low rumble from his chest signaling the pack members to change to human form.

Dropping his satchel to the ground, Dirk began the transformation and his coat of pure white turned to golden flesh. Shaking out a pair of jeans and a shirt, he couldn't mistake the feel of hungry eyes upon him. The coyotes were known for trickery and possible deviousness, so Dirk didn't trust them. He hoped they were not walking into a trap. However, Dirk trusted his alpha's judgment and knew reinforcements weren't far behind. Gionne didn't believe in taking chances. The Valde and the old Aden pack had bad blood between them from long ago. Dirk didn't know the whole story but he knew enough to be suspicious. Gionne believed in letting bygones be bygones and Dirk would follow his lead. This newly formed pack, made up of young coyotes who hadn't been around during the bad times, probably didn't know any more about it than he did.

Turning away from his pack, he began to dress. The small hairs on the back of his neck stood on end and he shivered. Be it fear or excitement, he didn't know but he had to tuck a painful arousal into his tight-fitting jeans. Leaving his shirt hanging loose, he hid his body's condition.

Dirk jumped as a firm hand settled on his shoulder. "Are you okay?" Gionne asked.

He shrugged. "Yeah, I'm fine." Looking up, he nodded his head toward the clearing. Four males awaited them.

"I see them." Gionne grinned. "Let's get this meeting over so we can get home."

Dirk couldn't agree more. Gionne had recently taken Jenna, a feline shifter as his mate. The joining had caused some unrest within the Valde pack and he didn't want to be gone long. Gionne had chosen him as his mate's protector and last night they had shared her in a claiming ritual. He could still feel the caress of her feline tongue on his cock. He had enjoyed many of the pack females since he'd come of age but Jenna was unique and he found great pleasure in taking her. Still there was something missing. He had enjoyed the couplings but she wasn't his mate and he hungered for more.

Shaking his loose hair out of his face, he attempted to clear his thoughts as he followed Gionne into the clearing. Four males stood side by side but Dirk's gaze riveted to the large bronze leader. A wave of heat washed over him as he neared the big male.

Introductions commenced but Dirk tuned it all out until the leader extended his hand to him. His heart thundered as the bronze hand engulfed his in a firm grip. The alpha's thumb caressed the back of his hand and his stomach muscles clenched. The dull, persistent ache that seemed ever present in his balls, ignited in fierce desire. With hands locked, Dirk raised his gaze to meet the other male's dark, hungry eyes and his world shifted.

Full lips curled up at the corners as the male spoke in a low, husky voice. "I am Rian. It is an honor to meet you."

Dirk breathed in a slow pant as his mind whirled with possibilities. *It can't be!* There had to be some mistake. Rian released his hand and he felt bereft at the loss of the touch.

A smug smile curled Rian's lips and Dirk's heart beat triple time. Lust, hotter than he'd ever felt, churned in his gut.

Conversation between the two alphas swirled around his head but he couldn't absorb the words. From time to time, Rian's dark eyes turned to him and he felt his gaze as a heated caress. The male's scent entranced him.

Taking a step backward, Dirk took a deep, cleansing breath as he tried to clear his mind. Turning away, he pretended vigilance to his duty as guard of the area. His eyes roved the darkened woods but his mind screamed with panic as he attempted to reason out his dilemma.

Dirk wasn't a scholar of philosophy or pack history. What he did know was that for the shapeshifting races lifemates were predestined. Times were changing, the breeds were mixing. He didn't know why the fates had chosen to mix the breeds—he only knew that they had. Gionne and Jenna were an example as was Gionne's sister, Riza and her mate, Leon the feline alpha. He had almost taken both of the females as mates but destiny had stepped in and united them with their true mates. Looking back, Dirk didn't know why he'd willingly wanted to mate with females he'd known were not his true mates.

Dirk sighed! Had part of him known what his future held? Was he trying to hide from a truth he knew within himself?

His gaze flashed back toward Rian. Had destiny chosen this male as his mate? He wasn't ready to accept it. Though the coyotes were known for trickery, he wouldn't fall easily for their games.

As the meeting came to an end, Dirk felt Rian's questioning gaze upon him but he did not acknowledge the connection.

His spine tingled. His beast wanted out. The call to mate was clear but he would fight it. Time would tell if this coyote was his true mate.

# Chapter One
*Faldron Mountains*
*Several months later*

&

A solitary howl shattered the peace of the evening. Dirk Valde raised his head from a science-fiction novel as the sound reverberated in his soul. Closing his eyes, he sighed. He was lonely, that was a fact. Laying the book aside, he stood and crossed to the cabin door. Lifting his head, he sniffed the cool night air. The coyote wasn't in Valde territory yet but it was close. Taking a seat in an old wooden rocker, Dirk propped his bare feet up on the top rail of the porch. It was fall in the Faldron Mountains and the ground was crisp with frost. A low moon hung over the trees, illuminating the clearing around the cabin. He watched as a young buck hugged the tree line, following the scent of a doe in heat. The deer was oblivious to anything but his potential mate. A smirk curved Dirk's lips. He could relate to the horny male.

The buck stopped and lifted his head. Taking a whiff of the air, he caught the scent of the coyote. Spooked, the deer bolted into the woods. The coyote wouldn't feast on that particular deer tonight.

The cabin was located on the lower ridge at the northeast corner of Valde territory. The Valde wolf pack was the largest, strongest wolf pack in the area. Their land was vast and protected at all costs. They were fortunate to have a friendly feline pack on their eastern boarder. The mating of Gionne to Jenna and Riza to Leon had solidified that relationship.

He had chosen to take over guard duty in this area. It was his responsibility to protect the Valde wolf pack's territory from invaders. The newly formed coyote pack pushed the boundaries daily. Yesterday, they had taunted him by leaving the remains of a fresh kill near the creek, behind the cabin.

It was a deliberate attempt to draw him out and he knew why. He would meet with Rian, their pack leader, when he was ready and not before then. The cabin had not been the best place to come to sort out his feelings, not with the coyotes so close. Temptation was just over the ridge. So far, Rian hadn't tried to force the issue but day by day his scent lingered closer.

Coming to the cabin had been a huge step for Dirk. Part of him knew he couldn't run forever but a knot of panic formed in his gut every time he considered his destiny. His worry was twofold. Having a male mate was a surprise but a coyote mate was a shock. He lived in denial. In fact, he'd almost mated twice in the last several months. Neither female had been his true mate but both were fine females and had aroused a need within him. Thoughts of Jenna and Riza made him hard. The scent in the air made him harder. Both females had moved on with their mates and it was time for him to move on with his life.

Standing, Dirk pulled the tie out of his long hair. The cool night air had little effect on him and he shucked the unfastened jeans that were his only covering. Darting into the yard, two legs turned to four as he took the shape of a white wolf.

In wolf form, he was free of the worries that consumed his human half. Picking up a hot scent he crashed through thick underbrush, almost stumbling as he came to a sudden stop on the frosty ground. In a knee-deep pool of the stream sat a coyote shifter. Wet, black hair fell over bronze shoulders. The wolf growled low in his throat as the coyote shifter stood on firm, sculpted legs. A sleek back led to a rounded ass a shade lighter in color. Twisting, the coyote turned to face him.

The scent of lust filled the air as his gaze met the gleaming brown eyes of the coyote shifter. Dirk's gaze traveled over the well-developed, lightly furred chest, the flat stomach and came to rest on the impressive erection jutting from the male's body.

"So you've come out of hiding," Rian Aden's husky voice teased Dirk. "Why don't you shift? I'd enjoy a back scrubbing and I'd return the favor."

In feral form, Dirk took a step forward, stretching his neck out as he scented the aroused male. Perking his ears, he flared his nostrils. The heady scent was like a flavor on his tongue and his mouth watered. Overwhelmed with need, Dirk's shiny coat stood on end as he struggled to contain his feral urge to mate.

"Come on Dirk. You know you want to." Rian's honey-rich voice teased as much as his soap-covered hand, which slid over rippling abs and encircled his erect cock. Dirk watched as the coyote shifter stroked his erection with a slow, firm grip.

Mesmerized by the beauty that was Rian, he took two steps forward. Dirk licked his lips hungrily. He was within touching distance of Rian and the coyote reached out his other hand. Startled, Dirk jumped back. The human within warred with his beast, fighting for control. He growled and darted back into the brush.

"Fuck!" The curse echoed in Dirk's ears as he headed for the cabin.

\* \* \* \* \*

Kicking the leg of a wooden chair, Dirk flopped facedown on the couch. Using both hands, he massaged his temples before running his fingers through his unbound hair. His thoughts turned to another time and place.

Several months earlier, Dirk had accompanied his alpha, Gionne to a meeting with the new coyote band. The unease of that day crawled up his spine once again as he remembered his first glimpse of Rian.

The meeting was fuzzy in his mind since he had paid little attention to what was going on. From the first glance, his mind had filled with Rian and Rian alone. Looking back, he wasn't sure if he'd returned the alpha's greeting, he'd been so overwhelmed by the shock of his touch.

Dirk sighed deeply. He had thought time and space would dull the need. He had returned to his pack and tried to carry on as before but always something was missing. To this day, his world hadn't righted itself. He stretched on the couch. The leather felt cool on his heated, naked flesh. He shifted his raging arousal against the smooth upholstery.

"Damn it," he cursed as he rolled to his side. He refused to hump an inanimate object. He wasn't a dog in heat. Breathing deeply, he closed his eyes and a picture of gleaming bronze flesh filled his head. In his mind, Rian's full lips parted and the slow smile softened his angular jaw. As it had many times before, the fantasy welcomed him with a mouth that was warm and hungry as it traveled his flesh.

Dirk groaned. He hated to think how many of his dreams the coyote had haunted in the last few months. Dirk's hand slid across his thigh to wrap around his cock as the image in his mind accepted his cock within his mouth.

He stroked his cock in a loose grip as his mind made love to Rian's mouth. Dirk's balls tightened as pre-cum leaked from his shaft.

It was time he faced what his body had known for months. Rian was his lifemate. He was tired of running from a truth he could not change. His lifemate was a male but not just any male. He was the alpha male of the coyote pack. "Rian is my mate," Dirk said aloud. It was a leap in the right direction. He'd always heard self-acceptance was the hardest step.

\* \* \* \* \*

Following the wolf's trail, Rian stopped outside the cabin window. Lamplight danced along bare, golden flesh. Involuntarily, his jaw dropped as he watched Dirk unawares. The other male lay naked and aroused on the couch and his raw beauty stole Rian's breath. From the tip of his golden head all the way down the length of his perfectly proportioned body, he was exquisite. From this angle, Rian couldn't see the blue-as-a-summer-sky eyes but he remembered how it felt to stare into them. Heat rolled off Rian. He wouldn't be surprised to see steam rising from his flesh.

Clamping his jaw, he silenced the low growl rumbling in his chest. He wanted Dirk. He wanted him with an obsession he'd never felt before. Clenching his fist, he fought the instinct to crash through the window. There was nothing he wanted more than to lie at Dirk's side. He longed to stroke the bare, golden body and taste the flavor of heated arousal on his flesh.

As he watched, Dirk's full lips parted on a pant just before he wasted a silvery stream of cum upon the floor. He'd wasted the heady fluid that should have been Rian's, should have been on his hands and lips.

Cursing beneath his breath, Rian turned from the window. A light snow had begun to fall but Rian barely noticed. His own stiff cock bulged behind his jeans but he wouldn't relieve himself. Now that he had found his mate, he would wait for him. Running a shaky hand through his hair, he sighed. He should take his small pack and leave the area before he destroyed Dirk's life. He should but he couldn't. There was one thing he wanted more than to possess Dirk and that was to see love and acceptance in the other male's eyes. Stepping off the porch, he headed for his camp but he knew he'd return early in the morning. His patience was near the end. It was time Dirk accepted their connection. Rian only wished everyone could accept it.

Heaviness settled over him. Sometimes, he missed the Aden pack or at least some of the pack. He missed the carefree days of his youth, before his sexual orientation had driven a wedge between him and his father.

He smiled as he remembered the first hunt he and his brother Mickal had gone on with their father. He remembered the exhilaration of the hunt but mostly he remembered how proud his father had been.

Rian grimaced as sharp words flashed in his mind. *"No son of mine is going to mate with another male. You've been groomed to become alpha. Are you going to pass that up for a piece of ass? Find a female to mate and breed. If you have to, stash a piece of ass somewhere."*

Rian's pain wasn't just for himself but for his sister and the others of his small pack. They deserved better. He did the best he could by them but times were tough. As he neared the clearing, he saw movement in his cabin. Jake was visiting his sister, Rosilee. She was the only female of his small pack, the only hope for a new generation of pack members.

\* \* \* \* \*

Within the tree line, a lone male watched Rian enter the cabin. He looked around in disgust. The small pack scrounged to make do on the fringes of the Valde properties.

From a distance he had watched Rian tonight, he'd seen his activities. He had hoped he wouldn't need to interfere but it appeared he had no choice. It was time to make plans.

\* \* \* \* \*

Dirk's stomach grumbled as he stirred the scrambled eggs. It had been a restless night and he had risen before the sun crested the mountain. The cabin was cool, he'd just added a log to the wood-burning stove but he barely noticed the temperature. Dressed only in a pair of worn, faded jeans, he shuffled to a tune he hummed under his breath.

Peace had settled over him last night as he'd made his decision. Actually, there was no decision to make, only destiny to accept. He wasn't fooling himself, there would still be issues but he was ready to face them. He wasn't a bigot. He had no problem with homosexuality. Hell, truth be known, accepting the fact that Rian was coyote was more difficult than accepting that his lifemate was male. Unknowingly, Gionne had helped him with his wary regard of the coyotes. As alpha, Gionne had met with Rian several times and through pack discussions, Dirk had learned that Gionne thought highly of Rian. He had gone so far as to say he was nothing like his father, Marcus. The words had helped him open his mind and heart to the coyote.

The creak of a loose board on the porch froze Dirk in place. Turning, he eyed the closed door. Something or someone moved outside that door. Turning off the gas stove, he silently crossed the room. Throwing open the door, he stopped in his tracks. "Rian?" The alpha's eyes skimmed his chest and reminded him that he stood half naked with his jeans unfastened.

"Weren't you expecting me?" Rian took a step toward him and the intoxicating musk of arousal surrounded Dirk, stealing his breath.

Easing back into the cabin, he allowed the other male to enter. The small confines of the cabin intensified Rian's masculine appeal. Tall and broad-shouldered, his presence filled the room. Dirk had wanted to see Rian today but having him come here threw him off balance. "I planned on coming to your camp today."

A smile played about the other male's lips before he spoke. "I'm pleased you wanted to come today."

Heat flushed Dirk's skin. He'd walked right into that one. "I was about to eat breakfast. Are you hungry?"

"Famished." Rian's eyes gleamed as they traveled his bare flesh.

Dirk silently cursed himself. Every time he opened his mouth, he put his foot in it. With a jerky movement, he turned away and hurried across the room. Reaching for another plate, he split the eggs and bacon in half. Setting the plates on the small pine table, Dirk turned back toward the sink.

He sensed the other male moving before he eased up behind him. Heat and hard-bodied male pressed to his backside as Rian peered over his shoulder. Despite the lust heating his blood, denial churned in Dirk's stomach and he leaned away from the contact.

"Impressive." Rian's hot breath bathed his cheek.

The metal pan clanked as he dropped it into the sink. "Rian?" Dirk gulped as arousal surged through his veins and filled his cock.

Strong hands settled on his waist as a denim-covered cock pressed against his ass. "Fuck! You feel good." Rian's chest vibrated with a low rumble of appreciation. "You feel good. You look good. I wonder if you taste as good." Warm breath bathed his cheek as Rian nuzzled his neck.

Dirk gasped, unable to speak as his hands curled against the ledge of the countertop. The feel of another cock pressed intimately against him gave him pause. Rian was the alpha of his pack. On some level, Dirk had expected Rian's aggressiveness but he'd avoided considering the mechanics of their relationship.

Biting his lip, Dirk withheld a groan of pleasure as Rian moved against him. Still, the other male's nearness inflamed his desire and his cock pulsed with need. The bulge in his pants proclaimed his want of Rian. He wanted to fuck him. He wanted a connection with the male but he wasn't sure he was ready to fulfill Rian's needs.

Dirk's experience with males was limited. In fact, there'd only been one encounter and though he hadn't initiated it, he had taken the aggressive role. The pitcher, if you will. Rian wanted him to be the receiver and he wasn't certain that was a role he desired to play. "Rian…hold on."

"You know you want me. You know I'm your mate." Confidence filled the dominant male's voice. "I can smell your desire." Rian sniffed and then trailed his warm tongue down his neck. "I can taste it."

His heart pounded at hearing himself called mate. "I'm not ready."

"You haven't been with a male?" The words, whispered into his ear, caused a shiver to ride down his spine.

"Not that way."

Rian's warm hand cupped his cheek and turned his head to mesh their gazes. A cocky smile lit his dark chocolate eyes. "Virgin ass!" Rian's tongue ran teasingly over his lips. "I like that. I'll give you more pleasure than you can imagine."

"I'm not an innocent." Dirk snorted. He was a few years younger than the alpha male but he was, in no way, a virgin.

"You've had females?"

"Yeah." Dirk tried to pull away but, pinned against the counter, he couldn't move without a fight.

"You haven't had a male?"

"One male. One time," Dirk replied and guilt filled his gut. He didn't know why he felt like he should apologize.

Rian's eyes narrowed to mere slits. "After you met me?"

Dirk looked away as a ribbon of regret sliced through him. "I didn't initiate it."

"You were curious? You wanted to know what it was like to fuck another male."

Dirk nodded. "I guess." He couldn't deny that meeting Rian had roused a curiosity in him. Rian's very existence made him admit something to himself. Something that he'd avoided for a long time. He was attracted to males. Over the years, he'd had the occasional homosexual wet dream but he hadn't allowed himself to explore those feelings. He had chalked them up to puberty, then curiosity. However, after meeting Rian, he'd acted on his curiosity. A submissive male had shown willingness and he'd taken him up on the offer. He didn't know what he'd expected but he'd been disappointed. It wasn't that he hadn't found pleasure in the act. He'd found the same type of fleeting pleasure he gained from joining with females but he'd hoped for more.

Rian's touch, however, ignited a fierce desire in his gut. A longing so strong it drove thoughts of others from his mind. Rian's touch promised satisfaction do a degree Dirk had never felt. "I needed to know," Dirk whispered softly.

Strong arms tightened around Dirk. "Did you like it? Did you think of me when you were fucking him? Did you wish it was my mouth on your body?" Rian's hand moved to cover Dirk's cock through his jeans and his knees weakened.

"Don't." Dirk twisted in Rian's arms. As good as Rian's touch was, he wasn't ready to go to his knees for him. Standing face-to-face with the alpha, Dirk didn't flinch. He wasn't intimidated and he wouldn't cower to the dominant male.

Rian's dark eyes blazed with heat, lust...fear. "Don't what? You're mine. As much as you don't want to admit it, it's true. We are mates. We can run from it. We can hide it but nothing will change. Fate made us mates but I can walk out that door and never come back if that's what you want. I won't lie to you. In some ways, your life will be easier if I leave now."

The words were a dagger of pain in Dirk's chest. He grabbed Rian's ass and squeezed the muscled flesh. "I don't hide from anything but I don't rush into anything either." He wasn't ready to roll over for Rian but he wasn't prepared to let him go either.

Toe-to-toe they stood and stared. Drawing rough, ragged breaths, he inhaled Rian's scent until he could taste the other male.

Pressed intimately against the male fate had chosen for him, Rian's lust rose hot and hard. Flaring his nostrils, he absorbed Dirk's scent, imprinting it on his soul. Growling low in his throat, Rian lowered his head the fraction of an inch it took to mesh their lips. Hot, hungry lips opened for him, stealing his breath, stealing his thoughts. Rian slipped his hand beneath Dirk's loosened jeans and squeezed the firm flesh of his ass. Damn, he felt good. Dirk's flesh was warm, smooth and firm. Rian wanted to strip him and taste every inch of his golden body.

Grasping the front of his shirt, Rian worked the buttons loose, managing to rip off only a few. Pressing closer to Dirk, he was thrilled to feel his naked, hard chest against his own. Dirk's chest hair tickled his taut nipples and he groaned as he ground their bodies together. Chest to chest and denim-covered cock to denim-covered cock, they rocked back and forth. Moaning, they found an erotic rhythm that pleasured them both.

Panting, Rian lifted his head. "I want you."

"Rian." Heavy-lidded blue eyes were full of lust but still held an edge of doubt.

Dirk licked his lips. "Fuck," Rian groaned. He wanted that tongue. Tugging on Dirk's long blond hair, he angled his face to accept his kiss. Dipping his tongue into Dirk's mouth, he received an ardent response.

Swallowing around Dirk's thrusting tongue, Rian pressed him against the counter. He was ready to mate, preliminaries be damned. Dirk had made him wait too long. He squeezed his mate's buttocks as he thrust his hips against him. Sharp teeth bit at his lips as Dirk pulled back.

"Damn it, Rian," Dirk growled.

"Let me touch you." He pulled at the zipper of Dirk's jeans. "I want to feel you against me," Rian rasped and unzipped his own pants.

Scorching hot, hard flesh rubbed against his cock. A red haze of lust clouded his thinking. He wasn't going to last long with Dirk in his arms. He was burning up. "If I can't have you, we'll have this." Rian bucked his hips against Dirk in a slow rhythm, his breath frozen in his lungs. It felt so good.

Shoving Dirk's jeans lower, Rian dug his fingers into the firm male ass. Increasing the tempo of their sexual dance, Rian promised, "Soon, I'll have you. I'll part these cheeks and take you. I'll make you mine. My mate!" He nibbled Dirk's throat and jaw. "You'll beg me to fuck you before I take you. I can't wait to taste your budded hole. I'll penetrate you with just a finger." Shifting his hands, he lightly brushed Dirk's anus. "Slow and deep. I'll finger-fuck your ass until you beg for my cock then I'll mount you and send us both to paradise."

Dirk growled but didn't argue. Rian felt him tense. He knew he was close to completion. Rian was shocked, yet pleased, to feel Dirk's teeth clamp on the skin between his neck and shoulder. Nipping hard, the male marked him with his teeth. Desire surged in Rian's veins.

"I'm coming," Dirk growled as he released Rian's neck.

"Come for me," Rian demanded. Using one finger, Rian rimmed Dirk's tight puckered hole. He wanted to penetrate him. Blood roared through his veins at the thought. Rian's balls tightened, ready to explode. Pressing his finger against the virgin hole, Rian bucked his hips against Dirk. He felt the other male's release surge through him and erupt against their abs.

"Fuck," Dirk shouted as the warm fluid coated them.

Growling deep in his throat, Rian allowed his own release and covered them with more sticky cream.

# Chapter Two

Sitting side by side on the couch, Dirk panted as he tried to regain his equilibrium. Dirk almost snickered. With his pants around his hips and their joint release smeared on his abdomen, he looked ridiculous. From the corner of his eye, he glanced at Rian. His unbuttoned shirt hung half off one shoulder. The top half of what appeared to be an impressive cock hung from his open jeans and a smear of cum covered his tight abs. Impatience had fired their lust so high neither of them had managed to undress completely. A slow burn of desire stirred in Dirk's gut and he jerked his gaze from the other male.

"I want you to meet my pack. Our pack," Rian declared.

The words were abrupt and unexpected but warmth settled over Dirk as he heard them. He knew in his heart he belonged with the alpha male. He wanted a future with Rian. However, as he turned the words over in his mind, Dirk became unsettled. He'd never considered leaving the Valde pack. Gionne had been his alpha the last few years and before that, Gionne's father had ruled. Since meeting Rian, he'd spent much time considering the personal aspects of their relationship. Somehow, he'd forgotten to consider the ramifications on the rest of his life. Rian had his own pack and it would follow that he would have to join it. He would become part of the coyote pack!

"Is something wrong?"

He felt Rian's gaze on him. "No. I just hadn't thought about leaving my pack." Typically the female left her pack when she joined with a mate. However, there was nothing typical about his relationship with Rian.

Rian nodded. "I understand how you feel but sometimes you have to make a hard decision to have what you want."

Rian's quietly spoken words made Dirk wonder. "Why did you leave your pack?"

"I wasn't welcome there. My followers weren't welcome. We're outcasts. I told you, life with me won't be easy."

Dirk's chest burned with empathy at the sad tone to Rian's words. "Why?"

"My father—my alpha—frowns upon homosexuality. I was given a choice. I could mate with a female or I could leave. I left. Are the Valde not the same?"

Dirk shook his head vehemently. "Gionne doesn't discriminate."

Rian sneered. "Does he know you're gay?"

"I'm not gay." Dirk jumped to his feet and pulled up his jeans, ignoring the sticky residue.

Rian cleared his throat and Dirk glanced at the male. Rian arched a dark brow over glittering eyes. "You prefer bisexual then?"

"We haven't discussed it. I didn't know…" Dirk's words trailed off as Rian teasingly ran a hand across his ripped abs, gathering their cream. Dirk struggled with a surge of desire as he watched Rian rub the cream into his smooth, bronze flesh.

Rian snorted. "You've known. You've known since the moment we met, you just didn't want to accept it."

Dirk shrugged. "It won't make any difference to the Valde or to Gionne."

One side of Rian's lip curled in a sardonic twist. "You'll see. My father ignored my preference at first. Eventually, he cast me out. He said I was useless since I couldn't produce an heir." A harsh laugh erupted from Rian's mouth. "He felt my sexual orientation made me too weak to rule. The role of alpha was not one I desired anyway. With me gone, rule will fall to my brother, Mickal."

"But you've taken on the role of alpha for your pack."

Rian stood and tugged up his pants. "I did not choose the role. We're a small group. Since we can't reproduce, we won't grow as a pack unless others join us. I do my best to lead them." Pulling his shirt together, he fastened the intact buttons.

"The others…are they all…?"

Rian cocked his head to the side. Narrowed eyes studied Dirk. "Gay? Or are you asking if they are my lovers?"

"I didn't mean…" Dirk hesitated. Yeah! That was exactly what he was asking. "Are they your lovers?"

A smug grin curled Rian's lip as he sauntered toward him. Stopping inches in front of him, Rian asked, "Jealous?"

"Maybe." Dirk shrugged, giving nothing away.

Skirting him, Rian turned to the window and looked out into the clearing. "As I said, it is a small group. I've been friends with Trey since childhood. He and his mate, Joel are part of the pack. Andre followed because he is looking for his place. I won't lie. I've been with Andre but it didn't mean anything to either of us and it ended long ago."

Pulling out a kitchen chair, Dirk sat and leaned forward, elbows on knees. "You don't have to tell me if you don't want to."

"I'm asking you to be part of my pack. You need to know where you stand." Rian cleared his throat. "Haron is a few years younger than me and I've had a relationship with him but it's over."

Something in Rian's voice made him uneasy. "Does he know it's over?"

Turning, Rian met his gaze. "Yes. He knew from the moment I met you. He has accepted it. The two remaining members of my group aren't gay. Rosilee, my sister, followed because she couldn't accept my father's way. Jake is another story. He's always been a rebel but I believe he followed because of Rosilee."

"Jake was with you the day we met. I remember that name."

"Yes. Jake, Trey and Haron were with me. I left Joel and Andre behind with my sister."

Looking at the plate of food, Dirk shoved it away. It was cold. "You didn't trust us?" Dirk thought it ironic that the coyote didn't trust the Valde. However, every story had two sides and who was he to say the Valde were blameless in the long-ago conflict.

"I've learned the hard way that it pays to be wary."

Wary. That would describe the look in the other male's eyes. He spoke of lifemates and futures but it was obvious he still held back. Was it his past that made him wary or was he hiding something? "It is hard to believe your pack would turn from you, especially your father."

"You don't believe the Valde will turn from you?"

Dirk shook his head. "No. I don't."

"It would be nice to have a good relationship with them but I am not counting on it."

"You'll see. I can trust Gionne." Dirk didn't miss the look of doubt on Rian's face.

\* \* \* \* \*

To anyone watching, the grayish-brown coyote and the white wolf would seem an odd pair. However if they watched for long they'd see how well the two worked together.

Rian held the young buck by the throat until Dirk charged in, adding his mouth and weight to the kill. Between them, they brought the deer down. The snow-covered ground turned red as the deer bled out and ceased to fight.

Rian had choreographed the exhilarating hunt with Dirk chasing the deer to him. Together they'd made the kill. Together they feasted.

A final lick to Dirk's coat and his white fur shone clean and shiny, free of the blood that had coated him. Shifting, Rian rolled to his side and watched the other male as he shifted from wolf to human. Healthy golden skin gleamed and Rian's eyes feasted on the sight. "Damn, you're hot."

Wide blue eyes met his. "Thanks."

"It's true. I've never seen a more well-formed male."

Dirk chuckled and stretched, teasing Rian with the play of muscle. "Have you looked in the mirror?"

Scooting closer to Dirk, he ran a hand along the other male's smooth, warm hip. "I enjoyed the hunt. We work well together." He could sense Dirk's nervousness. He could smell his fear. Rian knew Dirk wasn't completely comfortable with their relationship and he wanted to put him at ease. His fingers lightly trailed the golden flesh.

"Yeah. It was fun."

He leaned closer, inhaling Dirk's musky scent. "I owed you a meal since breakfast got cold." Heat surged in him as he remembered why the meal got cold.

"I didn't complain."

"No. You didn't." Scooting closer, the tip of his erection brushed Dirk's hip and he tried to roll away. "Let me see you." He grasped Dirk's thigh and held him in place. "I just want to look."

Dirk tensed and he tightened his grip. "Don't go cold on me. I'm not going to force anything." Lifting his hand, Rian brushed Dirk's long blond hair off his shoulder. "I want you but I won't force you." A nervous gaze flicked up to meet his. "Force isn't my style," Rian promised.

"Sorry!" Dirk pulled back. "The ground is cold."

Rian chuckled. "I didn't think the cold bothered you."

"Yeah. Well…" Dirk shrugged.

"So tell me, how did you deal with a female who played hard to get?"

"You expect me to give up my secrets?" Dirk laughed.

The sound delighted Rian and he grinned. "Sure."

"I suppose I sweet-talked her." Dirk's eyes softened.

Rian nodded. "Did you tell her how beautiful she was or that her body was perfect? Did you tell her you wanted to fuck her more than anything else in the world?" Rian skimmed his hands over flawless golden skin and watched as muscles rippled beneath his touch. Dirk's cock was long, thick and thankfully aroused. It gave him hope—hope that Dirk would accept him as mate. "Damn. You're perfect. Did you mention wanting to suck the most delicious cock you'd ever seen?"

"Fuck, Rian," Dirk murmured as he grasped Rian's exploring hand and held it still on his abs. "I don't think I ever told a female that I wanted to suck her cock." Rian could feel Dirk's possessive gaze roving his body. "But I can understand the sentiment."

"I guess I lost my train of thought."

"Yeah."

"Looking at you does that to me."

Blue eyes gleamed and Rian's heart soared. Things were looking up! He nearly groaned as he looked at Dirk's arousal. They were definitely looking up but before they went any further, there was something they had to do.

"I want to make love to you. I want to make you mine but first I need you to meet my pack. I need you to see your future before I make you mine." Rian needed Dirk to be sure before they became mates.

* * * * *

Lost in their own thoughts, the two males were oblivious to a presence watching them from a distance. The lone male growled low in his throat as he observed the two young lovers.

"Enjoy yourself while you can," he whispered. Soon, he would put an end to the relationship. The Valde and all their wealth thought they were better than the coyotes. They considered themselves the superior breed.

The male spit upon the frozen ground. "Superior! Humph," he huffed. Their choice piece of land made them seem superior. It was not the fault of the coyote that forest fires had ravaged their lands.

Raising his head, the male looked around. This land should belong to the coyote. His ancestors had fought for the land but had given up too easily.

The Valde had taken much from the coyotes and it sickened him to see Rian grovel at the feet of a wolf. Rian deserved better. Once the wolf was gone, Rian would realize it was for the best. Given time, he would accept the inevitable and bring his small group home where they belonged.

There was no room in a coyote pack for a wolf. Turning on his heel, the male stalked off.

* * * * *

Dressed in clean jeans and a cotton shirt, Dirk stepped out onto the porch where Rian waited. "My jeans won't fit you but I could get you a clean shirt," Dirk offered.

"I'm fine."

Dirk pursed his lips as he eyed Rian.

"Are you embarrassed to show up at my camp with me smelling like sex?"

Dirk's skin flushed. "If you don't mind..." He shrugged his shoulders.

"I don't mind my pack members knowing you belong to me."

Rian stepped off the porch and Dirk followed. Rian was right, the scent of their joining lingered on his clothes and teased Dirk's senses as they walked the short distance to the coyote camp.

At the edge of the tree line, Dirk and Rian stopped. Ahead was a small clearing that held three roughly built cabins. The frame was up on a fourth cabin and there appeared to be room to build a couple more.

"I told you, we are a small pack just starting out."

Dirk heard what he thought was apology in Rian's voice and he grinned. Rian's humble, almost shy declaration endeared him to his heart more than any riches could. "There's nothing wrong with that."

"I've heard of the Valde stronghold. I know it's massive…elaborate."

"It is but it's not mine." Dirk looked around, appreciating the hard work and craftsmanship that had gone in to building the cabins. Reaching out, he grasped Rian's hand. It was rough from physical labor. "Did I mention that I'm good with my hands?"

Rian snorted and squeezed his hand. "I expected as much."

Turning to face Rian, Dirk placed his other hand on his cotton-covered chest. Rian's heart pounded beneath his touch. "So you want me for my woodworking skills?"

"Hardly, though you can work my wood anytime." The corner of Rian's mouth curled upward and he winked.

Dirk felt a flush heat his skin. "I'll keep that in mind. Which one is yours?"

Rian's dark brows shot upward. "Excuse me?"

Dirk nodded his head toward the cabins. "Which cabin?"

"The larger one in the middle is mine. Rosilee lives with me. The cabin on the right belongs to Trey and Joel. The other is the bunkhouse for the single males."

Dirk stepped closer, his lips almost brushed Rian's mouth. "So, do I stay in the bunkhouse?"

Rian's arm came around his shoulders. "Fuck, no! They'd all try to fuck you. You might even convert Jake."

Dirk snorted. "What about your sister? What will she think if I decide to stay with you?"

"She knows about you. They all know about you. Rosilee will be happy for me...for us."

"What if they don't accept me? I'm not coyote."

Throwing his head back, Rian laughed. "The one thing my pack isn't, is prejudiced."

"Yeah! I guess not."

"Come. Let me introduce you." Rian pushed him toward the cabin. He jumped when a firm hand slapped him on the ass. "Hurry up." Rian took the lead.

Dirk had to force his feet to keep moving. Being with Rian was easy. This was the hard part, going public. Although, going public in this group shouldn't be so difficult and could be good practice for the future.

"Is something wrong?" Rian asked a lagging Dirk.

"No. I'm fine." He caught up to Rian as he opened his cabin door.

The door opened into a large, airy combination kitchen and sitting room. Four pack members, including Rian's sister, turned to face them as they entered the cabin. Rosilee stood in front of a wood stove, stirring a large pot. There was no mistaking the resemblance. Long, wavy black hair fell to her waist. As her gaze settled on him, a bright white smile flashed in a dark face that was just a shade lighter than her brother's. A male moved protectively to her side. Dirk assumed it was Jake.

"Rian, I'm so glad you're back and you brought your mate." Pulling away from the male's grip on her elbow, she swerved around the large pine table and ran into Rian's arms.

Her cheek pressed against her brother's chest but her warm, chocolate eyes, full of acceptance and joy, studied him. Her eyes were so similar to Rian's and he shifted uneasily under her gaze. He wasn't sure what made him more uncomfortable, having everyone know he was Rian's mate or realizing he wasn't attracted to one of the most beautiful females he'd ever seen.

"You're going to have to turn me loose if you want to meet Dirk."

Rosilee laughed lightly and stepped back. "Okay!"

Rian wrapped an arm around Dirk's shoulder, bringing him to his side. It was a show of ownership and possession. "This is Dirk Valde, my mate." The wealth of pride in Rian's voice caused a spike of heat in Dirk.

"Dirk, this beautiful female is my sister, Rosilee."

Unable to wait any longer Rosilee squealed and launched herself at Dirk. Closing his arms around the little spitfire, he met Rian's gaze over her head.

"She's a handful," Rian smirked.

"I'm happy you found your mate and he's pretty too." She smiled mischievously up at him.

Dirk felt heat flow up his neck and color his face as the other males in the room snickered.

"Don't embarrass him before he's met everyone." Rian tugged his sister away from Dirk. "Jake," Rian barked and the other male stepped forward. "Control this incorrigible girl."

Jake wrapped his arm around Rosilee but Dirk felt his gaze raking him. The brooding look was full of suspicion and jealousy. Rian had told him Jake was straight so he knew he wasn't jealous of his relationship with their alpha. As Dirk returned the level stare, Jake tightened his hold on Rosilee. So, Rian was right. Jake was here because of Rosilee. He had no interest in the female but she was Rian's sister and that made him feel protective of her.

"Dirk, this is Jake."

Holding out his hand, Dirk expected the firm grip but he hadn't expected the snide comment. "So, I guess you're the alpha bitch?"

Releasing Jake's hand, Dirk snarled and Rian quickly moved between them.

"Enough," Rian snapped. "That was uncalled for, Jake."

"Sorry," Jake snapped.

Rian spun on his heel. "I won't have that type of prejudice here. That is one of the reasons we left my father's pack. It was your choice to join us."

Jake shifted restlessly from foot to foot. "I know. I didn't mean anything by it."

Always a good judge of character, Dirk believed the words came from jealousy, not malice. "It's okay, Rian." He placed a soothing hand on Rian's shoulder.

Dark, angry eyes flashed in his direction, surprising Dirk with the change it made in Rian's appearance. Now he looked like a fierce alpha male.

"I can handle it. Why don't you introduce me to the others?"

A hand gesture from Rian brought the other two males forward. "Dirk, this is Andre."

A tall, sandy-haired male held out his hand. "Welcome to the pack." Taking the offered hand, Dirk nodded in greeting.

"And this is Haron."

Dirk expected animosity from this male but he hid it well or he was truly over Rian. "Welcome," Haron greeted him with a big smile. "Rosilee was right. You are pretty."

"Thanks, I think."

Laughter eased the situation and Dirk relaxed. The coyotes seemed to accept him, regardless of his Valde blood.

"Where are Trey and Joel?" Rian asked.

"Where else," Andre snickered.

A grin split Rian's face as his eyes once again danced with happiness. "Trey and Joel are newly mated."

"Oh." Heat crawled up Dirk's face. He knew they were all thinking the same thing about him and Rian.

Complete silence hung over the room until Jake spoke. "Maybe we should get out of here and give them some time alone."

"Good idea," Andre agreed.

"Th-That's not necessary," Dirk stumbled over his words.

"Oh but it is," Rosilee patted his hand. "I'll go take a run. I won't disturb you when I return."

"Jake." Rian didn't have to say anything else.

"I'll be on her tail."

Rian's eyes narrowed.

"Figure of speech. You know you can trust me. What I said before, it didn't mean anything." Turning toward Dirk, Jake added, "You're welcome here."

Rian nodded. "Jealousy does strange things to a male."

Jake's gaze darted to Rosilee. "Yeah."

# Chapter Three

ॐ

"Alone at last."

"Why do I feel like the virgin sacrifice?" Dirk tried and failed to hide the panic in his voice.

"Is that how you feel? I don't want to pressure you."

"You just want to fuck me?"

"I do, but I can wait. I'd like to touch you though. I want to learn your body."

Placing a hand in the middle of Rian's chest, he met his heated gaze. "I want to fuck you too." Rian's dark hand closed around his. "I'm ready to make love with you. I understand you want to fuck me because I want you too." Dirk sighed. "I can't be just your bitch. I'm not naturally submissive."

Rian lifted Dirk's hand to his lips and kissed his open palm. "You want us to be equals."

"I know you're alpha of the pack but in the bedroom…" Dirk licked his lips.

"In the bedroom we're mates…equals." Rian sucked Dirk's thumb into his mouth and heat shot straight to his cock.

"Damn," Dirk growled.

"We can do whatever makes us happy," Rian finished as he released his thumb.

"You're okay with it?"

"I've never let anyone mount me but just thinking about you inside me makes me hard."

The confession shot straight to Dirk's groin. "Fuck!"

"Yeah, let's fuck," Rian agreed.

Rian's heart pounded as he led Dirk down the hall to his bedroom. Damn, even his hands were shaking. He'd done this before so he didn't know why he was nervous. At the door, he stopped and glanced at an equally nervous Dirk. Wide, anxious eyes met his. Desire and trust warred with fear in their depths.

That's why he was nervous. He didn't want to disappoint Dirk. This time it really mattered. He was about to take his mate for the first time and he had to make it good. If he scared Dirk or hurt him, he'd never forgive himself.

"Are we going in?" Dirk asked.

"Yeah." He shifted his feet nervously. "I'm…"

"You're nervous. I can smell it."

Rian grinned. "You too."

Stepping closer, Dirk settled warm, firm hands on his shoulders. "It's going to be okay." Dirk's hot tongue licked him from collarbone to chin. His touch ignited his lust and Rian forgot his fears.

"It's going to be better than okay." Pushing Dirk against the door, he ground his erection against him. Tugging at Dirk's shirt, he got his hand beneath the material and touched his hot flesh. "It'll be awesome. I'm going to lick every inch of you."

If he worried that he would offend Dirk, he shouldn't have. Dirk's hands were busy unbuttoning his shirt and loosening his jeans. "I want to taste you too."

Rian's breath hissed from between his lips as a strong, warm hand gripped his cock. It was the first time Dirk had touched him so intimately and it almost brought him to his knees. He should have known that once Dirk accepted their relationship he'd be aggressive. "Keep touching me like that and it'll be over way too soon."

Dirk snickered. "I won't let you off that easily."

"We need to get to the bed."

"Yeah. Open the door."

Reaching around Dirk, he turned the knob and was very surprised when Dirk swept him off his feet. Dirk was a good two inches and twenty pounds smaller than he was but he had no problem throwing him over his shoulder. It made Rian wonder who would fuck whom first but then, did it really matter?

Rian's room was basic and dark toned but Dirk's only interest was in the bed. Crossing the room, he set Rian on his feet. Kneeling, he tugged the other male's loosened pants down. On eye level with Rian's cock, Dirk hesitated. During their earlier bump and grind, he'd seen Rian's half-clothed cock but hadn't gotten the full effect.

"Whoo," Dirk whistled through his teeth. "Impressive." He trailed a finger down the long, thick shaft. Rian had to be an inch longer than him and he wasn't exactly short. He'd expected dark pubic hair but found a groin shorn clean. The heavy sac was smooth and soft.

"Fuck," Rian moaned and rocked from heel to toe.

Dirk squeezed Rian's bulbous cock head, which leaked a stream of pre-cum. Inhaling Rian's musky scent, Dirk shifted nervously on his knees. He couldn't help but tighten his asshole. The thought of penetration by a monster cock was unsettling.

"Taste me," Rian whispered as his hand settled at the back of Dirk's head. "I'm dying here. Let me see my cock head disappear between your lips."

Rian's low whisper made him want to come. Dirk's nuts tightened as lust surged through him. Damn! Licking his lips, he leaned closer and the cushioned tip of Rian's cock brushed his mouth. His tongue darted out, tasting Rian's salty essence. Dirk's mouth watered and he swallowed. It was a pleasant flavor.

Opening his mouth wider, his lips slid over Rian's cock head. His tongue teased the heavy vein on the underside as he swallowed around the thick girth.

Rian moaned low in his throat and his hand tightened in Dirk's hair.

Encouraged by Rian's obvious enjoyment he wrapped his hand around Rian's lower shaft and stroked. Using his tongue, Dirk licked the underside and head. Every moan of pleasure sent a thrill through Dirk. He quickly found he enjoyed orally pleasing his mate. Having been on the receiving end of such pleasure he knew exactly what Rian felt. Dirk knew what each lick, nibble and touch did to the other male.

"Dirk," Rian called out. "If you don't stop, I'm going to come." Rian pumped his hips. "Do you want it? Do you want to swallow my cum?"

Dirk stroked at a firm, quick pace as he sucked on Rian's cock. He could feel Rian's release surging up his shaft. Swallowing deeply, he kept up the pace until he drained the other male.

"Damn it. It's too soon...too soon." Gasping for breath, Rian collapsed on the bed and leaned back.

On his knees, Dirk rested his head against his mate's inner thigh. Licking his lips, Dirk smiled. It wasn't at all what he had expected.

"Damn Dirk!" Rian panted. "I think you were born to suck my cock."

Dirk chuckled. "I didn't expect to enjoy it so much." Lifting his head, Dirk eyed Rian, whose thick shaft now lay limp against his stomach.

"I'm glad you did."

"Umm," Dirk replied as he cupped the heavy sac dangling between Rian's legs. He had temporarily sated his mate but his own cock ached with the need for release. Slipping his hand behind Rian's balls, he caressed the sensitive flesh. The muscles in Rian's thighs tightened and Dirk knew he fought an inner battle. The battle to submit to his mate.

After a moment of probing the area, Dirk rose to his feet and finished removing his clothes. "Do you have lube?" The question was direct and to the point. He had warned Rian of his needs and he wouldn't beg.

Rian's dark, penetrating eyes held his for a minute before roaming down his body. Dirk felt his gaze like a caress and his aroused cock twitched under Rian's stare.

Rian's eyelashes fluttered. "In the drawer." He pointed to the nightstand.

Dirk's heart jumped in his chest at Rian's acceptance. He knew and appreciated what a huge concession it was for Rian to submit to him. Retrieving the lube, Dirk asked, "You know more about this than me. What's the best way?"

Rolling to his side, Rian crawled across the bed. "The first time, it might be easier from behind."

Rian reached out and trailed a finger along Dirk's cock. The gentle touch stole his breath. "Okay," Dirk gasped.

"I'll need some prep to take you." Rian licked his lips suggestively. "In my ass, anyway."

Snickering, Dirk knelt on the bed and moved behind Rian. His rounded, light bronze cheeks were so tempting. He cupped a smooth, firm globe with one hand. "Don't worry, big boy. I won't hurt you." He slapped one cheek. "Much!"

"T-Tease," Rian gulped with a quiver to his voice.

"I'm not teasing." Leaning forward, Dirk nibbled the curve of Rian's backside. The scent of lust was hot and heavy in the air. His cock throbbed to get inside his mate.

"You sure you don't need me to show you how to do it first?"

"With that sated, limp cock?" Dirk joked as he parted Rian's cheeks for his first glimpse of the puckered hole. His hands shook as his heart thundered with excitement. This wasn't the first ass he had fucked but this was Rian, his mate. And his would be the first cock to penetrate him. He couldn't express what that meant to him.

"It's recovered!"

Dirk reached around and grasped the firm flesh. "So it has." He stroked the thick length. "You're excited to be taking my cock up the ass. You can't wait to feel me inside you."

"Fuck," Rian moaned. "You might be right."

Leaning forward, Dirk nestled his cock against Rian's ass and licked the back of his neck. "I know I'm right. You need to relax and let me have you." Dirk nipped at his shoulder. "I want to make you mine. I need to make you mine."

Moaning, Rian rocked his hips against Dirk.

Dick leaned back. "That's right. Show me you want me." Uncapping the lube, Dirk pressed it against Rian's hole and squeezed. "You're so fuckin' hot."

"Damn. That's cold." Rian jumped.

"It won't be for long." Dirk rimmed the puckered hole with one finger. "I don't want to hurt you."

"You won't," Rian released a shaky breath.

The tip of one finger penetrated Rian and rimmed the tight hole. "Tell me if there's any pain."

Rian nodded as a rumbling groan erupted from his throat.

"Fuck! You're hot. Hot and tight." Dirk slowly worked his finger in and out of Rian. "I could come just watching this. I wish you could see." Rian was so hot, his flesh so tender, that Dirk couldn't wait to get inside him.

"I'll see you spread for me."

Dirk growled. For the first time, he was anxious to feel Rian inside him, fucking him. "Oh yeah!" Plunging deep within the tight hole, Dirk withdrew to the tip of his finger. "Are you ready for more?"

Looking over his shoulder, Rian's dark hungry gaze met his and he nodded.

Adding more lube, Dirk inserted another finger and the tight hole closed around them. "You okay?"

Rian didn't answer but he rocked his hips backward in rhythm to Dirk's thrusting fingers. "Damn, this is so hot. I can't wait to get my cock in you." Dirk plunged his fingers deep and steady.

"Fuck me, Dirk," Rian growled and arched his back. For a minute Dirk thought he was going to shift to feral form.

Grabbing up the lube, he squeezed a generous amount on his cock and pumped several times. "Are you ready?"

Rian spread his legs wider and tilted his ass up. Dirk almost erupted in his hand. Holding his cock head against Rian's hole, he pushed forward and watched the tip disappear inside him.

"Dayumm," Rian drew the word out in a low, rumbling voice. "It's a hot, sweet burn."

Dirk pushed deeper. "You are burning me up." Grasping Rian's hips, he rocked forward. "I want to bury my cock in your ass."

"Do it. Fuck me. Fill me up."

Bucking his hips, Dirk pressed deep and hilted his cock. Gasping for breath, he blanketed Rian. "I've never felt anything like this," Dirk whispered near Rian's ear. "I could stay inside your throbbing heat forever."

Rian squirmed beneath him. "You have to move. I want to feel you move inside me. I want to come with you in my ass."

Dirk growled as he shifted his hips. He knew what was different. Besides the fact that Rian was his mate and they shared an emotional and physical bond, it was more carnal. With another male, especially another dominant male, sex was carnal and base. There was little need for the niceties required when fucking a female. There were no games. They both wanted to connect in the most primal, elemental way two males could join.

"I'm going to fuck you. I'm going to fuck you so long and hard you'll feel me for hours."

Rian snickered. Bucking his hips, he squeezed and Dirk almost lost it. "You won't last. I'm going to milk your cock."

"Milk me. Make me come." Slowing his thrusts, Dirk prodded Rian's prostrate. "Is that the spot?" Slow thrusts contorted Rian's body beneath him. Reaching around, he grabbed Rian's cock and stroked the heavy length. Gritting his teeth, Dirk held back as he shoved Rian over the edge.

"Fuck," Rian growled as his cock erupted on Dirk's hand and the bed.

Pushing deep, Dirk held himself in place and let his cum fill Rian's ass. "My mate," he whispered as he blanketed Rian and they both crashed to the bed.

* * * * *

A knock at the door startled Rian and he sat up in the bed. A sleepy Dirk stretched at his side. "What is it?" Rian asked.

"It's me, Jake. Sorry to bother you but a pack member is at the Valde cabin looking for Dirk."

"Shit," Dirk mumbled as he sat up in the bed and brushed his long, blond hair across his shoulder.

"Did you talk to him?" Rian asked Jake through the door.

"Yeah, I told him Dirk was talking to my alpha. He's waiting for Dirk at the cabin."

"I have to go." Dirk shoved the sheet to the side.

Rian nodded but he anxiously watched Dirk as he hopped from the bed. He had hoped for a little more time before reality collided with their paradise.

"Do you want me to accompany you?"

"No!" Dirk replied quickly. "I mean, there's no need." He tried to soften the refusal but Rian had expected it.

It wasn't the refusal that hurt so much but the fact that Dirk never looked at him. From the time Jake had knocked on the door, Dirk had avoided his gaze. Just now, he stared out the window as he fastened his pants.

"Are you coming back here tonight?" Rian bit the inside of his jaw and cursed himself for sounding needy.

"I'm not sure about tonight. I don't know who's at the cabin or how long they'll stay." Dirk picked up a discarded shirt. He started to put it on then stopped and just held the crumpled shirt.

"Aren't you going?"

"I just figured I'd bathe in the creek before I go to the cabin. I'm kind of…" Finally, Dirk raised his gaze to meet his.

"Yeah. You could probably use a bath." Rian grinned as he thought of why Dirk needed to wash. For a moment, their eyes held and Rian felt the connection as strong as ever but reality settled in quickly. "Well, you better go." Pain lanced through Rian's chest but he wouldn't let it show.

"Okay. I'll see you…" Dirk hesitated at the foot of the bed. "Later." He raised the hand holding the shirt in a salute as he walked away.

The door closed behind Dirk and Rian fought the urge to howl in rage. Of course Dirk wanted a bath. He wanted to wash away all traces of him. He'd thought Dirk had accepted their relationship, but obviously he hadn't. Certainly, he wasn't prepared to go public, at least not with his pack. Part of Rian didn't blame him. He knew what would happen when Dirk's pack discovered his secret.

Rolling to his side, Rian felt the sheet crinkle beneath him. It was stiff with cum. The scent of sex filled his senses. Dirk would come back. He had to.

# Chapter Four

෪

Leaning against the corner post of his cabin's porch, Rian stared out into the night. The frosty ground crunched under a heavy foot and he spun to find the source. Excellent night vision immediately homed in on the new arrival. His shoulders sagged, if only slightly, as Jake neared.

"Good evening," he greeted the other male.

Jake nodded. "Dirk's company just left."

"You don't have to spy on him."

"I wasn't…exactly."

"Do you think he'll come here tonight?" Rain cursed himself for asking.

A deep sigh escaped Jake's lips and he shook his head. "It appeared he was staying there for the night." After his company left, Dirk had added wood to his fire pit. Jake didn't think he'd do that if he planned to leave soon but he didn't pass the extra info along.

Rian nodded. "I figured as much." He wished Jake would go. He didn't want to appear vulnerable to the other male.

"Go to him," Jake urged.

"No. I won't pressure him. My responsibilities are here."

"You can leave for the night. I'll keep an eye on Rosilee. You'll only be a howl away."

"He needs time!" Rian argued.

"He's had time. He's your mate. Don't let someone get in his head and convince him otherwise. Fight for him. Otherwise, he'll ruin both your lives."

"I can't force him…"

256

Jake stepped up on to the porch. "Did you force him earlier? Did you make him get in bed with you?"

"No."

"Did you claim him as your mate?"

"Not exactly." Rian stared out into the darkness as he shifted from foot to foot. He was still tender from joining with Dirk. It was a constant reminder of their lovemaking. Turning, he met Jake's gaze and wasn't embarrassed to say, "I let him claim me."

Silence hung in the air. Finally, Jake spoke, "Then you must really love him."

Rian nodded. "He's my mate." The words were plain and simple and said it all. Hearing the words aloud made him realize what needed to be done. "It's time I claim my mate."

Jake smiled. "Sounds like it."

"Rosilee…"

"I'll watch out for her."

Rian narrowed his eyes on the other male. "Who'll protect her from you?"

Jake grinned. "She's safe with me, at least until her first heat cycle."

Rian knew that. He knew Jake was an honorable male. "What if she's not your mate?"

"She is." Jake sounded certain but Rian knew he couldn't be positive until her first cycle.

"You don't know for sure." Coyote breeds didn't recognize their mates until they reached sexual maturity, which happened in females after their first heat cycle. Rosilee hadn't come into heat yet so there was no way Jake could be positive, though some males claimed to know earlier than first heat. Some were correct, some weren't. He had discussed Jake with Rosilee. She thought he was possessive and arrogant but he had the feeling she was attracted to the male. However, only time would tell if they were mates.

"I'd never hurt her. If she's not my mate, I'll let her go, but I know she is. I know it."

Rian sighed. He wished he were as confident as Jake sounded. "For your sake, I hope she is."

\* \* \* \* \*

From inside the tree line Rian could see Dirk standing at the stove with his back to the window. It was a good thing Dirk liked to cook because he didn't and he didn't always want his meat raw. Currently, Rosilee cooked for him but she wouldn't be around forever, especially if Jake had his way.

He slowly neared the cabin, never taking his eyes from Dirk. He liked to watch him unawares. Dirk moved gracefully for a male. He was never flatfooted, always moved on the balls of his feet. He spun to set a dish on the table and Rian knew the moment he sensed his presence. Dirk's head tilted up and his nose flared. His laser blue eyes stared at him through the window but Rian knew he couldn't see him. Dirk's lips curled in a slow smile as he raised a hand, motioning him forward.

The door was unlocked. Rian let himself in and dropped his bag to the left of the opening. A delicious aroma of roasted meat greeted his entrance. He immediately noted the table set for two.

"Your company left. Is he coming back?" He gestured toward the table as doubt knotted his stomach.

"No." Dirk slowly shook his head. "I knew you'd show up eventually."

"You did?"

"If nothing else, I assumed you'd come to retrieve your shirt." Dirk tugged at the collar of the shirt he wore.

"My shirt?" For the first time he noticed the shirt that hung loosely on Dirk belonged to him."

"You didn't notice I left with it earlier?"

"No. I had other things on my mind." Rian refused to acknowledge that he had been so devastated he'd noticed very little.

"So, I assume Jake told you I was alone."

"You spoke to him?"

Dirk shook his head. "No. I sensed his presence."

"I didn't send him. I don't need another male to watch out for me."

"Didn't say that you did. He probably feels protective of his *alpha bitch*."

Rian chuckled. "You're not my bitch. Not yet anyway."

Dirk arched a brow. "Is that a promise?"

"Oh yeah." Rian wagged his eyebrows suggestively.

"Then sit down and eat. I didn't cook these steaks to let them get cold. Besides you'll need the energy."

Rian scooted the bench seat away from the table. "They smell delicious."

"So do you."

Rian met Dirk's piercing gaze. "When you left earlier…"

"You were worried."

Rian shrugged. "More concerned than worried. It's my responsibility to protect you even from yourself. I know you think your pack will be accepting but I want to be there for you if they're not."

"I don't need protection. I'm an adult."

"I noticed." Rian ran his gaze over Dirk's form.

Noticing his gaze, Dirk shook his head. "If this is going to work, I have to be honest. I can't be the submissive mate waiting to be told what to do."

Rian nodded. "Fair enough. I can give you some space. This is new for both of us. I'm not asking for obedience, just respect." Rian studied Dirk's tense stance. He wanted to make things right for them.

"I do respect you but leaving the Valde is a big step for me and the rest..." Dirk sighed as he ran a hand through his hair.

"I realize that. I'm sorry I don't have more to offer. I wish I wasn't subjecting you to scorn and hatred."

"What you offer is more than I've ever known in my life."

Rian gulped and blinked rapidly as he felt his heart turn over in his chest.

Dirk grinned as he read the raw emotion in Rian's gaze. Opening two beers, he handed one to Rian and set the other one on the table. Taking a seat on the bench next to his mate, he cut a chunk of his steak. Picking it up between two fingers, he offered it to Rian.

Full, dusky lips parted and he fed his mate. Leaning forward, he licked the juices from Rian's lips. "Umm, I'm an excellent cook."

Rian nodded as he chewed. "You definitely know how to heat things up."

"If you're hot, you should take off that shirt."

"I will as soon as I feed you." Dirk licked the fingers that presented the food. Between bites, they discarded shirts and pants. Soon, two naked and aroused males straddled the bench and sat face-to-face, feeding each other.

"You're a messy eater." Dirk smirked as he trailed his tongue down Rian's neck and across his chest. Drops of juice glistened on his chest and clung to the smattering of dark hair.

"Umm, it's by design. I'm sure my cock is covered in juice."

Dirk snickered as he nipped a peaked nipple. "Oh it's juicy all right. Did I tell you that I love the way you shave your groin?"

"I'll let you shave it from now on and I'll shave yours."

"Damn," Dirk groaned. "Take me to bed."

"Lead the way." Rian scooped up the bag he'd dropped when he entered and followed Dirk down the hall. The bedroom was small but thankfully the bed was large and sturdy. Dirk had never shared this bed with anyone and he was glad.

"I brought you a present." Rian stopped just behind him and the tip of his cock brushed Dirk's ass cheek. Dirk laughed and shifted against him. "I bet you did."

"Several actually." A firm hand between his shoulder blades propelled him forward. Dropping the bag on the bed, Rian reached into it and pulled out a curved dong. "I'm going to prepare your ass with this."

Dirk gasped. "Shit."

"You're going to be so ready for my cock when I fuck you."

"Rian…" He gulped and tried to still his rising panic.

"I want to claim you as mine."

Dirk nodded. He knew the need that drove Rian but he'd never used toys.

"I know you've never been taken. I know you're hesitant to belong to another male but I'm going to make it so good."

"I'm just nervous." Dirk chuckled. Years of denial didn't just vanish.

"There's nothing to be nervous about. I'll take care of you." Cupping Dirk's chin Rian brushed his lips across his.

"Tonight you'll learn what it's really like to make love."

"We made love earlier." Dirk gasped as Rian's lips trailed down his neck. Sharp teeth closed on his erect nipple as Rian palmed his ass.

"Umm, this will be even better."

"Damn, Ri, can it get any better?"

A growl rumbled in Rian's chest as he rhythmically rubbed their cocks together. "Oh yeah. It can." Rian shoved him to the bed. "Lie on your side. I want to insert this before we begin."

"Begin?" Dirk questioned as he stretched out and rolled to one hip.

"Umm," Rian murmured as his hands roamed Dirk's perfect ass. Parting the cheeks, he saw the tight puckered hole and he couldn't stop from lapping Dirk's crack.

Dirk whimpered and he chuckled.

"Damn, you're sweet." He lapped Dirk again from balls to anus.

"Jesus, Rian," Dirk croaked.

Rian laughed. "Bend your knee and put your foot down on the bed. I want room to play." Reaching for the lube, Rian coated his fingers. "I have to finger-fuck you first. I want to feel how hot and tight you are."

Dirk growled as he squirted the cool lotion on his hot, sensitive flesh.

Rimming the hole, Rian inserted his finger to the first knuckle and Dirk's sphincter clamped down tight. "Relax, babe. Let me fuck you."

Circling his finger, Rian pushed deeper into the hot, tight flesh and Dirk's muscles tightened.

"Oh my god," Dirk called out.

"Are you okay?"

"Y-Yeah. It's just different."

Rian pumped slowly in and out. "You like?"

Dirk nodded.

Rian's hands shook. His blood roared in his veins. He couldn't believe the day had come. He was about to take his mate for the first time. "Just wait until it's my cock in there stretching you wide and filling you up." Running his lips along Dirk's hip, Rian closed his eyes. He had to control himself. He didn't want to spoil the moment by rushing it.

"Shit."

"You're going to love it just like I loved feeling you inside me." Pulling his finger out, he lubed the small dong. "I'm going to insert this and then I'm going to play some more. The small curved dong inserted easily enough and Rian pumped it in and out, being sure to run the curved head over Dirk's prostrate. Each time he hit it, Dirk jumped. "Sensitive?"

Dirk's eyes flashed as he nodded.

His pale ass looked so good, spread for the dong. It would look even better spread for his cock. Rian shook his head to clear his thoughts. He couldn't go there, not yet. "Enough of that." Rian left the dong in Dirk's ass as he rolled him to his back. "Now I'm going to taste every inch of you." His hungry gaze traveled Dirk's breathtaking form. "Some inches I'll taste several times."

"Tease," Dirk grumbled.

Rian grinned and stretched out on top of the other male. Lowering his head, Rian nipped Dirk's lower lip. "I'm not teasing."

It felt odd but not unpleasant to have a dong in his ass but Dirk gave it little thought as Rian stretched out on top of him. The other male's flesh was hot and smooth. Wrapping his arms around Rian, Dirk's hands ran from shoulder blades to waist. Roaming lower, his hands cupped Rian's ass and shifted him against him.

Dirk growled as Rian's mouth settled over his. He wasn't going to be able to take a lot of this teasing, not with that dong buried in his ass.

Turning his head to the side, Dirk gasped for breath. "Damn, Rian. You are killin' me."

"I'm just getting started."

"I might finish before you're ready."

Rian chuckled and rolled to the side. "You are beautiful."

"Males aren't beautiful."

"Hey!" Rian protested.

"You are hot, sexy and handsome, not to mention built, but most importantly…mine." Dirk reached out and trailed a finger along Rian's aroused cock.

"Hands off. This is my turn to play," Rian commanded as he shoved Dirk's hand away. "Reach up and grab the bed posts."

"Rian," Dirk protested.

"Do it or I'll tie you up."

Dirk wrapped his hands around the cold metal bars just as Rian nipped a peaked nipple. "Fuck," Dirk muttered and shifted restlessly on the bed.

"Spread your legs and I'll fuck you with that dong while I devour your body."

Dirk anxiously complied and his reward was a slow thrusting penetration as a hot tongue circled his bellybutton. Sweat broke out on his body as he tried not to beg.

"You like this don't you?"

Groaning, Dirk managed to nod.

"I love seeing you writhe beneath me, knowing that soon you'll writhe beneath my cock."

Rian's hot breath bathed Dirk's groin as he spoke and his cock jutted upward, begging for a touch. "Rian," Dirk croaked. His whole body jerked in response to the swipe of Rian's tongue around his cock head.

Lifting his head, Dirk watched, transfixed, as the dark-haired male lapped at his cock. His balls tightened. Fuck! He wanted to come. Gritting his teeth, he held back. It felt too good to let it end so soon. Rian's hot mouth engulfed the head and slid down his cock as he pushed the dong deep into his ass. "Jesus," Dirk roared as he pulled at the bars. He wanted to cup Rian's head and fuck his mouth.

Dark, hungry eyes lifted to meet his. "I'm going to come," he told Rian.

Releasing his cock, Rian gasped, "Not yet." He shifted to kneel between Dirk's splayed thighs. "I want to watch you come while I take your ass." Removing the dong, Rian reached for the lube. "I'm going to take you like this so I can see you come for me. I want to look into your eyes as you take my cock for the first time."

Dirk swallowed deeply and nodded. He thought of how much he'd enjoyed taking Rian and how much Rian appeared to have enjoyed his cock.

"Are you okay?"

Dirk licked his lips as he watched Rian lube his cock. He was almost surprised that he felt no fear, only need. "Yeah. I'm ready. I'm ready for you to fuck me."

"That's what I want to hear." Rian lifted his legs toward his chest. "Relax for me."

He felt the thick head at his opening and his cock throbbed. "Take me," Dirk begged.

"Look at me," Rian growled as he pushed forward.

Dirk held the deep penetrating gaze as his breath seeped from his lungs. Rian was thick, much thicker than the dong, and the possession filled him with sweet pain. Neither male blinked as Rian slid deeper and deeper. Buried to the hilt, Rian leaned forward and meshed their lips. Their tongues tangled as Rian penetrated his mouth with hungry possession. Dirk gasped for air, stuffed full as he was each breath was a struggle.

"My mate," Rian gasped as he slowly bucked his hips. "My mate...always."

The fire of desire quickly replaced the burn of possession. Dirk's balls tightened with each thrust and he knew he wouldn't last long. "I'm coming," Dirk gasped.

"Come for me." Rian leaned back and he could feel the dark eyes watching him. Watching him at his most vulnerable moment.

# Chapter Five

### ୬

"Go talk to Gionne. He's in his office with Leon. We'll be more than happy to keep your mate company," Jenna told Dirk. Rian had heard of Jenna, Gionne's mate and Riza, his sister and he was glad to meet them.

Dirk laughed and looked uncertain for a moment. Rian smiled at him. He had been surprised how easily Dirk had introduced him to the females as his mate.

"Go ahead. We won't eat him, even though he is tempting." Gionne's sister, the one called Riza put her arm through his and began tugging him toward a seating area. He had heard much about the Valde palace and from what he had seen so far, it was all true. On first glance, the huge stone palace had stolen his breath and the interior was just as impressive. He stretched his legs as he took a seat in a heavy pine chair that sat in front of a floor to ceiling creek-stone fireplace.

He smiled at the females. Rian had been prepared to feel jealous of the two females Dirk had almost mated, but after meeting them, it was nonexistent.

"Don't believe anything they tell you," Dirk shouted as he headed down the hall.

"Don't worry, Dirk. We won't tell him all your secrets," Gionne's mate promised.

"So where did you meet? When did you know?" Both females threw questions at him.

Rian chuckled. "I thought you were going to tell me about Dirk."

Riza scooted closer. "We will after we get the scoop."

He nodded. "We met several months ago when the Valde came to my camp and I knew immediately."

"Then why'd it take so long? Why didn't you claim him?" Jenna asked.

"I wanted to but I could tell Dirk was in denial and after everything I had just gone through with my alpha..." Rian shook his head. "It's not an easy path we chose. I was banned from my pack for choosing to be gay, as if I had a choice."

"That's horrible!" Riza was aghast.

"Unbelievable," Jenna chimed in. "It's different here. Gionne will welcome you as Dirk's mate."

"Leon will be supportive." Riza spoke for her feline mate.

Dirk had told him it would be so but he hadn't believed him. Now, after meeting these females and feeling their acceptance, he had hope. The last thing he wanted was to alienate Dirk from his pack. "I hope you're right." It seemed the Valde were accepting. They'd accepted a feline as the alpha female. And in turn, Gionne's sister, Riza had mated with the feline alpha. If any pack would accept homosexual mates, it would be this one.

"I am." Jenna patted his arm. "We'll have a big celebration in honor of your joining."

"An adult celebration." Riza winked. "I can't wait to see you take Dirk."

Rian guffawed. "What?" The words shouldn't have taken him by surprise. Dirk had warned him about Riza's mischievous side.

"Dirk didn't mention the public mating?" Riza asked innocently.

"No." He shook his head. He had mentioned the claiming ceremony with the females though.

"That's odd because he often enjoyed it," Riza replied and wagged her brows suggestively.

"I bet he did."

"It's not mandatory but usually new mates claim each other publicly," Riza offered.

"Usually the male shares his female with another male to ensure her safety. It is an honor for the female. It proves her mate values her safety above all else. I'm not sure that males do that though." Jenna turned her gaze to Riza and both females shrugged.

"Your mates shared you with Dirk," he stated and momentarily silenced the females.

They glanced at each other and laughed. "We weren't sure if you knew that," Riza replied.

Rian grinned. "I know all the juicy details."

The loud slamming of a door echoed down the hall and all three heads turned. Rian heard Dirk's angry stride before he saw him. Jumping to his feet, he watched Dirk approach. The expression on his face told the story and Rian's heart sank.

"Let's go," Dirk demanded.

"What happened?" Rian asked as he moved to Dirk's side.

"I was wrong."

"Hold on Dirk." Jenna grasped Dirk's arm. "I know Gionne —" Jenna protested.

"Apparently not as well as you thought."

"Did Leon side with him?" Riza questioned whether her mate sided with Gionne.

"You could say that."

"Oh, I'm gonna whip that lion's ass all the way home." Riza charged down the hall.

"There has to be some mistake. Gionne has no problem with homosexuality."

"I'm sorry, Jenna." A wry grin curled Dirk's lip as he shook her loose from his arm.

Jenna threw her arms up in the air. "You're sorry? Why are you apologizing? I'll talk to Gionne."

"Don't bother. If he can't accept Rian, I can't be part of the pack." Dirk turned and headed for the door.

Rage boiled in Rian's gut but he followed his mate down a cobblestone walkway.

"Why don't you say 'I told you so'?"

"Because I hoped it wouldn't be true. I didn't want this for you. I'm sorry." Guilt gnawed at Rian. Dirk's pain was his fault.

Dirk stopped and turned to face him. "I'm not. I'm not sorry I chose you over hate. We'll make our way without them."

"It's a hard road without a large pack."

"You chose it."

Rian sighed and shook his head. "I had no choice."

Dirk grabbed his upper arms and meshed their lips. It might be a slap in the face of the Valde but regardless Rian returned the kiss hungrily.

\* \* \* \* \*

A somber Dirk returned with Rian to his pack. It was not that he minded living with Rian and his pack but he had expected more from Gionne and his gut churned with disappointment. As his alpha, they shared a bond. Gionne had chosen him to protect his mate. He had thought Gionne would accept Rian and welcome him as his mate. He had clearly heard Gionne speak well of Rian. He'd said he wasn't at all like his father. He didn't understand why there was a problem.

Crossing to the stove, Dirk lifted a steaming kettle and poured the hot tea into a mug. Sniffing, he inhaled the fragrant brew and stirred in a generous amount of honey. He sighed as he rested his hip against the counter. The cabin was quiet. Rian had gone hunting with the pack but he'd stayed behind. He wasn't in the mood to hunt, though at the moment, he wouldn't mind biting something.

Today's meeting with Gionne and Leon lay heavily on his mind and heart. Lost in thought, he stared at the cup as he continued to stir. He had been nervous going into the meeting. Confessing his sexual orientation to the two alphas had been a daunting task. Not because he had feared they wouldn't accept his mate but because he had feared they'd see him as less of a male.

Tension had filled the room before he'd even begun to speak. Looking back, he realized they had already known about Rian. They had judged their relationship without hearing the facts. Did Gionne think he had been derelict in his duties as a guard? Had something happened? In his haste to get away from Gionne he hadn't questioned his reasoning for not accepting their union. Was it because Rian was male or because he was coyote?

Dirk chewed the inside of his lower lip as he considered the questions swirling in his mind.

A knock at the door brought Dirk's head up. Two males entered and he didn't recognize either of them. The tall, thinner male smiled. "I'm Trey."

Recognizing the name, he nodded. "Then you must be Joel. I'm Dirk."

Closing the door behind them, they stood quietly, looking expectantly at him.

"If you're looking for Rian, he's on a hunt."

"We know. We came to see you."

Arching a brow, Dirk gestured at the table. "Have a seat. Do you want some tea?"

"No thanks," Trey replied as they sat at the table. "We heard about your pack."

Dirk inclined his head. Bad news always traveled fast.

270

"It might not be my place to speak but I've know Rian my whole life." Trey hesitated. "We've been best friends since we were weaned. Anyway, what I wanted to say is, Rian has a big heart. He's hurting because you're hurting. He blames himself for your pack turning on you."

"It's not his fault." He didn't blame Rian for the prejudice of the Valde pack.

"We know that but Rian thinks he pushed you into this relationship."

Setting the mug of tea on the counter, Dirk approached the table. "What? I don't want him to feel that way." He furrowed his brow as he considered what Trey had told him.

"He just wants to protect you. That is what Rian does. He protects everyone. He'll give you up if he thinks that will make you happy." Two pairs of worried eyes studied him.

Dirk sighed and shook his head. "That's the last thing that would make me happy."

"Glad to hear it because Rian cares deeply for you. The last few months have been hell waiting for you to come to grips—to come to Rian. If it was up to me I would have just kidnapped you but Rian wouldn't hear of it."

Dirk snickered. "I might not have reacted well to that."

Trey shrugged and lifted his hand, showing his fingers entwined with his mates. "Aww, hell. You'd have come around quickly enough. There's nothing like the touch of your mate."

Dirk smiled at the obvious look of love that passed between the two males.

"I just wanted you to know that two males can be as happy as a male and a female. They say love is colorblind. It's also gender blind and in your case species blind." Joel spoke for the first time.

"Thanks guys. I appreciate your concern."

They stood and turned toward the door. "Dirk?"

Dirk lifted his head to meet Trey's gaze. "Welcome to the pack."

Dirk nodded. "Glad to be here." The two males left and Dirk retired to the room he shared with Rian. His mind churned. He needed to show Rian that he was here by choice, because he was. This pack was small but it wasn't short on love or acceptance.

* * * * *

The hunting party returned and the quiet disappeared.

"Hi Dirk," Rosilee called out. "You missed a great hunt."

"Don't worry. I saved you a choice piece of meat," Rian promised.

"Really?" Dirk smirked and ran his gaze over his mate. "Which piece is mine?"

Stepping closer, Rian wrapped an arm around him. "All of it, baby."

"Aw, fuck. You need to take that to your room." Jake walked toward the bunkhouse as they entered their cabin.

Rosilee added wood to the cookstove as they closed the door. "How do you like your steak, Dirk?"

"Medium is good for me." He leaned over and whispered to Rian. "Actually, I like mine raw. How about you?"

"You're killin' me," Rian groaned. "I'll make you pay later."

"Why don't you come to the bedroom for a minute? I want to show you something."

"Baby, it'll take longer than a minute." Rian slapped his ass as he pushed him toward the other room.

"Didn't say I was going to let you touch your present."

"You're such a fuckin' tease." Rian closed the door behind them just as the front door slammed.

"Rian," Rosilee called out.

"Fuck!" They both cursed.

"Rian?" Rosilee spoke from just outside the door. "Jake just came in. A group of Valde is in our territory but only four approach our camp. He says it's Gionne and his mate plus his sister and her mate, Leon."

Rian's troubled gaze turned his way. "Do you think they want us to move away from their land?"

Dirk shrugged. "Gionne wouldn't bring Jenna and Riza if he was looking for trouble."

They headed for the door with Rosilee on their heels. "Go to the bunkhouse," Rian ordered his sister.

"But—"

"Don't argue with me," Rian snapped. Dirk hated to see what the pressure was doing to his mate.

Rosilee scurried out the door and Rian turned to him. "Why would they come here?"

"Let's find out." Dirk stepped out of the cabin just as Gionne and company stepped into the clearing. He could feel Rian tense at his side. "Gionne," he addressed the alpha of the Valde.

"Dirk. Rian." Gionne nodded. "We've come to talk. I don't want any trouble." Gionne held up both hands as a symbol of peace.

Dirk didn't doubt his word, not with his mate at his side. "I would protect Jenna and Riza with my life. I pledged that to them and I never go back on *my word*."

Gionne nodded his head. "I know you don't."

"I think there might have been a misunderstanding," Leon spoke up and Dirk's gaze moved to the feline alpha. He had had his differences with Leon, mostly over Riza, but they'd put that behind them and until the earlier meeting he had thought of the male as a friend.

"I misunderstood? I understood perfectly that you aren't accepting of my relationship with Rian." As Dirk spoke, Rian settled his hand on his shoulder. It was a declaration of their bond.

"It was not the two of you as a couple." Gionne hesitated. "Marcus, Rian's father came to see us."

"Fuck," Rian cursed. "What did he say?"

Gionne's gaze flashed to Rian. "He said you were using Dirk to get in with his pack."

Rian's laughter was dark and humorless. "How did I convince Dirk he was my mate."

Gionne shrugged and turned his gaze back to Dirk. "I should have listened to you. I should have remembered Marcus' devious side. I had thought the old rivalry was behind us but I was wrong." Gionne stepped forward. "I had time to think and talk with my mate and a few other key people."

"I threatened to cut him off if he didn't listen." Jenna winked and Dirk's mood lightened. He was sure she'd given Gionne hell.

Gionne smiled. "Females are insightful."

"We listen with our hearts." Riza flashed a bright smile.

"We are here to offer an apology. Your small band is welcome in my pack."

"Or mine," Leon offered.

"At the very least we would like to have good relations," Gionne offered.

Rian turned to meet his gaze before he answered Gionne. "I'm not sure the others would want to join a wolf pack or feline pride but the offer humbles me. We will discuss it with the pack."

Gionne nodded. "My concern is for Dirk's safety."

"You do not trust the coyote?" Rian asked.

Dirk read the indecision in Gionne's gaze before he spoke. "I do not trust your father."

"Throughout my life, I have heard whispers and hatred spewed toward the Valde but never have I heard the reason. Do you know why the hatred exists?"

"I was told that long ago the alphas fought over land and a mate."

"A mate?" Jenna gasped. "Was she lupine or coyote?"

Gionne's lip curled up at the corner. "Did I never tell you that I have some coyote blood in my veins?"

"I guess that means the Valde won," Dirk replied.

"And for generations my pack has resented yours."

"It's time for it to end," Gionne declared.

"I wish I could tell you my father has put it behind him." Rian sighed. It was unfortunate but he did not trust his father either. The past few years, his temperament had changed. Rian had thought at times the alpha coyote seemed unbalanced but no one dared question him. Maybe he shouldn't have left. Maybe he should have spoken to the council. He would have to give serious thought to approaching the council or his brother. He hated to think the other shifter breeds looked warily upon his father's coyote pack. "Let me offer you the hospitality of our house. It is not grand but it is home." Rian gestured and moved to the side. He held the door and Dirk preceded the small group.

Rian stood his ground as they filed into the cabin. When Jake and Trey hesitantly approached, he told them to stay outside but keep a watchful eye. His stomach fluttered nervously. His father's attempt to separate them worried him. He would protect his mate with his life.

As Rian entered the room, Riza approached. "I told you it would work out. You just need faith."

He took the hand she offered and held it for a moment. "Thank you for your part in convincing your brother and your mate. I know it means much to Dirk."

Riza grinned. "You're welcome but remember you owe me."

He nodded. "I do."

"I know how you can pay me back," she whispered and wagged her eyebrows suggestively.

"I can only imagine." Rian chuckled.

"Don't worry. You'll enjoy it and so will I."

"Trying to steal my mate?" Leon joked as he approached and held out a hand.

"No. Lovely as she is I prefer...blonds." Rian joked as he winked at the big, blond feline and held his hand a moment longer than necessary.

Riza guffawed. "Oh, interesting!" she exclaimed.

Leon coughed and shook his head. "She's untamable."

"Is this a private conversation?" Dirk asked as he walked over, followed by Gionne and Jenna. Rian's heart fluttered as Dirk joined the group. Dirk's smile was contagious and he couldn't help grinning. He hadn't felt this good in a long time.

"Nope. I was just telling your mate we need to have a celebration in honor of your taking a mate," Riza answered.

"Definitely," Jenna agreed.

"Why do I get nervous when you two start scheming?"

"We just want to show you how much we appreciate you. We want to repay you for your years of concern and protection."

"If you two are thinking up some kind of claiming ceremony involving other males..." Dirk shook his head. "I don't need protection."

"We aren't thinking that!" Jenna exclaimed in mock horror.

Riza rolled her eyes. "What kind of perverts do you think we are?"

Dirk narrowed his gaze on the two females and Rian wrapped an arm around him, tugging him close. "They just want us to join in an after-dinner party so they can watch me fuck you."

"Jenna!" Gionne exclaimed.

"It wasn't my idea."

Leon roared with laughter. "I'm sure I know whose idea it was, though I have to admit that I might find perverse pleasure in watching Dirk get fucked."

Gionne chuckled but didn't comment. Rian had to believe part of the alpha would enjoy it too. It had to have been difficult for either male to share their mate with Dirk and to see him mated might soothe some male pride.

"With little ones waiting at home, we cannot stay. Can you come to the compound tomorrow to discuss your father?"

Rian nodded. "We'll come."

"It's settled then. We will see you tomorrow." Gionne hesitated at the door. "Take care. Your father is an angry male."

"We'll see you tomorrow." Dirk clasped Gionne's shoulder and Rian saw the real affection between the two males. "Get the females home to the babe's. I'm anxious to see how much they've grown."

"Watch it. Jenna will stick you with diaper duty." Gionne winked.

"Any time." Dirk grinned.

Pleasure soared within Rian to see his mate so happy. "Well, that was a surprise," he commented as he closed the door behind their guests.

A bright smile spread across Dirk's face. "No. The earlier meeting was a surprise. This is what I expected of my pack."

Fierce heat assaulted Rian and he battled his inner beast. "Do you feel like a run?" The coyote within wanted out. It wanted to play with his mate. He leered at Dirk in a way he couldn't miss.

"Sure. I could use the exercise." He unsnapped his jeans and let them drop.

"Fuck! You shaved," Rian immediately noticed the absence of the golden hair that usually surrounded his mate's cock.

"Umm. My present to you and I expect you to show your appreciation."

"I'll go to my knees right now if you want me to." Rian tingled from head to toe. The coyote wanted its mate. He wanted his mate.

"Later…in bed. Right now my wolf wants out."

\* \* \* \* \*

In feral form, Rian followed the wolf along a small deer trail. The underbrush was heavy so they walked single file. The wolf's white tail swished back and forth in front of his face, stirring up the musky wolf scent.

Rian inhaled his mate's scent. It was fresh, clean…arousing. He hoped to make a quick kill and then lift his mate's tail. He sniffed again. Maybe they'd skip the kill. The wolf's tail brushed across his snout and he playfully nipped the furred tip.

At the edge of a clearing the wolf stopped. His head went up as he sniffed the air. Rian took another whiff of his mate before lifting his head. Sniffing, he smelled a familiar scent. Coyote!

Rian caught Dirk's look of unease just a moment before he felt a blow from behind. Shoved into the clearing, Rian rolled to his feet.

Growling, Rian turned to face the attack. The attackers were of his father's pack. They were coyotes he had considered family. Surrounded, he stood back-to-back with a feral Dirk. Rian considered shifting and trying to talk the coyotes down but he didn't hold out hope of being successful. The attack came as four coyotes charged him. Grabbing the first coyote by the scruff of the neck, he shook him. However, the weight of three coyotes drove him to the ground. His neck and legs held in powerful jaws, he was pinned.

Horror filled him at the sounds of a nearby fight. From the corner of his eye, Rian could see three coyotes circling the white wolf. Dirk was larger than the coyotes but he was outnumbered. Blood-red spots covered the white fur as the coyotes took turns charging the wolf.

Dirk! Rian's mind screamed in agony as he witnessed the attack. With strength born of fear, Rian began to thrash. He had to protect his mate. Disregarding the pain, he rolled to his feet. By this time, Dirk was on the ground. His coat was more red than white. Crouching down, Rian lunged and shook his body attempting to dislodge the coyotes. The one clinging to his neck fell under his feet and Rian trampled him.

Grabbing another coyote by his neck, he locked his jaw and tugged. He felt the coyote's teeth tear into the flesh of his leg before he loosened his grip. Rian flung him to the side. Not bothering to dislodge the last coyote, he charged the three surrounding Dirk.

A crash in the underbrush drew Rian's gaze. Two more coyotes charged up the trail, followed by a wolf and a lion. Jake, Trey, Gionne and Leon exploded onto the scene and some of the coyotes turned to face the new arrivals. As the battle intensified, Rian's only thought was for Dirk. Turning, Rian saw a large coyote lunge at Dirk's throat. He was going for the kill. Too far away and hindered by a clinging coyote, Rian feared he wouldn't make it in time. Rian's forward momentum halted as a huge lion straddled the downed wolf. One massive paw batted the charging coyote. Not willing to stop, the coyote charged again and the lion grabbed him by the neck. Lifting the coyote in the air, he shook the flailing body. Bones crunched in the powerful jaws. Flinging the broken body to the side, the lion roared.

A chill traveled down Rian's spine as a chorus of roars, howls and growls filled the air. The remaining coyotes fled the scene. The lion stepped aside as Rian reached his mate. He sniffed the wolf and licked a gash in his right shoulder. Dirk lay limp and bloodied from head to toe.

A whimper of pain escaped Dirk's lips. At least, he lived. Rian licked his muzzle.

Male hands ran over his mate and Rian growled. Looking up, a naked Gionne knelt at his side.

"Rian, we need to get Dirk to the stronghold where he will be safe."

Understanding what needed to be done, he moved to the side. Rian shifted to human form as Gionne lifted a feral Dirk in his arms. Standing, Rian held out his arms. "I'll carry him."

Gionne hesitated only a moment before handing him over. "He'll survive but we need to make him comfortable."

"Rian," Leon called his name from behind him. "The large coyote—"

"Was my father," Rian finished the sentence as he looked over his shoulder and met Leon's gaze.

Leon nodded. "I killed him."

Rian was too numb to feel pain for a father who had emotionally abandoned him years ago. Reading the concern in Leon's eyes, he nodded. "I need to take care of Dirk."

"I'll gather the bodies. The pack will want to have a burial," Jake commented.

Rian nodded his agreement. "Rosilee and the others?" he questioned.

"They are safe at the Valde compound." Gionne place a comforting hand on his shoulder. "We scented the coyotes on our way home and doubled back to your camp. When we discovered you two were gone, I had my guard and the rest of your pack take the females to safety."

"Thank you. I'll never be able to repay you."

A smile split Gionne's face. "There is nothing to repay. Dirk is one of ours. We love him too."

"Rian, with your father gone, rule of the pack falls to you," Trey commented.

"No. Mickal will rule the pack."

"Your brother wasn't here," Jake said as he looked around the clearing.

"I know, and for that I am thankful, but for now Dirk is my only concern." Turning on his heel, Rian carried Dirk away from the bloodbath.

# Chapter Six

෨

A shadowy figured moved in the stillness of the night. Tensing, Rian squinted as he watched the movement. Sighing deeply, he relaxed. It was just a Valde guard. He was probably the only person awake besides the guards. Gionne, Jenna and the others had retired for the night once the healer confirmed Dirk would recover. Moving to the fireplace, Rian added a log. He didn't want Dirk to get chilly. He had kicked his covers off a short time ago as he thrashed on the bed in the midst of a nightmare.

He glanced at the bed. Dirk's naked flesh gleamed golden in the firelight. Only a few abrasions marred the perfect body. Just an hour earlier, he had recovered enough to shift to human form. Dirk would recover fully but he was still weak. It had only been about six hours since the attack. Amazingly enough, no one had argued about him taking care of Dirk. They had welcomed Rian into the Valde compound as one of their own. It was a unique feeling of belonging and acceptance. It was a feeling that he hadn't enjoyed in a long time.

Rian rubbed the injury to his wrist. It was sore but compared to Dirk's injuries, minor. He would give thanks daily that Dirk's life had been spared. He only wished no one had died. Sitting on the edge of the bed, Rian wrung out a warm, wet rag. Dirk moaned as he wiped his brow. Dirk's body was blood splattered and when he felt up to it, Rian would bathe him.

A smile pulled at Rian's lips. He'd enjoy bathing the gorgeous male. For the next few days, Dirk would receive nothing but tender loving care.

Dirk's blue eyes fluttered open and Rian cupped his cheek. "Hey, beautiful."

Dirk licked his dry lips. "I thought I told you, males aren't beautiful."

Rian chuckled. "I've never seen anything more beautiful."

Grimacing, Dirk tried to sit up. "Fuck," he cursed.

"Hey! Take it easy."

"Damn. I feel like a tree fell on me."

"Nope. Just a few coyotes."

"What happened? I passed out at the end." Dirk coughed then grimaced.

"Relax." Rian patted Dirk's shoulder. "Let me get you some tea." Rian crossed to the fireplace and picked up the kettle he had warming on the hearth. Pouring the hot brew into a cup he asked, "Do you want some honey?"

"You know I like it sweet."

Dirk's smile did crazy things to his heart and he hurried back to him. Sitting on the edge of the bed, he placed the honey on the nightstand. Holding the cup to Dirk's lips, he warned him, "Careful, it's hot."

Holding Rian's gaze, Dirk blew into the cup then took a small sip and licked his lips.

"You're such a tease."

Dirk chuckled. "That's about all I can do right now."

"Is it sweet enough? I have more honey."

"I'd rather taste your sweetness."

"Damn!" The cup clattered as Rian set it on the nightstand. Leaning across Dirk, he supported his weight on his arm. Pressing his cheek against Dirk's, he whispered in his ear, "I don't want to hurt you."

Dirk's teeth closed on his earlobe, nipping the tender flesh. "My mouth isn't sore."

Turning his head, he met Dirk's lips. They were hungry and sweet with honey. Dirk's tongue thrust into his mouth and he pressed up against him.

He stroked Dirk's cheek. "Easy," he whispered against his lips.

Dirk's blue eyes widened as he gasped a breath. "I thought I'd never touch you again."

Rian groaned. He wanted to scoop Dirk up in his arms and hold him close but he couldn't. Pressing his mouth to Dirk's, he parted his lips with his tongue. With slow, easy thrusts, he made love to Dirk's mouth. A shiver shook Dirk and he raised his head. "Are you okay?"

"Yeah! I just keep thinking— How did you save me?"

Shifting position, Rian stretched out next to Dirk on the bed. He hated telling him the sordid details. He didn't want him upset further. "Jake, Trey, Gionne and Leon showed up. Sorry, I couldn't do a better job of protecting you."

Dirk frowned. "I told you before. It's not your job to protect me."

"You're my mate."

Dirk grimaced as he rolled onto his side. "And you're my mate, but I'm a big boy. I can take care of myself." Dirk groaned. "Usually." He forced a grin that didn't show in his eyes. "They were from your father's pack!"

It wasn't really a question but Rian nodded anyway as he lowered his eyes.

"He sent the coyotes to get rid of me?"

"He was there too," Rian confessed and glanced back up at Dirk to see his expression cloud with anger.

"Was anyone else hurt?"

"None of the rest of us were hurt seriously."

"And the other coyotes?"

Rian hesitated. "My father and two of the others were killed."

Dirk gasped, his eyes widened. "You didn't..." Dirk's hand closed on his shoulder.

Rian shook his head. "Leon killed my father."

"I'm sorry." Dirk swallowed deeply.

Fresh anger bloomed in Rian's gut. Dirk had no reason to be sorry. It was his father's fault. It was his fault for putting Dirk at risk. "I'm not. He intended to kill you. If Leon hadn't killed him, I would have." He hated to think that but he knew it was true. He would have killed his father to save Dirk.

"I'm glad you didn't have to kill him." Dirk ran his hand down his arm and linked their fingers. "If it makes you feel any better, your father must have loved you to go to such lengths."

"In his own twisted way, I think he did, or at least he loved the image he had of me."

"I'm sorry it couldn't have ended differently."

Shifting closer, Rian whispered, "You need only concern yourself with recovering."

"What happens now?"

"I take care of you—"

"I meant what happens to your father's pack—your pack?"

"They're not my pack anymore. My brother can rule them. I couldn't return, not after all that has happened."

Dirk squeezed his hand. "Are you sure? You have family and friends there."

"Positive. We could never be happy there. There would always be some resentment. Three pack members died because my father couldn't accept our relationship. We did nothing wrong but there would always be bitterness over the situation." There was no doubt in Rian's mind. He would rather be here or anywhere with Dirk than back with his pack. His place was with Dirk, his mate.

Dirk sighed and his warm breath fluttered across Rian's cheek.

"Are you okay?"

"I'm just tired and sore."

"Are you up to a sponge bath?"

"I don't know if I'll be *up* for it but I'd enjoy the feel of your hands on my body. At the end, I remember regretting that we didn't have more time together. I wasted so much time."

"We have the rest of our lives."

His leg ached and his head throbbed but it didn't stop Dirk from enjoying the sight of his mate crossing the room. Wearing only a pair of tight jeans, Rian was a remarkable sight. When he leaned forward to fill the bowl with warm water, Dirk groaned. Rian had a sculpted back and a fine ass.

"Are you okay?" Rian asked. Twisting his upper body to look at Dirk, he smiled as he saw the real reason for Dirk's discomfort.

Dirk felt his dark gaze like a warm caress that sizzled as it stroked his cock. "I'm good."

"You are that!" Rian returned to the side of the bed and set the bowl of heated water on the nightstand. "Damn," he cursed as his eyes lingered. "You're making this hard."

"No. You're making it hard." Dirk trailed the tip of his fingers up his aroused cock. He didn't miss the thick erection pressing at the front of Rian's jeans.

Rian chuckled. "I just wanted to give you a bath. I don't want to risk hurting you."

"You won't hurt me. I'm just sore. I'll be fine by tomorrow."

Rian gripped the fingers of his left hand and lifted his arm. The cloth-covered hand trembled as it reached out to bathe him. "Then we should wait until tomorrow."

Dirk snorted but didn't reply. It would be a long bath. Before Rian was finished, he was confident he could persuade him that some gentle lovin' was just what he needed. Shutting his eyes, Dirk enjoyed Rian's touch. His hands made quick work of his arms, shoulders and chest but when Rian reached his waist, he stopped.

"Don't stop now," Dirk groaned. A firm hand gripped his left foot and lifted as Rian resumed his bath. "Fucking tease."

"Mmm-hmm," Rian agreed.

Dirk's body jolted as a tongue followed the cloth down his calf. Rian's lips caressed the back of his knee as his hands washed his thigh. Damn! Rian looked hot bent over him. The other male's heavy-lidded eyes opened, meeting his gaze. Love and need showed openly in his gaze. "Fuck, Ri. Take off your pants and love me."

Rian shook his dark head. "Today is just for you." Nipping the inside of his thigh, Rian smiled and lowered his leg. "One to go and then…" Rian licked his lips as his gaze ravaged Dirk's cock.

Dirk gasped. "You can skip my leg."

"Nope."

"Fuck! Then hurry it up," Dirk pleaded as Rian lifted his other leg and began the slow torturous strokes.

It seemed like hours but was probably minutes until Rian announced, "I'm done."

"Thank god." He wasn't sure he could last much longer. He'd just found his mate and almost lost him. Just the touch of his hand was like a flame to dry tinder.

"I need fresh water to bathe your cock." Rian stood and walked away.

"What?" Dirk sat up too quickly and had to suppress a groan of pain.

Rian looked over his shoulder and his dark eyes danced mischievously. "You don't want me to use cold water do you?"

"I don't want you to use water at all."

Rian chuckled. "Don't worry. I intend to blow it dry."

"You're killin' me," Dirk sighed.

"Just wait! Those shaved balls will be very sensitive. You'll love the feel of my tongue lapping them."

The low, seductive words sent a shiver down his spine and Dirk gripped the sheet beneath him.

Crossing to the bed, Rian knelt at his feet. "Spread your thighs. I want between them."

Dirk readily complied and was surprised when Rian set the bowl of water on his abs.

"You'll have to stay calm or you'll soak the bed." Rian dropped the warm cloth over his groin.

"You don't play fair."

"I'm not playing." Rian clinically washed his lower stomach, his shaft and balls. He even lifted him enough to wash his bottom. Throwing the cloth into the bowl, Rian set it aside. "Now, I intend to play."

Rian circled his cock head with his tongue and Dirk's abs flexed so hard, he felt a twinge of pain. However, no force in nature would make him complain. "Damn, that feels good," Dirk gasped as Rian engulfed his cock.

Rian took him deep, swallowing around him and Dirk arched up, cupping the back of his head. The pain in his side was minor compared to the pleasure. "Suck me," Dirk murmured. A firm hand cupped his balls, twisting and rolling them as only another male knew how to do. "I'm going to come. I'm going to come too soon if you don't stop."

The pressure eased up and Dirk lay back on the bed. He wanted to take pleasure in his lover's mouth for a while before he came.

"Enjoying yourself?" Rian panted as he crawled over him.

"Oh yeah!" Running his hands up Rian's smooth back, he lifted his head and grasped a peaked nipple between his teeth. The light covering of chest hair tickled his nose.

"Not yet, babe." Rian cuffed him lightly on the chin.

"Hey.

"Just getting my honey." Rian held up the bottle. "I'm planning a feast."

"Hope you like cream with your honey." Dirk smirked.

The cool syrup stuck in globs as Rian squeezed the bottle. "Now you know why I want you clean shaven."

Closing the cap, Rian licked his fingers. "Tasty." He smacked his lips together. The honey was tasty but Dirk looked even better stretched out on the bed with a king-sized erection waiting for satisfaction.

Lowering his head, Rian lapped the thick vein that ran the length of Dirk's cock. Dirk's hips bucked and he grinned. "Like that?"

"Oh yeah."

"Mmm, me too. My honey-drizzled cocksicle." A snicker from Dirk turned into a moan as Rian sucked his smooth left nut into his mouth. Stroking Dirk's shaft, he alternated between sucking his nuts and shaft until Dirk writhed in near ecstasy. Wiping his hand on the sheet, Rian circled the fleshy glans atop Dirk's cock.

"I can't take much more," Dirk warned.

"Then give it to me." He swallowed Dirk's cock. Taking him deep in his throat, he tongued the thick vein. Dirk tensed and Rian felt his cock get ready to explode. Liquid heat bathed his throat in cream sweeter than the best honey. Lapping Dirk's cock, he drank the essence sweetened by love.

Resting his head on Dirk's abdomen, Rian asked, "Are you okay?"

"Oh yeah!"

Stretching out along Dirk's side, he gathered him close. "I'm sorry."

"Sorry?"

"Sorry about my pack. Sorry that loving me almost cost you your life."

"Ri." Dirk rolled to his side and held him tight. "Even if we only had a few days or a few weeks, I'd never be sorry. I love you."

Burying his head in Dirk's long, blond hair, Rian murmured, "I love you too." His voice sounded hoarse to his own ears.

"Make love to me."

"Dirk, I don't want to hurt you."

Dirk's hand cupped his cheek. "You won't. I need to feel you inside me. I need the connection. I can handle it. I'm a wolf."

Turning his head, Rian kissed Dirk's palm. Moving on he kissed Dirk's cheek and ran his tongue along his jawline to his chin. "I want you too," he whispered against Dirk's mouth.

Dirk tugged at the closure to his jeans. "Take these off and show me."

Rolling from the bed, Rian shucked his jeans and found a tube of lube. "We'll take it easy." With a loose grip, Rian coated his cock with lube.

"Okay."

Circling the bed, he crawled in behind Dirk. "Stay on your side and we'll take it nice and slow." Lifting Dirk's top leg, he bent his knee. "Nice and easy." A lube-coated finger rimmed Dirk's anus. "You're still so tight." He pressed a fingertip inside. "So new to this." Dirk's inner muscles clamped on his finger.

"But it feels so good," Dirk groaned.

"It will feel even better when I'm inside you." Rian gritted his teeth as Dirk's hot, tight hole sucked at his finger. It was all he could do to hold back. Circling his finger, he pushed deeper. "Are you ready for me?"

"Please."

Pre-cum leaked from his cock head as he pushed it against Dirk's opening. "I love you," he said as he watched the dark flesh of his cock disappear inside Dirk's paler body. "I love you. I love fucking you." Rian slowly pressed forward.

"Yes," Dirk hissed as his blue eyes flashed with pleasured pain.

"Stroke your cock. Let me see you touch yourself while I fuck your sweet ass." Holding Dirk's leg up, he pushed deeper.

Dirk's back arched. "Sweet."

His heart pounded and blood roared in his ears. He wouldn't last long. He was too worked up. Pumping his hips a little harder, he lowered his head. Licking the back of Dirk's knee, he nipped the tender flesh.

"I'm coming." Rian heard the words over the roar in his ears but he wasn't sure if he or Dirk spoke. His balls tightened as he began to spurt and Dirk's hole contracted around him.

\* \* \* \* \*

Dirk woke up alone in his big bed and sighed. Throwing the covers to the side, he stretched. He was a little sore but he felt good. Crossing to the fireplace, he added a log. His stomach grumbled nosily. He hoped Rian was getting breakfast. He'd worked up an appetite. He rubbed his stomach and his cock twitched. Actually, he had an appetite for a couple things.

The door opened and he turned, sporting a smile and a hard-on. Gionne and Leon stood inside the room. Heat flushed his skin as his erection waned. "Sorry."

The two males smirked and he crossed to the bed and tugged on a pair of discarded jeans. They sagged low on his hips. Obviously, they belonged to Rian.

Gionne cleared his throat. "How are you?"

"I'm good."

Taking a step forward, Leon stopped and bent over. Picking up a tube of lube, he handed it to Gionne who threw it on the bed.

"Are you sore," Leon asked, then coughed into his hand as he tried to hide his chuckle.

Gionne snorted, though he obviously attempted to control himself.

"Funny." Dirk narrowed his gaze.

Leon shrugged. "Sorry. Couldn't help myself."

Dirk nodded.

"It doesn't matter to us what you do in your bedroom."

Running his fingers through his loose hair, Dirk asked, "Do you know where Rian is?"

"He came down to get a tray for breakfast but Riza waylaid him," Gionne answered.

"Good thing he's gay. I don't like competition and your mate's just a little too…"

"Hot!" Dirk added with a wink. "I never said he didn't like females too."

"But he likes blonds," Gionne inserted into the conversation. "I think he was checking out your ass when we were leaving." Gionne looked at Leon.

"Fuck you, Gio."

"Just kidding." Gionne winked. "I think he's a one-male kind of guy."

"You want to come down and have breakfast with us?" Leon asked.

"I better since you can't control your mate's plotting. She'll be trying to convince him to share my ass."

"You don't want to share? Not even with Leon?" Gionne wagged his eyebrows.

Dirk shook his head. "Hell no. I don't like blonds. I prefer dark hair."

Leon smirked in Gionne's direction. "I always knew you two had something going on."

"Yep. You caught us," Dirk agreed as he waved them toward the door. "I'm about to change pants so unless you all want to ogle my cock again, I suggest you go."

"We better get out. Don't want your mate getting jealous."

* * * * *

The breakfast conversation hushed as Dirk entered. The chatter resumed as the food hit the table but he couldn't help feeling that they were keeping something from him. The feeling grew throughout the day.

"What were you discussing with Jenna and Riza?" Dirk asked as they headed out into the yard. Rian had finally agreed that a little exercise would be good for him. If it was up to him, he'd work out with the Valde guard but he knew better than to push his luck.

Rian reached for his hand and interlocked their fingers. "Just the usual. They're happy you recovered so quickly."

"Anything else."

"Nothing important." A slow smile spread across Rian's face.

"Are you going to tell me what they have planned?"

"I don't know what you mean."

"Fine! Whatever. Keep your secrets." Dirk sighed. "Have you considered visiting your brother?"

Rian shook his head. "While you were recovering Jake and Trey delivered the bodies of my father and the others to the pack."

"And?" Dirk stopped walking.

"And nothing. My brother has no animosity toward you or me. He told Jake that any or all of us were welcome to return."

Dirk raised his brow as he waited for Rian to continue.

"I'm not interested. The others can make their own decision."

"Did you make that decision because of me?"

"I could never live anywhere that I wasn't sure you were safe." Rian grinned. "You're the most important thing in my life."

"I love you. If you want to return to your pack —" Rian pressed his fingers against his lips cutting off his words.

"I don't. I talked to Gionne while we waited for you to wake up. I like him."

Dirk grinned. "Guess it's my turn to say 'told you so'."

"I agreed to live on the border. We'll act as guards and be part of the pack but not under Gionne's thumb."

"The best of both worlds. Safety and freedom."

"I think so."

\* \* \* \* \*

By dinnertime, Dirk was like a caged animal. Everyone was pampering him and conversations stopped every time he entered a room. He could hardly eat. He just wanted to get it over. He felt as if he should just rip off his clothes and bend over for Rian. That's what everyone wanted — to see him getting fucked.

The dinner was over and the table cleared. As a pitcher of ale was set on the table, Dirk lunged to his feet and turned his back. Dirk had grown up in the midst of public joining and he'd often participated but now he felt pressured. He had admitted and accepted that he was gay. Hell, he didn't mind his pack knowing. He was proud of Rian. He didn't really care if a million people watched them make love but he didn't want to feel like he was performing.

Rian's hand landed on his shoulder and he turned to face his mate. "I guess I'm supposed to go on my hands and knees for you."

"Always," Rian whispered as he wrapped his arms around him. Rian's warm hand slipped under his hair, cupping his head and Dirk relaxed into Rian's arms. As their lips met, thoughts of an audience slipped away. Held in Rian's arms, nothing else mattered.

Gionne cleared his throat and Dirk opened his eyes. He blinked to clear the haze of lust from his mind. The pack had assembled and they all stood watching. Gionne, Leon, Jenna and Riza stood at the front of a group that included Rian's pack members and even his sister, Rosilee.

Dirk gulped as he looked at them.

"Have a seat." Gionne motioned to two chairs sitting side by side.

He had no idea what they had planned but with Rian at his side, he took a seat. "Relax," Rian whispered as he rested their joined hands on the armrests between them.

Riza smiled at him and that made him nervous. If she was happy, he was in trouble. His discomfort grew as Riza and Jenna stepped forward.

"Dirk, this is a special day for all of us. We want to welcome all the coyotes. We especially want to welcome your mate, Rian." Riza winked in Rian's direction.

Dirk shifted nervously as Jenna stepped forward and took his hand. "You're my protector and Riza's and for that we will always owe you. Tonight we pledge our protection to you. We might not have the physical strength to protect you but we pledge not only our strength but our mate's, as well."

"Jenna," Dirk gasped as he turned to Riza. He furrowed his brow as he watched her.

"Dirk, you've always looked out for our pack. It's our turn to look out for yours."

Gionne and Leon stepped forward. "Our packs," Gionne gestured to Leon. "We stand behind you whatever happens."

Dirk blinked rapidly. "I can't believe this." He turned to Rian. "Did you know?"

Rian inclined his head. "Your pack is as you said — accepting, loving…a family."

Lunging to his feet, he wrapped his arms around Jenna and Riza. "I love you," he whispered.

"We love you too," Jenna replied as they both kissed him on the cheek.

"Now, let me go so I can greet your mate." Riza playfully pushed him away and approached Rian.

Standing behind him, Rian was tall and gorgeous in a tight formfitting shirt and low hip-hugging jeans. Just looking at him made Dirk horny. Rian lowered his head as Riza approached and she planted an affectionate kiss on his cheek. As her lips pressed against Rian, she winked at her mate.

"Damn. I'm glad he's gay," Leon joked.

"So am I." Dirk agreed. "So am I." Later he would show Rian how glad.

# Also by L.A. Day

∽

# About the Author

ℰℑ

L.A. Day exists only in the mind of Laura. An avid reader since early childhood, she began writing romance in her teens. Now, 20+ years later she's progressed to erotic romance. Supported by her husband of many years, she spends most of her time in front of a computer weaving tales of love and lust.

Multi-published in erotic romance, her stories have been tagged imaginative, steamy, and even one of the most erotic stories ever read. Her favorite genre is erotic romance with a paranormal or sci-fi twist. She feels that if you're going to create an alpha male character, why not make him bigger, stronger, more well endowed than any human man could ever be? It is fantasy after all.

Remember, alpha males are only a "Day" away.

L.A. Day likes to hear from her fans, so email her and let her know what you think.

L.A. Day welcomes comments from readers. You can find her website and email address on her author bio page at www.ellorascave.com.

## Tell Us What You Think

We appreciate hearing reader opinions about our books. You can email us at Comments@EllorasCave.com.

# Why an electronic book?

We live in the Information Age—an exciting time in the history of human civilization, in which technology rules supreme and continues to progress in leaps and bounds every minute of every day. For a multitude of reasons, more and more avid literary fans are opting to purchase e-books instead of paper books. The question from those not yet initiated into the world of electronic reading is simply: *Why?*

1. ***Price.*** An electronic title at Ellora's Cave Publishing and Cerridwen Press runs anywhere from 40% to 75% less than the cover price of the exact same title in paperback format. Why? Basic mathematics and cost. It is less expensive to publish an e-book (no paper and printing, no warehousing and shipping) than it is to publish a paperback, so the savings are passed along to the consumer.

2. ***Space.*** Running out of room in your house for your books? That is one worry you will never have with electronic books. For a low one-time cost, you can purchase a handheld device specifically designed for e-reading. Many e-readers have large, convenient screens for viewing. Better yet, hundreds of titles can be stored within your new library—on a single microchip. There are a variety of e-readers from different manufacturers. You can also read e-books on your PC or laptop computer. (Please note that Ellora's Cave does not endorse any specific brands.

You can check our websites at www.ellorascave.com or www.cerridwenpress.com for information we make available to new consumers.)

3. *Mobility.* Because your new e-library consists of only a microchip within a small, easily transportable e-reader, your entire cache of books can be taken with you wherever you go.

4. ***Personal Viewing Preferences.*** Are the words you are currently reading too small? Too large? Too… ANNOYING? Paperback books cannot be modified according to personal preferences, but e-books can.

5. ***Instant Gratification.*** Is it the middle of the night and all the bookstores near you are closed? Are you tired of waiting days, sometimes weeks, for bookstores to ship the novels you bought? Ellora's Cave Publishing sells instantaneous downloads twenty-four hours a day, seven days a week, every day of the year. Our webstore is never closed. Our e-book delivery system is 100% automated, meaning your order is filled as soon as you pay for it.

Those are a few of the top reasons why electronic books are replacing paperbacks for many avid readers.

As always, Ellora's Cave and Cerridwen Press welcome your questions and comments. We invite you to email us at Comments@ellorascave.com or write to us directly at Ellora's Cave Publishing Inc., 1056 Home Avenue, Akron, OH 44310-3502.

Cerridwen, the Celtic Goddess of wisdom, was the muse who brought inspiration to storytellers and those in the creative arts. Cerridwen Press encompasses the best and most innovative stories in all genres of today's fiction. Visit our site and discover the newest titles by talented authors who still get inspired - much like the ancient storytellers did, once upon a time.

Cerrídwen Press
www.cerrídwenpress.com

Discover for yourself why readers can't get enough
of the multiple award-winning publisher
Ellora's Cave.

Whether you prefer e-books or paperbacks,
be sure to visit EC on the web at
www.ellorascave.com

for an erotic reading experience that will leave you
breathless.